DESPERATE

A chilling mystery with a huge twist

PATTI BATTISON

(DETECTIVE MIA HARVEY THRILLERS BOOK 1)

D1596929

Revised edition 2019
Joffe Books, London

**Please join our mailing list for free Kindle crime
thriller, detective, mystery books and new releases.**
www.joffebooks.com

ISBN: 978-1-78931-207-2

PROLOGUE

And so it was done.

How did he feel now? Elated? Frustrated? No, strangely disappointed, as a matter of fact. It had all been so easy. Too easy. He'd wanted more of a battle. Oh, she'd struggled, and he'd enjoyed that struggle. It was bliss. An exquisite torture.

A raucous laugh escaped his lips. The torture might have been exquisite for him but he surmised that the girl would have disagreed.

He stirred his coffee with a languid ease, looking beyond the liquid, seeing instead the abject terror in her lovely hazel eyes and feeling again the quickening pulse points beneath his fingers as he held her wrists in a vicelike grip.

Getting her there had been so easy, like guiding a child. Indeed, he'd surprised himself; his nerve, his ingenuity had known no bounds. Of course, the uniform helped. Women always trusted a man in uniform. Stupid cunts.

Anyway, easy or not, it was mission accomplished.

Now he knew it all.

Now he knew how the human body responds to prolonged and excruciating pain, how the muscles spasm. Now he knew that blood doesn't gush when a blade slices through dead flesh, however deep the wound. And what a pity that was. How much more exciting it had been to witness her warm blood spurting in the wake of the Stanley knife. How dramatic; how visually satisfying that had been.

Now he knew that the lungs constrict and push out shallow, frantic breaths during excessive torture, causing the victim to hyperventilate to such an extent that her cries seem to be carried along on one continuous exhalation. A frown creased his brow at the memory. She'd been noisy, all right, but he'd soon put a stop to that.

And he could have done without the shit. Now he knew from bitter experience that extreme circumstances could put too heavy a strain on the human digestive system, causing the bowel to evacuate forcefully. She'd shit herself, poor cow, all over the area he'd so carefully prepared for their lovemaking. He'd made her suffer for that. Oh, yes.

It had detracted from his pleasure, that stink, that mess. His orgasm, when it came, was powerful, but he would have liked more time to savour its aftermath; perhaps using her mouth as a way of extracting every last drop of pleasure from his cock. As it was that sickening stench had turned his stomach and he'd hurried the fuck.

Then, frustrated beyond measure, he'd wrapped his powerful hands around the delicate softness of her neck and proceeded to squeeze away every last vestige of her useless life.

He'd expected her actual elimination to be the easiest part of the experience. She had, after all, endured the most abhorrent torment that could possibly be dredged from the murky depths of a twisted imagination, and her energy levels were dropping fast. Even so, when his eager fingers curled around her neck with such an insidious determination, she found from somewhere a second wind and thrashed beneath him with all the strength of a slippery eel that was fresh out of water and planning to return forthwith. He'd held on, though, straddling her writhing body like the rider of a bucking bronco, relishing their deadly battle of wills until, finally, thankfully, her movements began to grow weak, then weaker still … and then she was dead.

He should have cut her throat, he realized that now. It would have been much safer and a hell of a lot quicker. Still, no experience was ever wasted; next time he'd be able to avoid those niggling little irritations.

Suddenly the breath caught in his throat and a delicious shudder ran through his body, causing the coffee to spill over on to the breakfast bar.

So, there might be a next time? He might kill again?

He grinned. Why the hell not? After all, theory was fine, up to a point. But, let's face it, only practice makes perfect.

CHAPTER ONE

Detective Sergeant Mia Harvey followed her mother's slow progress along the corridor at St Stephen's nursing home with all the diligence of a mother watching the first uncertain steps of a precious child, her hands never more than a few inches away from the woman's skeletal waist in case she should stumble.

'She's doing just fine,' said Janet Munroe, the Home's senior manager, with a practised cheerfulness that Mia found hugely comforting. 'You'd outrun me, wouldn't you, Barbara?'

Barbara Harvey made no reply, her concentration being wholly focused on the double doors at the end of the corridor and the day room beyond, but her mouth broke into a crooked, self-satisfied smile that would have reached her eyes had her mental faculties still been intact. Her thin, blue-veined hands gripped the stainless steel walking-frame with such a strength that the knuckles showed white, while Mia's concern now grew too heavy to bear.

'That's enough,' she said. 'Let me get the wheelchair, now.'

Behind her mother's back Janet gave Mia a chiding look. 'It's best to let her walk. She'll let us know when she's had enough.' Then, with a supporting arm around the woman's shoulder, 'You'll let us know when you've had enough, won't you, sweetheart?'

Barbara nodded and chuckled wildly, her demeanour like that of a child. Mia had to look away briefly as tears threatened without warning. The last thing she wanted was to break down in front of Janet. And, what good would it do, anyway? It was plain, old-fashioned guilt that was disrupting her equilibrium, not some finer emotion like compassion or – God forbid – love.

Mia had always been a daddy's girl. Her father, Robin, had also served in the police force, rising slowly through the ranks to finish as chief superintendent. He had been a formidable taskmaster, but he had served his officers well, arguing with his superiors almost to the point of dismissal if he believed one of them had been treated unfairly by the system. Some of his more colourful arguments had since passed into station folklore, to be repeated with relish for the benefit of any new recruit who showed an interest.

Mia had worshipped at his feet and had decided that she, too, wanted to be a police officer, even before she could spell the words. They were besotted with each other, Mia and her father, and Barbara could only watch from the margins, a contented smile on her lips more often than not. She was the archetypal mother figure, there to serve, to nurture, to provide comfort. If her family was happy, then so was she.

And they were happy until Robin Harvey suffered a massive heart attack and died instantly. Mia was just seventeen years old, too young to know how to manage the pain, and too blinkered by grief to see that her mother was suffering, too. She followed the wrong path for a while, mixed with the wrong crowd, and compounded her mother's anguish in as many ways as she saw fit. But time eventually worked its magic; Mia's heartache did eventually decrease and she was able to realize, for the very first time, how intolerably she had behaved. So she set about making amends, seeming to hold her mother dear while striving to enter her father's world, a figurehead to his memory.

This change in Mia's affections was without substance, however. The vagaries of youth instilled in her a cockeyed view that Barbara was too willing to forget the abominable behaviour, and altogether too eager to embrace their newfound closeness. She saw her mother as weak, ineffectual: a clinging encumbrance that had to be tolerated for the sake of the status quo.

It was during this period of sustained cheerfulness that Barbara succumbed to a monstrous stroke which left her virtually helpless. The road back to full health was long and riddled with obstacles, and Mia had been warned that her mother might never complete its course. She could say the odd word, when she felt like it, and she managed those painfully slow jaunts to the day room; but that loving and nurturing woman whom Mia had spurned and patronized in equal measure was gone for ever. Now, gazing at her mother, the tears at last suppressed, Mia contemplated all that was lost. We none of us knew what we had until it was gone. That old song said as much and it was spot on.

Janet continually reminded Mia that Barbara was content. Mia would simply have to take the words on trust. The important thing now was to get her mother sitting down.

The day room was almost within reach and, inside it, the safety of an armchair. Mia rushed ahead to open one of the doors, leaving a free path for her mother to negotiate. Janet stayed glued to the woman's side, softly coaxing her along.

The residents watched television, played dominoes or simply chatted amiably in comfortable recliners clustered around small tables scattered across the room. It was a far cry from those places where poor souls sat in hard chairs lining the walls, facing no one, pumped full of drugs to keep them quiet while they counted the days before death.

Mia had chosen St Stephen's specifically because of Janet's vision of a happy and relaxed establishment. Responsibilities were shared amongst those still capable, and brain cells exercised daily with games and activities ranging from bingo and baccarat to difficult quizzes.

After successfully negotiating the doorway, Barbara Harvey aimed her walking-frame at the nearest table and launched herself off at a near trot, causing Mia to glare pleadingly at Janet to intervene.

'Isn't she doing well?' said Janet, without the slightest hint of condescension. Then, to the ladies seated around the table, 'Shove up, you lot, Barbara's on her way.'

A series of hellos and welcoming smiles, a chair pulled out in readiness, and Mia was subjected to a number of inquisitive glances that took in her casual clothes, her hairstyle, the thickness of her make-up. She gave them all a ready grin while attempting vainly to fit names to the faces.

She was plumping up the cushion on her mother's chair and offering flustered small talk to the other ladies when her mobile phone rang from the depths of her bag. Shrugging the bag from her shoulder, she moved a discreet few feet away from the table.

'DS Harvey,' she said, her voice low.

It was Detective Chief Inspector Paul Wells. 'Mia, drop what you're doing and get over to the landfill site at Stratton End. We've got a body. Terrible mess, apparently.'

'I'll be right there. What about Nick, sir? Does he know?'

'I've been trying to get hold of him,' Wells scowled. 'His phone's switched off.'

Mia mentally tut-tutted. She had a good idea where Nick Ford might be and the DCI wouldn't like it one bit. 'Oh, well, sir, it is his day off—'

'No excuse. I'll have his bollocks when I find him.'

'Leave him to me,' she said, cringing at his tone. 'I'll track him down.'

'Make it quick. That crime scene needs to be made secure – pronto.'

Mia said her goodbyes, gave her mother a heartfelt hug, and headed for the door, silently thanking Wells for giving her a means of escape. It was just a pity someone had had to lose their life in the process.

Lisa Mackey broke open the condom packet and tossed it across to Nick. The gesture held little grace, but he was a regular and niceties had long ago ceased to feature in their sessions. Only crudity and mild violence got a look-in nowadays, and the smallest hint of satisfaction if he was in a giving mood.

Detective Inspector Nick Ford was a handsome man and outsiders might have wondered why he needed to exploit the talents of a prostitute when girls must surely be lining up to offer him sex. Lisa knew why. She'd witnessed the demons that drove him on. She'd been privy to the tears, the tantrums, the shocking self-loathing that ate away at his soul. Nick was damaged goods, and he came to her for solace and repair. It was Lisa's job to fix him, to apply the balm that would allow him to function in the real world for a little while longer.

'Hurry up, gorgeous,' she said, her fingers brushing his face as she sashayed towards the bedroom. 'I'm so wet I can hardly wait.'

Her tongue licked cherry-red lips; her blue eyes showed longing … but, inwardly, she cringed. It was all so pathetic, this game that was played out twice a week. So pathetic, and so bloody tiring. Nick was too needy, too much like hard work, but he paid well and she needed the money. Lisa had her sights set on art college as soon as she'd earned enough. Nick could get lost, then. They all could. But for now she'd pander to his bruised ego, make him believe he was the best, even when he couldn't get it hard enough for the condom. And what did it matter if he sometimes lost control and got a bit too physical with his fists? She'd had worse.

Lisa dropped her dressing-gown and climbed on to the bed, arranging her shapely body to its best advantage. 'I'm ready, baby.'

In truth, she was anything but ready. She felt jaded, out of sorts, and sex with a psychotic copper was the last thing she wanted. But Lisa was a professional; she always gave value for money. Writhing passionately on the bed she begged him to end this wonderful agony.

And then he was in the doorway. 'If I'd wanted all this chat I'd have called a sex line. Give it a rest, Lisa, for Christ's sake.'

So, he was in that mood, was he? She'd have to work hard for her money today, and she could forget all about foreplay. As Nick straddled her body Lisa noticed that his erection was far from solid and her spirits sank. It was usually when he failed to climax that he became too frisky with his fists. She writhed beneath him, attempting to turn him on, while Nick made a grab for her bra and tore it from her body. Lisa winced but said nothing. Then, caring not the slightest for her comfort, he ripped away the tiny thong and tossed it on the floor. The elastic cut into her flesh, drew blood. And she stifled a cry, but opened her legs nevertheless.

Nick entered her roughly, his thrusts deep and painful, but Lisa had learned the art of dissociation and was able to switch off the hurtful and sordid reality that seemed to go on for ever. He had a tight hold of her wrists, his fingernails digging into her flesh, his hot breath stinking of garlic and tobacco. She wanted to retch and, feigning ecstasy, her groans loud and enthusiastic, she turned her face away in search of cleaner air.

When he was finished Nick rolled off and lay at her side. With other punters Lisa would be on her feet immediately. Clothes would be on and money changing hands even before the sweat had dried on their bodies. But Nick was allowed special dispensations on account of the fact that he was a detective and he could make her working life hell if he felt like it.

Eventually Nick left the bed without a word and wandered into the other room for his clothes, stopping only briefly at the door to give her a look that said … what? Thanks? Fuck you?

Lisa scrambled to her feet and reached for her dressing-gown, thankful it was over for another day. He had been quite restrained for once. She might only have a handful of bruises this time. Nice one, Nick. And luckily the cut made by her thong had stopped bleeding, so she'd be able to camouflage it with a little make-up before her next client arrived.

She was on the verge of offering him coffee, but his expression told her to think again. His face had a mean look that she'd seen countless times, a look that didn't bode well for the future of her own complexion. It would be better to get him out, and she was wondering how best to achieve this when the intercom buzzed. Nick shot her an enquiring look, and she shrugged in reply. Her next client wasn't due for another hour.

She depressed the button on the intercom. 'Who is it?'

'Is Nick there?'

His face clouded in recognition of the voice, and Lisa marvelled inwardly as his cheeks flushed.

Pushing her aside Nick reached for the button. 'Mia?' His tone was incredulous.

'Who the fuck's Mia?' said Lisa, pretending to be indignant.

'Nick, there's no time for delicacy,' said Mia. 'We've got a job on. A big job. Wells wants us, like, yesterday, so get your knickers on and hurry up.'

Nick bristled, but said nothing. He looked like a small boy caught with his hand in the sweets jar, and Lisa wanted to laugh out loud.

'Trouble?' she said, her face showing concern.

He skimmed her a look, but kept quiet. Instead he pulled a wallet from his inside pocket and tossed five twenty-pound notes on to the nearest chair and let himself out of the flat.

Lisa followed him to the door. 'Will I see you on Wednesday, Nick?'

'How the fuck should I know?' he said, disappearing down the stairwell. Stopping abruptly, he looked up. 'You're getting too clingy, Lisa. You'd better watch that.' Not much of a parting shot, but it was better than nothing.

'I can't help it,' she said, pouting. 'I need you, Nick. I need you, baby.' But, he was already gone. Lisa shut the door and leant against it, eyes closed. 'I need you, Nick,' she said, mimicking her own voice. 'Huh, like I need a hole in the head, you prick.'

CHAPTER TWO

They arrived at the landfill site to find uniformed officers conducting a rigorous fingertip search amongst the mouldering mounds. One area was cordoned off with yellow police tape. Mia cut a determined path towards it and found herself staring at the naked body of a young female crammed into a heavy-duty green-plastic refuse sack, chin touching knees, heels kissing buttocks.

Part of the sack was all but destroyed now, exposing fully the right side of the corpse. Mia's gaze took in the shreds of green plastic littering the immediate area and she imagined, with rising horror, the large number of hungry rats needed for such carnage. They had gorged ferociously on the pliant flesh, chewing down to bone in a few places on the face, torso and upper arms, creating problems galore for the pathologist unlucky enough to be assigned to this case.

Turning up her coat collar against the biting February wind Mia concentrated for a moment on the skyline of industrial chimneys and tired 1960s tower blocks that served as a backdrop for this depressing place before returning her attention to the girl.

She had been pretty, according to what was left of her face. Early twenties? The auburn hair was thick and glossy; the bronze tan either fake or the result of an early foreign holiday. It was impossible to see what wounds there might be – if any – given the position of the body and the damage caused by the rats. Mia turned to a fresh page in her notebook and started to describe, in words that would never be adequate, the scene before her eyes.

Nick stood close by, shoulders hunched against the cold, in brisk discussion with Police Constable Andy Taylor whose job it was to secure the crime scene. Beyond them, a line of panda cars formed a visible barrier between evil and the rest of society, their flashing lights stark and dismal in the cloying winter gloom. The first car held the two men who had stumbled across the body. Both stared straight ahead, their faces blank with shock. Mia pocketed her notebook and trudged towards them with Nick at her heels.

'This is DS Harvey,' he told the men as they scrambled into the front seats of the vehicle. 'Mia, this is Steve Palmer....' He indicated the older of the two. 'And, that's his brother, Johnny.'

Mia gave a brisk nod, her nose wrinkling in disgust at the rank body odour emanating from the pair. 'Pity she wasn't dumped somewhere a bit warmer,' she said, trying to breathe some warmth into her freezing fingers.

'It weren't nothing to do with us,' Johnny Palmer said, clearly agitated. 'We was just looking for stuff to sell ... honest.'

'Relax,' said Nick.

'I can't, that's the trouble. I need a wet really bad.'

Nick muttered an oath. 'Have one, then. Only do it away from the crime scene. The boss'll have your balls if you piss all over the evidence.' He tapped on the side window and motioned to PC Taylor. 'Andy, he wants a piss. Go with him, will you?'

While Taylor escorted Johnny to a suitable spot, Mia studied his brother. 'Come here often, Steve?'

'You chatting me up?' he said, grinning. Mia gave him a look that would shatter cement and the grin evaporated. 'Most weekends, yeah,' he said, suddenly serious. 'It's surprising what you can pick up here.'

Mia's gaze took in the acres of rubbish, the rotting organic matter strewn around in unhygienic mounds. Even in freezing temperatures the stench was almost unbearable. 'A number of fatal diseases for a start,' she said, with a shudder.

Steve shrugged. 'It's a living.'

'Tell us about when you found the body,' said Nick, pen poised over paper. 'And, don't leave anything out. You never know what might be significant.'

Steve twisted in his seat, his flustered gaze searching out his brother. Cosy chats with the police didn't feature in the life of Steve Palmer. He was more used to hostile interrogations, and he needed his brother's comforting presence to bolster his flagging bravado.

'Not much to tell,' he said, eventually. 'We got here about twelve o'clock, as usual. Weekly loads get dropped off late on Friday afternoons, so Saturday's the best time to come looking….'

Before he could continue, Johnny was back. 'Bleedin' hell,' he said, climbing into his seat. 'I thought little Johnny was gonna drop off, it's so bleedin' cold.' He made a face at Mia, a grubby hand shooting towards his mouth. 'Excuse my French, ma'am.'

Mia smiled. 'I'm not the Queen, Johnny.'

'Oh, I know … you're too pretty. More like Princess Di, I'd say. She was nice, weren't she?' He turned to his brother, an excited expression on his face. 'Weren't she nice, Steve … Princess Di?'

Steve sighed loudly. 'Shut up, Johnny, there's a good lad.'

'Will do.' He turned to stare out of the side window, his expression one of total compliance.

Nick said, 'So you got here at twelve o'clock, Steve. What happened, then?'

'We worked our usual area….' He pointed towards the site. 'Starting from the east side, we'd gone maybe seventy-five to a hundred yards across, and then we just … well … found it.' He gave a half-hearted shrug.

'Was it hidden under anything, or exposed, as it is now?'

'Like it is now. We didn't touch anything.' He shuddered. 'Well, who would? Know what I mean?'

'Where's your car?' said Nick, scribbling furiously.

'We ain't got no car,' said Steve. 'We use a wheelbarrow for everything but the biggest stuff. It's over there.' He pointed out of the back window.

'And, which way did you come in? From Dyson Lane, or Wallbrook Street?'

'Dyson Lane.'

'OK.' Nick flicked the page. 'Did you see anybody – either here or in Dyson Lane? Anybody acting suspicious?'

Steve gave a vigorous shake of the head. 'No, mate, there was just us.'

Nick thought for a moment. 'Where do you live, Steve?'

'Staples Brook.'

When no further information was forthcoming, Nick aimed a quizzical glance at the man. 'I want your full address.'

Steve hesitated. It didn't do for the police to know too much about a person's business. It didn't augur well for the future, when he might want to bend the law a bit. He sighed and let out a silent curse. Why did the fucking body have to be on their patch, anyway? Didn't he have enough on his plate, having to drag his piss-brained brother around all the time?

Nick said, 'Hurry up, Steve. You must realize that we'll need your details, if only for the court case.'

Steve's eyes widened. 'What fucking court case?'

'The one for the nutter who's killed the girl.'

'But, why will you need us for that? It's nothing to do with us. We only found the fucking thing.'

'It's a girl, Steve, not a thing,' Mia pointed out. 'And she didn't deserve what she got. Surely you want to do all you can to help her?'

'It won't do her much good now, will it, so what's the point?'

'You're all heart,' said Mia. 'Now, give us your address.'

'Steve, shall I tell them?' said Johnny, trying to be helpful.

Steve glowered at Mia, then at Nick, and said in a sullen tone, 'Number twelve, Thistle Close, Staples Brook. And, I don't know the fucking post code, so you'll have to look it up.'

'You both live there?' said Mia while Nick took down the details. Johnny gave her an eager nod.

'OK,' said Nick. 'Did you see anybody between Thistle Close and here?'

'No, can't remember seeing anybody.'

'Nobody?' Nick's tone was unbelieving. 'You walked about a mile and a half on a Saturday lunchtime and you didn't see anybody?'

'I said so, didn't I?' Steve jerked his head towards the side window. 'Hardly walking weather, is it?'

'What about cars? Did any cars pass you on the way?'

'Oh, yeah, there was plenty of cars.'

'Good. Give me makes, colours … anything.'

Steve huffed. 'How the fuck should I know? You think I've got total recall or something?'

Nick was about to protest when the fast-gathering dusk was sharply illuminated by a pair of swerving headlights. As they watched, a black Ford Sierra was brought to an abrupt halt a few feet away and DCI Paul Wells emerged from the driver's side, his face wearing its usual cocksure expression. More vehicles followed, bringing scene-of-crime officers, the police doctor – whose job it was to certify that the girl was indeed dead – and lighting equipment to brighten the crime scene so that work could continue well after dark.

At six-foot-five, Paul Wells stood head and shoulders above the rest of the group tiptoeing around the crime scene as though the ground was constructed of broken glass. He was a brash in-your-face Cockney with a soft centre that was rarely revealed. His clothes were the finest that Oxford Street could offer, but Wells, with his lack of finesse, made them look like leftovers from a charity shop jumble sale. A master of political incorrectness, and a firm upholder of the maxim, *do as I bloody well say and never, ever, as I do*, Wells was, however, fair and always good to his team. They could all do a lot worse.

They left the car and approached the DCI, both of them leaning into a gusting wind that was determined to have them off their feet.

'Hello, sir,' said Nick. Mia nodded an acknowledgement.

'What have we got, kiddies? And don't say "nothing, Daddy", unless you want to get me narked before we've even started.' He glared down at them, his face holding an open dare.

Nick offered him the tiny morsels of information they'd dragged out of the Palmer brothers, then they tramped, with heavy steps, towards the body.

Twilight was falling in fast. Ahead of them torches illuminated the dusk, arcing above the piles of rubbish like giant fireflies as officers took advantage of the last dying embers of daylight, their busy silhouettes etched against the brightness of the horizon. At the immediate crime scene officers raced against time to erect the spotlights needed before forensics could begin to photograph the body and its surrounding areas. The air buzzed with tense activity, and a stealthy wind continued to gust, bringing with it the first heavy raindrops that had been threatening for hours.

Pulling his scarf tight around his scrawny neck DCI Wells hastened towards the SOCOs. The professionals moved with incredible efficiency. Working in unison and barely uttering a word they looked as though they communicated on a purely telepathic level. With movements both fluid and firm they erected a tent and the lighting system in no time, ensuring a safe and dry environment in which to fish for those vital clues.

Just then Phil Williams, the police doctor, emerged from the tent and started towards them, pulling off his surgical gloves with a languid ease as he walked.

'I can't tell you much, Paul,' he said, acknowledging Nick and Mia at the same time, 'but she's definitely dead.'

The DCI managed a smile. 'I told you this man was brilliant, didn't I, kiddies? Detect any rigor, Phil?'

'Only a little. She wasn't anywhere near fully stiff.'

'What does that tell us about time of death?'

'Not a lot.' Williams glanced around. 'This cold weather, lack of protection from the elements … these would grossly hinder rigor mortis. She could have been murdered recently and it hasn't set in yet. Or it's just as likely she's already passed through the rigor stages and flexibility has started to return.'

'Not much help there then.' Wells huffed.

The doctor looked towards the tent, his fingers brushing back the few remaining hairs on his shiny scalp. 'Who'll be doing the post-mortem?'

'Don't know. I'm hoping we'll get John Lloyd.'

Williams snorted. 'Rather him than me. It looks like the killer had a field day with that body. Then add the damage done by the rats….' He spread his hands. 'It won't be easy, whoever does it.'

'Is it ever, Phil?'

'Anyway,' said Williams, 'I've done my bit. I'll be off.' He headed for his car, a hand raised in farewell. 'Best of luck.'

They watched him go, Mia marching on the spot to force life back into her frozen feet, Nick toying with the cigarettes in his coat pocket because he was itching for a smoke.

DCI Wells took in his surroundings, his scowl deepening. 'I can't see us being inundated with witnesses on this one. Nearest residential area a couple of miles away. Nobody coming by the place outside working hours.' He shook his head wearily. 'If the Palmer brothers hadn't been foraging she might never have been found.'

Out among the mounds of waste, uniformed officers were calling it a day. Visibility was nil; they'd be better employed elsewhere. So they headed back to the cars, their torch beams bobbing with every step. When the last man had returned Wells motioned for them to group together within the glow of the arc lights. Their freezing faces were pinched, their breath fogged the air, but all stood steadfast and resolute, eager to avenge the horrific slaying of a young girl.

Wells said, 'I know the light wasn't brilliant out there but did anybody see anything suspicious? The smallest thing that looked out of place?' The officers could only shake their heads, their negative replies uttered in hushed, apologetic tones. 'Her clothes must have been dumped somewhere. Why not here? Any signed confessions lying about? No? What about a bag or a container of some kind?'

More negative replies. Wells sighed heavily, was about to stomp off back to his car when Police Constable Daniel Rose stepped towards him and raised a hand, intent on having his say. Wells took in the young officer's eager stance, the enthusiasm that glowed from his face. It was no coincidence that Rose had been the last officer to give up the search that afternoon. Wells knew him to be an ambitious and diligent young man and, to his mind, the force needed more like him, especially in today's politically correct climate. At a time when dangerous crimes were on the increase and the perpetrators of those crimes had far too many rights, recruitment levels were at an all-time low, particularly in small semi-rural areas like Larchborough. It was good to know that enterprising individuals like Daniel Rose could still be attracted to the job. Wells nodded for him to speak.

'Sir, I know you're looking for volunteers to join your team and I want to be the first to apply. I'm fit, sir, and I'm hard-working. I'd search this landfill site on my own, if I had to. I don't mind getting my hands dirty, sir.'

The DCI hid a smile. 'Well, Rose, this is hardly the time but … all right, you're in. I'll square it with your superior officer and I'll see you in civvies as from tomorrow morning.' His gaze took in the rest of the group. 'If anybody else wants to come to Daddy, leave your names on the notice board and I'll sort out who's doing what tomorrow.'

Just then the piercing note of a car horn cut through the night air and Steve Palmer threw open the door of the police vehicle. 'Remember us,' he shouted, hotly. 'We're freezing our fucking balls off here, and all you lot can do is chat.'

DCI Wells held up his hands in a placating gesture. 'Apologies, Mr Palmer, no doubt you have a champagne party to attend this evening and you have a horror of being late.' He turned back to the group. 'Mia, get the brothers back home. The rest of you, back to the station. We'll be using the board room – the superintendent shouldn't object. I've left young Jack sorting out computer terminals and phone lines. He's always boasting about his technology skills – it's about time he showed us just what he's capable of.'

As the rear lights of Wells's Sierra disappeared into the distance Nick lit a cigarette and inhaled gratefully, his back towards Mia. She knew he was still smarting from the humiliation of being caught in Lisa Mackey's flat but she wasn't in the least concerned. Nick knew as well as she did that Wells would have his warrant card if he ever found out about their relationship. The DCI was no prude; he'd be the first to call a spade a shovel or a penis a prick. But there was a line and if any of his officers put so much as a toe across it they were out.

'I'll get the Palmer boys home,' she said, 'and I'll leave you to sulk in peace.'

'Who's sulking?' he said, flicking his cigarette butt into the darkness. It hit the floor in a cascade of sparks.

'It speaks,' she said, arms stretched wide as she looked towards the heavens. 'Hallelujah and God be praised.'

Nick skimmed her an irritated look. 'One of these days you'll start treating me like your senior officer.'

She huffed. 'One of these days you'll start behaving like my senior officer.'

He had to stifle a curse. This was neither the time nor the place for a major row. He could just imagine Wells's face if they both went off on one within spitting distance of a young girl's tortured corpse.

Determinedly ignoring her, Nick crossed to Johnny Palmer. The young man was jumping around in an agitated manner on the back seat of the panda car, his hand raised for attention. When he saw Nick approaching, Johnny opened the door a notch and stuck his head through the gap.

'What's up?' said Nick.

'We don't want a lift home,' he said, with a worried frown. 'I mean, thanks all the same, but we want to walk. Don't we, Steve?'

Steve bent forward, his features set in weary resignation. 'He's worried about the wheelbarrow. He doesn't want to leave it here overnight.'

Johnny nodded. 'It might get pinched if we leave it here all night. Eh, Steve?'

Nick let out a sigh. 'It'll be safe here, Johnny. I'll have a policeman keep an eye on it all night. Come on, mate, let us give you a lift home.'

'No, it's OK, we'll walk,' said Steve. 'He'll only whittle otherwise.'

Johnny clambered out of the car and hung around, shivering, while his brother swiftly followed. They hurried to the wheelbarrow, pulling their thin jackets tight, a friendly banter playing between them.

'We'll be in touch,' called Nick.

He watched them go, breathed a relieved sigh. Now they were alone he could at last tackle Mia. He needed to know how she had found out about Lisa. He was always discreet – or so he believed – and he always made sure his tracks were well covered. His stomach gave a sudden roll. If the DCI got to hear about this there'd be accusations of split loyalties, warnings of flammable information likely to be transferred during the heady moments of shared passion. Wells did his best to come across as a wide boy, one of the lads, but it was pure copper's blood filtering through his veins.

He lit another cigarette and took a long drag, surprised to find that his hand was shaking. Mia was opening the door of her car. He needed to act quickly. He cast a glance at the forensics team to make sure they were still engrossed, then he edged towards her, his mind in turmoil. It was now or never. He took one last nervous drag of the cigarette and tossed it aside.

'Mia …' he said, 'how did you know where I'd be – this afternoon?'

She leant against the car and met his stare, her smile contemptuous in the faint glow from its interior light. 'Let's just say I'm psychic.'

Nick grabbed her arm, his teeth clenched. 'Just tell me … please.'

Mia nodded towards the SOCOs; that smile still visible at the corners of her mouth. 'Careful, Nick, they'll see.'

He let go of her arm, uttered an explosive curse under his breath, and started towards his own car.

'If you must know, one of my girls told me,' she called to his retreating back.

Nick stopped abruptly and turned towards her. 'Which girl?'

'As if I'd tell you,' she huffed. 'And she didn't find out from Lisa, so don't start using your fists.'

He frowned. 'What's that supposed to mean?'

Mia pushed herself away from the car and reached for the door handle. 'I know it all, Nick. I know about the black eyes, the bruises, the violent sex. Of course, some girls like that sort of thing. It's just a pity Lisa isn't one of them.' She gave a shrug. 'I wonder what Wells would say if he knew his blue-eyed boy was just a few steps behind the sick pervert who dumped our girl here.'

Nick stared at her, his laugh sceptical. 'What the bloody hell are you talking about now?'

'Think about it,' she said, stepping into the car. 'Anyway, I'll see you back at the station. And, don't worry, I won't tell the DCI … yet.'

CHAPTER THREE

Larchborough was an old Saxon town, famous the world over for its boot and shoe industry until the 1970s, when short-sighted politicians thought it cheaper to buy abroad and effectively sounded its death knell. The factories that had stood empty for years were now expensive apartment blocks housing those rich city types who thought nothing of commuting the sixty miles to London every day and paying small fortunes for two bedrooms and no garage. Modern housing estates were popping up, virtually overnight, and eating into the surrounding countryside with all the devastation of a rogue virus.

The original part of the town, the nucleus, was an eclectic mix of architectural styles. Gothic revival rubbed shoulders with Victorian terraces; elegant Regency townhouses looked down on tiny workers' cottages.

Silver Street was home to the Church of the Holy Sepulchre – one of only six round churches in the whole of England. And, across the road, casting an ugly shadow over all it beheld, was the police station, all crumbling sandstone and decaying wood.

Silver Street was a busy thoroughfare as a rule, but on this sleepy Sunday morning nothing stirred except for a rickety old milk float rattling noisily across the snow-covered cobbles. It was a different story inside the station, however.

Up in the board room, now the hub of the murder investigation, nerves were jangling. Ordinary officers were normally barred from that most sacred of places. Superintendent Shakespeare saw to that. The board room was his special haven of peace, a space where he could forget about the ugly day-to-day details of police work and enter into companionable discourse with those individuals in local council and the like who had to be appeased if the police service was to get the small crumb of government money that was its due.

When DCI Wells had first hinted at using the board room as his incident centre Shakespeare's hackles had risen sharply, as his mind threw up ominous images of coffee rings on highly polished walnut and curry sauce in the shag pile. Even so he'd relented and, swallowing those words of protest that were jostling for pole position on his tongue, he'd nodded and muttered amiably that all resources would of course be at the DCI's disposal.

As a result, the once pristine condition and comfortable conviviality of the surroundings had now been devastated by the heavy hand of Detective Constable Jack Turnbull, the youngest member of CID; the room was now equipped to deal with all eventualities that might occur in the race to catch their killer.

It was 8.35 a.m. and the team eagerly awaited the arrival of DCI Wells. Those officers seconded from uniformed division stood stiffly in awkward groups, made stilted small talk, fidgeted with ties and stroked lapels with nervous little gestures. They looked more like job applicants waiting to be called in for interview than experienced police personnel there to start a murder hunt.

Mia was hovering by the refreshments table, having her ear bent by Jack. The young DC, red-haired and fiery, was newly separated from Michelle, his wife of five months. He'd returned home from work one day to find his suitcases out

24

on the street and now saw Mia as his very own agony aunt, a willing receptacle into which he could pour his considerable scorn and resentment for marriage and women in general with tedious regularity. It would take more than the brutal slaying of a young girl to divert Jack Turnbull from his egotistical mind-set.

Nick Ford had ensconced himself in a corner, hoping for a quiet moment to go through his notes but, instead, was having to answer a multitude of questions being fired in rapid succession from the mouth of Danny Rose, and his patience was fading fast. A well-chosen expletive was on the tip of his tongue, but before he could let it rip DCI Wells came blustering into the room, a bitter breeze travelling in his wake. A deep hush descended immediately and all that could be heard was the constant rumbling from a decrepit central heating system.

'Right, kiddies, listen up,' he barked, coming to a brisk halt on the dais at the head of the room.

To his left was a table with a large whiteboard beside it. Wells deposited his briefcase on the table and moved the board to the rear of the dais, allowing extra room for his gangling body. Then he faced his team, his scrawny features as near to euphoric as they were ever likely to get.

'It's a bit of a long shot,' he said, 'but I think we might just have a name for our murder victim.'

That dazzling piece of news was met with much murmuring and opening of notebooks. Those officers still standing now pulled up chairs and sat facing the DCI, their moods expectant. Mia threw her shoulder bag to the floor and perched on the edge of a table housing computer equipment. Jack sat beside her, his attention now caught, for the moment, at least.

Wells pulled a 10 x 8 colour photograph from his briefcase and pinned it to the whiteboard. It showed the head and shoulders of a young auburn-haired girl in formal pose. Her large oval eyes were deep brown and brimming with life; her nose straight and finely drawn; her lips full and pulled back in an energetic smile that showed straight white teeth. Those officers at the front craned their necks for a better look at the face that would soon become imprinted on the cinema screens of their memories.

'Meet Hannah Bates,' said Wells, writing the name in large capitals above the photograph with a black marker pen. 'She's been missing since 5.30 on Friday afternoon. Now, I know we haven't got time of death, yet, but I reckon that fits in OK with the timescale of our murder.'

While the DCI ruminated, Mia approached the dais and studied the girl closely. It was hard to say for sure whether the face in the photograph resembled the poor wretch in the rubbish sack. For one thing, the position of the body had been such that the face was mostly hidden. And, by the time they arrived at the landfill, what little light there was had started to fade fast. Nevertheless, if pushed, she would have claimed that the girl in the photograph bore more than a passing resemblance to their victim. She said as much to DCI Wells.

'Couldn't agree more, love,' he said, rapping a knuckle against the photograph. 'The hair's the same ... the deep tan....'

When Nick moved his chair to the edge of the dais Danny Rose moved too, as though connected by an invisible thread. Nick took in a long breath and, silently counting to ten, exhaled slowly in an attempt to rid himself of the irritation that had been building steadily ever since Danny had started his painstaking attempt to pick apart the DI's brain.

Nick said to Wells, 'What have we got on the girl so far, sir?'

'Not much,' he said, making a face. 'We know she's twenty-one years old and lives at home with both parents. We know she works at the Angel Mood shop in Argyle Street and that she left there after work on Friday to meet a bloke in town. We don't know who he is or where they were going to meet. She didn't even confide in her mates at the shop.'

He raised an inquiring eyebrow. 'Now, why is that? Is the bloke married? Is he a wrong 'un?' He shrugged. 'Anyway, the parents phoned in next morning at around eight o'clock when they realized Hannah had been out all night.'

He pointed a long bony finger at Mia. 'I want you to go and see them, darling. They don't know we've got a body yet, so go easy. And take Ginger with you.' Jack's smooth features reddened to match his hair when he caught a couple of the new boys sniggering surreptitiously behind their notebooks.

Nick glanced across at Mia, his eyes narrow slits of loathing. He was just as capable of relating disturbing information in a gentle and reasonable manner. Furthermore, he was the senior officer. Mia had called him Wells's blue-eyed boy but, if anything, the reverse was nearer the truth. In the six months that Nick had been serving in Larchborough Mia had repeatedly been given the best assignments, the cushiest hours, leaving him to fit in where appropriate.

The DCI didn't like him and he wasn't averse to making his feelings known. On one occasion, after Nick had been subjected to a particularly spiteful dressing-down by the DCI in front of half a dozen uniformed officers, Nick had taken him aside and respectfully pointed out that such open displays of disfavour did little to bolster his authority with the rest of the staff. Wells had looked at him aghast, had berated Nick for daring to imply he was anything but fair when dealing with his officers. And he'd advised Nick to take any misgivings he might have about his tenure within the division to Superintendent Shakespeare. He'd done no such thing, of course. Snivelling to the boss would solve nothing. In any case, since then Wells had clearly been trying to soften that tempestuous attitude of his in an effort to raise their working relationship to a more reasonable level. It would be fair to say that a new – if uneasy – truce was now in place.

Even so, Nick's professional ego still smarted whenever Mia was given an unfair advantage. He was smarting now but Mia was unaware. She was conducting a whispered conversation with Jack and scribbling notes furiously.

Nick returned his attention to the DCI. 'What do you want me to do, sir?'

Wells perched on the edge of the desk. 'You're going to the morgue, Nick. John Lloyd's about to do the post-mortem as we speak. John's a good bloke. He knows we're working against the clock. He said I could send somebody round instead of having to wait for his report.' He raised his eyebrows questioningly. 'How's your stomach? Up for it?'

'Don't worry about me, sir, I'll be fine.' Nick was well pleased with that assignment. Observing the dissection of a body in full dazzling Technicolor beat giving routine news of a death any day of the week.

'Good. Who wants to go with him?'

Danny Rose jumped to his feet, arms waving with enthusiasm. 'I will, sir.'

Nick muttered a silent 'fuck' when Wells acknowledged the DC.

'Right, Nick, you'll be taking Danny with you.'

'Yes, sir.'

Wells reached into his briefcase for a thin manila folder and briefly scanned its contents. 'Now, before Hannah Bates left to meet Mr Mystery on Friday she changed out of her work stuff and here's what she was wearing the last time anybody saw her.' He picked up the marker pen and wrote quickly on the whiteboard.

Blue denim straight-cut Levi jeans.(Size 8)

Black woollen polo-neck sweater. (H&M Size 8)

Black lace bra & black lace thong. (M&S Size 32B)

Black knee-length socks.

Black ankle boots. (Office Size 4)

Dark-blue padded coat with hood. (H&M Size 10)

Black woollen gloves.

Black leather shoulder bag.

He turned to face his team. 'Finding these items is a priority,' he said, glad to see they were all adding the list to their notes.

'She was so tiny,' said Mia. 'The bastard doesn't have to be much of a he-man to subdue somebody that small.'

'No, he doesn't,' growled Wells. 'That's another reason to believe the dead girl's Hannah. Both are around the five-foot-one mark. Now, we'll need to do a fingertip search of the whole area. I've asked the super for officers to be brought in from Northampton division. It'll take bloody years to cover that site otherwise. With a bit of luck, they'll be arriving in the next hour or so.'

He wrote SEARCH OF LANDFILL SITE on the whiteboard and, directly underneath, added HOUSE-TO-HOUSE ENQUIRIES. He turned back to see a number of frowns and quizzical expressions. 'Yes, kiddies, I know there're no houses in the immediate area of the landfill, but we'll need to question all those living around the entrances to the site at Dyson Lane and Wallbrook Street. Somebody might have seen something suspicious.'

Wells glanced at his watch. It was almost 9.30 a.m. Time to get things moving. 'OK, all you with jobs, get off now. Everybody else wait behind. We need to decide who's doing what.' He clapped his hands briskly. 'We'll meet back here at five o'clock sharp. And all of you ... bring me something we can use.'

CHAPTER FOUR

Janet Munroe was an angel. Everybody said so. She was a ministering angel whose every waking moment was taken up with thoughts of others less fortunate, whose every working day consisted of one selfless act after another.

In her dual role as senior manager and head nurse at St Stephen's nursing home, Janet tended the sick until they reached some semblance of health. She listened to the world-weary and the depressed until they found their way again. And she offered succour to all those who had loved and lost.

Nothing was too much trouble. She emptied bedpans and commodes, administered drugs and blanket baths, offered encouragement and a shoulder to cry on. She did all this with a sparkle in her eye, a smile on her lips, and love in her heart. Then, at the end of each long day, she went home to her disabled mother and started the whole routine all over again. And she was happy to do it.

Janet's relationship with her father, Frederick Bowman, might occasionally have been fraught and volatile, but she had always been close to her mother, Edith. And, after nursing college, she had started her career at Larchborough General Hospital so they could remain close, both emotionally and geographically.

When Janet's involvement with Robert Munroe – head of the hospital's physiotherapy unit – culminated in marriage during the hard winter of 1973, it was Edith who had kept the train of her dress from dragging across the dirty slush-covered pavements. It was Edith who had made up the bed in their new home prior to their return from Antigua, where they had honeymooned for two glorious weeks.

It was Edith who had held Janet's hand while they waited – hardly daring to breathe – for the pregnancy test to show its tell-tale line. And, it was Edith who had dried her tears after the miscarriage that had devastated them all.

So, when Robert declared eight years ago that he loved another and perhaps they should part Janet went straight to her mother. Frederick was long dead and Edith was lonely, her arthritis steadily worsening. Sharing the house seemed like the perfect option, the only sensible recourse in the whole sorry situation. They could help each other; the two of them against the world.

Even now Edith had the constitution of an ox and a will to match. But she was almost eighty-three, and the years were beginning to tell. Her skin was paper-thin and always ripping, especially on the shins; and her bones were softening rapidly, so breakages were a constant threat. The arthritis now raged through her body, rendering useless all pain-killing regimes. And the scary bouts of breathlessness that she had stoically kept to herself had recently been diagnosed as angina.

In an effort to appear still useful and independent, Edith would grit her teeth and work through the pain. She would ignore the constant complaining of her heart and will it to keep on beating. But Janet could read the signs; she knew well enough that Edith would soon need constant care. And, it was this one particular worry that kept her awake at night.

No one could continually give of themselves, as Janet did, without some sort of comfort zone on which to fall back. Some chose drink to bolster their flagging spirits. Others favoured drugs. Janet's addiction of choice was gambling – on-line betting, to be precise. And her habit had accrued large debts that loomed before her like a black pit into which she threw most of her salary every month.

She had, so far, managed to assuage the monster that lived at the bottom of that pit. But, Janet knew there'd be no hope of pacifying her creditors should she have to give up her career in order to nurse Edith full time.

All she needed was the one big win that had so far remained elusive. With just one lucky turn of the card, one propitious throw of the dice, her worries would be over for ever, and she could give Edith the care she deserved.

And so she kept on betting.

Most evenings, after her mother had gone to bed, Janet would connect to the Internet and gamble into the small hours – winning some, but losing more. She'd had the computer installed in her bedroom for privacy and during her weekends off the connection remained open, on permanent standby, ready and waiting to offer its perfidious entertainment whenever she had a moment to spare.

On that Sunday morning, while Edith enjoyed a lie-in, Janet was well into her second hour of French roulette; her losses for the session now totalled £673. Her optimism remained strong, however, even though her favourite bets – the *cheval* and the *sixaine* – had produced nothing. On a whim she'd transferred to the one number bet – the *en plein*. Number seventeen was still to show itself. Number seventeen wouldn't let her down.

No one knew about her secret vice and Janet wondered sometimes what her mother's reaction would be if she discovered the extent of her borrowing.

A nervous, but wholly enjoyable anticipation usually preceded the application for a new loan. But there was nothing remotely pleasant about the boiling-hot shame that always accompanied the opening of a final demand for payment from whichever loan shark she needed to pacify next. She inhabited a seesaw world of good and bad times, of rewards and forfeitures, and her frazzled emotions followed the same path – drunkenly euphoric after a win; depressed and irritable after a loss.

The latter applied this particular morning, and a crotchety frown crinkled her forehead as she watched the screen, willing the ball to stop with a satisfying rattle at black, number seventeen. It chose red, number thirty-six.

Janet flounced out of her chair in disgust and wandered across to the window for a moment or two of tranquil contemplation. The countryside around Larchborough was typical of the area: flat fields interspersed with the occasional gravelike grassy mound or menacing stony outcrop, creating an illusion of subtle foreboding across the barren landscape. Her bedroom was at the back of the house and looked out on a panorama of frozen fields, resplendent in their coats of undisturbed snow. It was a wonderful view, and one that lifted her spirits as a rule. Today, however, it only served to strengthen her feelings of irritability.

That gang of yobs was there again.

For the past few months, ever since the local youth club had been razed to the ground under the most suspicious of circumstances, the kids who normally patronized the club had taken to congregating in the fields behind Janet's house for their illicit smoking sessions and under-aged drinking bouts.

Janet despised them all, with their loud mouths, their volatile attitudes, and their ridiculous uniforms of oversized jackets and baggy denims with crotches that hung low around the knees like nappies heavy with urine.

If Freud were alive today he might allude to the fact that Janet was using the boys as a focus at which to aim her feelings of anger and helplessness that were generated daily by her gambling addiction. Perhaps, without them, she would have to face the fact that her habit was out of control.

To admit that the boys were simply feeling their feet, practising for future adulthood; to conceive that they were to be pitied instead of derided because the establishment had let them down was simply not an option. They were yobs and she wanted them removed from her sight. She'd mention the problem to Mia Harvey the next time they met at St Stephen's. Maybe she could offer a solution.

The decision made and her emotions once more under control Janet returned to the computer screen and that bashful number seventeen.

Russell and Shirley Bates lived at number 45 Larchwood Lane, in an area known as Stratton Heights. It was a fairly recent addition to the town, mostly brick-built semis inhabited more often than not by those from the council houses and starter homes who viewed themselves as upwardly mobile. The more generous plots accommodated timber-framed detached properties, mostly commissioned by the richer contingent, and openly lusted after by those in the semis.

While she negotiated the narrow country lanes leading into Stratton Heights, Mia speculated with Jack as to the property most likely to be purchased by a factory worker and a doctor's receptionist, whose two children, while still living at home, were grown up and in full-time employment.

Those few scraps were all the information they had, so far, on the Bates family. Should it turn out that their daughter, Hannah, was the corpse at the landfill, however, every tiny detail of their existence would soon become available for the police to pick over and dissect.

Mia hated those first few days of a murder investigation, when everyone involved was working blind and all that could be achieved was the annihilation of everything that was good in the lives of those closest to the victim. She had given news of death on many occasions, but each time was as difficult as the first. No one was ever prepared for the worst, no matter how long the person had been missing. They all clung to hope with such tenacity, as though to do otherwise would anger the ancient God whose job it was to deliver, intact, all innocent beings to the bosoms of their families.

She could well imagine Russell and Shirley Bates, pacing the floor as they waited for news, edgy and argumentative from too much coffee and not enough food; each one silently blaming the other for the predicament in which they now found themselves.

No doubt they believed life couldn't get more desperate, more frightening, than it was now. How wrong could they be? In no time at all their desperation was set to increase a hundredfold. Mia was filled with dread at the thought of what lay before them, and all she could do to keep that dread at bay was make banal comments about the Bateses and the type of property they might favour. It was shallow small talk, and totally unsuitable for the occasion, but absolutely necessary because it helped to keep her mind away from the inevitable.

Neither Mia nor Jack was familiar with Stratton Heights – Larchborough's criminal element tended to break the law in close proximity to the town centre – but they decided, after much deliberation, that the Bateses probably lived in one of the semis.

A discussion about exorbitant property prices followed, leading Jack into a rant about selfish and rebellious Michelle, who still expected him to pay the mortgage every month, not to mention half of the rest of the bills, even though she was still living in the house and enjoying the new furniture, new white goods, etcetera, while he was having to make do with a put-you-up in the spare bedroom at his sister's house.

Mia sighed inwardly. Why did their every conversation have to end with a monologue about Michelle? She wanted to scream at him to give it a rest but she restrained herself and, staring doggedly ahead, steered the car around a tight left into Larchwood Lane, only to find that number forty-five was a Victorian end-of-terrace cottage.

It was a large place, double-fronted, with pink rendering that gave it a warm look even on a freezing February morning. There was no front garden, only a thin strip of pavement, so the white double-glazed door opened directly on to the road. A pair of brown ceramic pots, each holding a dwarf evergreen tree, flanked the door. Mia noticed that the nets hanging at all four windows were gleaming white, and that the black gloss on all guttering and downpipes looked newly applied. Number forty-five was easily the best maintained in the row. The other three cottages, although not neglected, looked tired in comparison, as though a little tender loving care would not go amiss.

They parked a short distance along the road, in front of a tall untidy hedge of hawthorn and brambles that helped to keep from view a dilapidated hay barn and a second building, used to house pigs if Mia's sense of smell was to be believed.

They left the car and took in their surroundings, careful to avoid the patches of ice that made lethal the slippery tarmac. The four cottages stood alone, apart from the farm buildings and a monstrous viaduct, a mere 200 yards to their right, which allowed the safe passage of trains on the Silverlink line from London's Euston station to Birmingham New Street and beyond.

Clutching her shoulder bag as though it were a lucky talisman, and wrapping her black woollen scarf more tightly around her neck, Mia nodded to Jack that now was the time and marched smartly towards the pink cottage.

There was no bell, so Jack grabbed the brass-plated knocker and rapped it firmly three times. Almost immediately the door was pulled ajar by a small blonde-haired woman whose attractive features showed the ravages of a sleepless night.

'You're the police,' she said. It was a statement, not a question.

Mia gave a nod. 'I'm Detective Sergeant Mia Harvey,' she said, offering the woman her warrant card. 'And my colleague is Detective Constable Jack Turnbull.' She stood stiffly on the threshold, willing her apprehension to subside. 'May we come in? There's been a development.'

CHAPTER FIVE

Without a word the woman pulled open the door and stood aside for them to enter the narrow passageway. The space was dark, its low-wattage bulb failing miserably to throw any light beyond a sturdy shade of pink plastic. The walls were covered with an embossed paper sporting an intricate pattern in greens, pinks and purples on a background of white.

Mrs Bates ushered Mia through a door to their right and she found herself in the living area, a long thin room with tall windows at either end. The room was drowning in various shades of pink. The carpet was pink, the curtains, the cushions scattered in untidy abandon upon the three-piece suite which, in order to fit into the greater picture, held threads of pink within the overly fussy pattern of its upholstery. As her fleeting glance took in everything, Mia fancied she was sinking fast into a nightmare world of sickening candyfloss, and she wondered briefly where the husband and son fitted into this predominantly feminine environment. Any further thought was put on hold, however, by the sudden appearance of Russell Bates, who stumbled eagerly through a door at the end of the room, his face a picture of hope.

Mia stepped further into the room, allowing space for Mrs Bates and Jack, and they all stood silent for a long moment, a motionless tableau of undisguised dread.

Mrs Bates was the first to speak. She said, 'Please … make yourselves comfortable,' and proceeded to plump up the cushions on a pair of armchairs that stood on either side of a teak fireplace which was home to a number of china ladies, their crinoline skirts resplendent in green and, of course, the obligatory pink. While Jack settled into one of the chairs, Mia took the other, thankful for the warmth emanating from the lively flames, licking and darting around in a grate full of artificial coals that dutifully glowed red for realistic effect.

Russell Bates sat huddled close to his wife on the settee. He was a short, squat man, with the broad powerful shoulders and bulky thighs of one who revelled in physical exercise. He was around the middle forties but already his closely cropped hair was showing signs of grey. His features were pleasing, his eyes a warm brown; and he gave off an aura of quiet authority. Mia saw a man who was totally secure in his masculinity; a man who would enjoy indulging his wife, even to the point of existing in a world of girly pink.

Shirley Bates had the look of a woman used to having her own way, a woman who wanted for nothing. She wore expensive clothes, even for sitting around the house. And it was clear that image was of great importance for, even today, with the disappearance of their daughter weighing heavily on their minds, she had still found time to fix her make-up, to style her hair.

They made a handsome couple, and as they clung together, totally secure in their love for each other, Mia felt the faint stirrings of envy. There they sat, on the threshold of probably the worst disaster ever to befall a human being, but she knew instinctively that they would be all right. They would pull through. They would draw upon the other's strength, display a united front, and overcome all eventualities. Would she ever know such love, such devotion? She hoped so.

For now, though, Russell and Shirley Bates remained silent, strangely reticent, fearful of furthering the conversation in case the content was not to their liking. Mia took a few moments to unravel her scarf and unbutton her coat. When she spoke her voice was steady although her heart was pounding.

She said, 'I'm afraid there's been a development—'

'Yes,' said Mrs Bates, 'you said as much at the door.'

Mia leant forward, hands together, forearms on her knees, her gaze sympathetic. 'A body has been found.'

All at once Shirley Bates collapsed against her husband, face in hands. 'Oh, God … oh, my God,' she groaned into his shoulder.

He held her tightly, whispered loving words of support into her hair, but all the time his enquiring eyes held Mia's. He, for one, needed to know the truth. He was desperate to know the truth.

He said, 'Is it Hannah?'

'We don't know, yet, Mr Bates. But the girl does fit Hannah's description.'

Russell Bates glanced from Mia to Jack, his expression a puzzled frown. 'We gave you Hannah's photo. You must know if it's her.'

Mia took in a long breath. 'It's not always that simple, I'm afraid. Sometimes….'

She paused for a moment, her thoughts in turmoil. How could she tell them that rats had made a meal of their daughter's face? That diabolical image would live with them for ever.

'Let me see her, then. I'll soon tell you if it's our Hannah.'

Shirley Bates looked appalled. 'No, Russell, you can't—'

'Listen, love, they're not sure it's her. They've got the photo and they're still not sure,' he said, holding his wife at arm's length. 'So, chances are it's not. It's better to know … eh, love?'

Mia pictured again the damage done by the rats, and she shuddered. 'We'll know more after the post-mortem. At the moment, there's nothing to say for sure that the girl we've found is Hannah. We're here to get as much information as possible so we can find out for sure.'

By now Shirley Bates had pulled herself together. She sat quietly at the husband's side, gripping his arm tightly, as though even the thought of letting go would be enough to court disaster.

Mia delved into her shoulder bag for notebook and pen, all the while conscious of the mordant ticking of a tall grandfather clock standing sentinel against the wall behind her.

She found a fresh page in her notebook and turned her solemn glance towards them. 'If we could go back to Friday … We need to know everything that's happened since then.'

'But we've already been through it once,' said Russell Bates.

'I know.' Mia's tone was apologetic. 'And I know it's not easy for you to go over it all again, but we need to do this, Mr Bates, in order to get the investigation started properly. Do you understand?'

He gave a hesitant nod and patted his wife's hands as they tightened their grip on his arm.

'Hannah works at the Angel Mood shop in Argyle Street – yes?'

Mr Bates nodded. 'She's been there about five months. She likes it. There's four of them working there. They go out at weekends. You know … nightclubbing … having a good time….'

'Did they plan to go out on Friday night?'

'No,' said Mrs Bates. 'Hannah told me not to get her any tea on Friday. She said she was meeting somebody straight from work. A friend of her fiancé, Colin, she said. He was going to help with Colin's case, apparently.'

For the first time during this encounter Russell Bates's genial features dissolved into an angry mask. 'That bugger,' he huffed, his brow creased disapprovingly. 'Why does she

40

want to marry him? A lovely girl like our Hannah…. She could have anybody, and she goes and picks him.'

Mia said, 'Why don't you like Colin, Mr Bates?'

'Because he's a bloody thief, that's why. He's inside now, on remand, the bugger.'

'What? In the Marshcroft Remand Unit, over at Stratton End?'

'That's right. He's being done for aggravated burglary this time. He'll get about three years, if there's any justice.'

'Russell … love….'

'I'm sorry, Shirley, but it's got to be said. The lad's no good, and I don't want him sniffing round our Hannah.'

'Well, it's too late for that. The service is booked, and the reception's all organized.' She turned on him, her expression an open rebuke. 'You know as well as I do, Russell, that Hannah can wrap you round her little finger. She always gets her own way, so stop pretending you're in charge. You're not helping matters.'

Mia had the distinct impression that this was an old argument. It had a repetitive, well-worn air, and it was holding up the interview. She needed to get things back on track.

She said, 'This mysterious person who was supposed to be meeting Hannah after work on Friday – he was going to help with Colin's court case?' Mrs Bates nodded vigorously. 'And you're sure it was a man she was going to meet?'

'I'm positive. Hannah said he was in a position to help, but she didn't say how, or who he was.'

'Would any of the girls at the shop know?'

'We've already asked them. They don't know any more than we do.'

'Is Hannah usually so secretive?'

'We always tell each other everything in this house. It's just that … well … if we'd known this was going to happen, we'd have quizzed her more. As it is….' Her voice trailed off and she gave a pathetic little shrug.

Her husband pulled her close, uttered comforting sounds. He said, 'We've tried ringing her mobile, but it's dead.' His face contorted in misery. 'It's not like our Hannah to be without her mobile.'

Throughout the conversation Jack had been making his own notes. He leant forward, perplexed. 'What's Colin's surname?' he asked.

'Fowler,' said Russell Bates. 'Colin Fowler.'

The name rang no bells. 'You said he was up for aggravated burglary this time. So, this isn't his first brush with the law, then?'

Mr Bates made a face. 'It's his third time in front of the magistrates, but it'll be his first time in crown court, if it gets that far. He's been arrested for nicking stuff twice, but the CPS never had enough evidence. That lad was born lucky, if you ask me. Of course, Hannah doesn't believe for one minute he's guilty. She reckons he's been set up.' He gave a derisory snort. 'But, I mean, two different firms in different parts of the country? It's hardly likely. The lad's a thief, and not a very good thief either, otherwise he wouldn't keep on getting caught. Try telling that to our Hannah, though.'

'He stole from work?' said Jack.

Mr Bates nodded. 'He's in the security business. Started off in Birmingham. Got himself a group of lads he hired out to firms. He'd do a bit himself when he was short-staffed. He's not frightened of work, I'll give him that. But he got greedy. He was guarding a firm that made sun-beds and he decided to help himself to a few, but he got spotted on the CCTV and that was it.'

'What happened then?' asked Jack.

'He's got the gift of the gab, that lad, and the nerve to match. He moved here, recruited another load of lads, and started all over again. But the stupid bugger hadn't learnt his lesson – he started pinching again, didn't he?'

'We don't know that for sure,' his wife said, hurriedly. 'They couldn't prove it.' She favoured them with an eager look, completely without guile. 'I don't want you thinking

42

our Hannah would waste her time on a good-for-nothing. Colin's a lovely lad, really. He came clean to us about his past, didn't he?' She shot her husband a scathing look. 'Trouble is, nobody's good enough for her in Russell's eyes.'

'Now you know that's not true. I just don't want her throwing her life away on him.'

'Precisely,' said Shirley Bates.

Mr Bates bristled. 'And what's that supposed to mean?'

'You can't for one minute believe that Colin might be good for our Hannah. You'd hate to believe she might have made the right choice for herself. Like I said, you don't think any lad's good enough, so there's no point in talking about it.'

'No, you're wrong there, Shirley. I'd—'

'If we could please stay on track,' said Mia. The pair fell silent immediately, their expressions contrite.

'Sorry,' said Mrs Bates. 'It's just that … well … you know.' She gave a slight smile and lifted her shoulders in a sweet coquettish gesture.

The moment Mia glimpsed that small and seemingly insignificant movement, her spirits sank and she pitied the woman desperately. For it told that the burden of grief was slowly lifting. Shirley Bates was taking comfort from their chat about her daughter. She was seeing hope where there was none. She was allowing herself to become lulled into a sense of security that was as false as it was temporary.

Mia was convinced that the post-mortem report would conclude that their body was, indeed, that of Hannah Bates, but she had allowed the girl's parents to believe otherwise. Her own cowardly reticence had prevented Mia from carrying out her duties properly and, as a result, the couple sitting opposite and watching her with such hope and expectation would soon experience a despair so terrifying in its intensity that the breath would be sucked from their lungs and the strength from their limbs. And she alone was to blame. She should have come clean at the outset and prepared them for the worst. She cast a surreptitious glance towards Jack. God alone knew what he must be thinking about her expertise; she had hardly set the best example for him to follow.

She sighed heavily. 'We'll need to interview Colin Fowler. But for now, if we could just have a few more details about Hannah….'

'OK,' said Mr Bates. 'Although I'm certain she'll turn up. I mean, you've got the photo and you're still not sure. It's somebody else's poor kid, I'm certain of it.'

'Let's hope you're right,' she said, unable to meet his eyes. 'Does Hannah wear an engagement ring?'

'Yes,' said Mrs Bates. 'It's a nice little ruby surrounded by a circle of diamonds. It's a pretty little ring. Colin chose it, and I must say, he chose well.'

Mia made a note. 'Does she have any distinguishing marks? Tattoos? Birthmarks?'

The blood ran from Mrs Bates's face as the full significance of that question registered in her mind. 'No … no birthmarks. But she has got a tattoo. It's a little black mouse, just above her right hip. Russell went mad when he found out she'd had it done.'

'How old is Hannah?' Mia asked.

'Twenty-one,' said Mrs Bates, increasing the grip on her husband's arm. 'She'll be twenty-two in May – the fifth.'

'And the wedding's all booked, you said?'

'Yes, for August the fourteenth.'

'Unless the groom's banged up for three years,' was Mr Bates's unhelpful aside.

'Russell … please,' said his wife, visibly relaxing as she focused for a moment on happier events. 'They're having the service at St Matthew's, over at Stratton End. Do you know it? The graveyard backs directly on to the River Stratton. Got flooded a couple of years back after those heavy storms. Everybody was up in arms because the council said they couldn't do anything to stop it happening again.' She stared into the middle distance, a faraway look in her eyes. 'They chose St Matthew's because that's where we got married. The photos should look lovely with the river in the background.'

'I'll bet,' said Mia. It was all she could think of to say.

Jack had started to fidget. A discussion about weddings, marriage, or anything even loosely associated with the subject of matrimony was the last thing he wanted, given that his new bride had proved, so early in their union, to be such a self-willed and cantankerous bitch. But, to have to sit there, listening to a proud mother outlining the details of her daughter's big day, when there was more than a passing chance that the body of that daughter was, even now, being meticulously dissected on a marble slab in the local morgue was too much, even for his callous soul.

He was on the verge of diverting the line of questioning towards safer ground when a faint rumbling began in the distance and the walls of the cottage began to vibrate. He aimed a frown at Mia as the rumbling quickly increased in volume, and was about to make a comment when the rhythmic clatter of a train reached deafening proportions and the house shook with an intensity that made him fearful for the future of the foundations.

Russell Bates cast a fleeting look at his wristwatch. 'That'll be the 9.30 from Euston, due in Edinburgh at precisely 6.50 tonight.'

'He's a train enthusiast,' said Mrs Bates, in answer to their questioning glances. 'That's why we chose to live here.' She managed a smile. 'His anorak's hanging up, isn't it, love?'

In a matter of seconds the din had receded into the distance and a peaceful silence reigned once more. 'I hope your walls are solid,' said Jack, with a wry smile.

'Don't you worry about this house,' said Mr Bates. 'It was built well over a hundred years ago, and the viaduct's nearly as old. They built things to last in those days. This block'll still be here long after we're all dead.'

His last words hung in the air with an awesome resonance, and the breath caught in his throat as he forced himself to face the true reason for the police visit, and the question they were all pussyfooting around with such skill. Was their precious Hannah already dead? The possibility that she was hung over them with all the heaviness and foreboding of a thunder cloud, causing a painful constriction in the middle of his chest.

A telling silence had settled in the room and Jack was about to break it when they heard the sound of a key in a lock and the front door was thrown open.

'That'll be our Tom,' said Russell Bates, thankful for the interruption to his disturbing line of thought.

'Oh, good,' said Jack. 'I was going to ask about him.'

Shirley Bates mouthed, 'He's been out with Candy, our Yorkshire terrier,' and settled back on the settee to await his entrance. 'We're in here, love,' she said, with a lightness that failed to show on her face.

They heard the sounds of trainers being kicked off, the heavy panting of a well-exercised dog, and then Tom Bates filled the doorway with the tiny Candy tucked neatly under his right armpit. They made an incongruous pair, given that Tom must have been all of six-foot-two and weighing around sixteen stone, while the dog was about six inches tall and a couple of pounds at the most. Jack wondered how the boy could possibly want to be seen with a dog that was no bigger than a rat, especially as its long blonde fringe was tied back with a ribbon of shocking pink.

And what made the coupling all the more surprising was the fact that Tom was an all-out Goth. He wore, with obvious pride, the usual uniform of mismatched, oversized garments of regulation black to which all self-respecting charity shops would give a wide berth. His lank shoulder-length hair was dyed a dull matt-black to match the liner around his eyes and his face was painted a deathly white, giving him the look of an anaemic vampire in need of a drink. A touch of lipstick, so dark that it exaggerated horribly the redness of his mouth, completed the look.

The detectives stared, wide-eyed, until Tom said in a quiet voice, 'I'll take her in the kitchen, Mum. Her paws are filthy.'

'All right, love.'

They watched him tread, with steps surprisingly light for one so large, towards the door at the end of the room, all the while muttering good-naturedly to Candy as she put up a constant and monumental struggle for her freedom.

Mia was the first to speak. 'He's a big lad, your Tom.'

'Isn't he?' said Mrs Bates, with pride in her voice. 'But he's a sensitive soul, a real gentle giant.'

'He takes after his mum,' said her husband. 'Hannah's more like me.'

'She's a proper Daddy's girl, is our Hannah,' said Mrs Bates, patting her husband's knee. Suddenly, her face fell. 'Tom's taking all this really badly. We've hardly had a word out of him since we realized our Hannah was missing.'

'How old is Tom?' asked Jack.

'He's just turned nineteen,' said Mrs Bates. 'We had a party for him at the community centre, and about—'

'And where does he work?' Jack continued, smartly.

He didn't want to appear rude but there was no time for chat. Shirley and Russell Bates were of the type that was only too eager to relate anything and everything about the day-to-day minutiae of their lives. For anyone working in the police service and similar professions such openness was a refreshing change from the reticence of those tight-lipped individuals who made the retrieval of even the smallest fact an epic battle.

If Mrs Bates was at all put out by the sharpness of Jack's tone, she didn't let it show, and her manner remained genial as she said, 'He works for Tesco's at the moment, in the loading bay. It's only temporary, mind. He's having a year out. He's got a place at Oldham University, starting in October. He'll be doing optometry.'

Mia grinned. 'Let's hope he drops the Goth image before then. He looks awful.' As the last word left her mouth, she grimaced. Had she really made such an ill-mannered remark? 'No disrespect intended, of course.'

'None taken,' said Mrs Bates. 'Russell was a punk when I met him – safety pins through his earlobes and trousers halfway up his shins. My dad nearly had a fit the first time I took him home. And now look at him.' She nodded towards the kitchen. 'All kids go through phases. Tom's a lovely lad, basically, so I'm not going to worry about a bit of make-up and some hair-dye.'

'Right, then,' said Mia, pocketing her notebook and pen. 'I think you've told us everything we need to know for now. Do you think we could just have a quick word with Tom before we go?'

They found him leaning against the sink, arms folded, glumly watching the tiny dog as she pounced on her biscuit treat with all the gusto of a lion attacking its kill. After the perfunctory introductions, Mia sat at the kitchen table with the boy's parents while Jack bent down to pat the dog.

Candy recoiled from the intimidating stranger, her lips pulled back to show a row of surprisingly sharp little teeth. Then she growled, the sound holding about as much menace as a cat's contented purr. When Jack jumped to his feet, feigning terror, they laughed. Even Tom, whose white mask looked as though it might crack at the slightest twitch, managed an uneven smile. The little dog had broken the ice beautifully.

Mia said, 'Do you know why we're here, Tom?'

His nod was brisk, causing the mane of hair to fall across his face. 'It's because Hannah's pissing about,' he said, pulling the fringe to one side with fingers that were surprisingly long and elegant.

'Tom,' said his mother, sharply. But the word was loaded with too much affection for it to be seen as an actual rebuke.

'Do you know where Hannah went after work on Friday?'

'Mum and Dad have already asked me that,' he said, clearly annoyed. 'If I knew, don't you think I'd have said?'

'Of course, you would,' said Mia, in a placating tone. 'That's the trouble with our line of work. We have to keep going over the same stuff. It does my head in, sometimes.'

The boy shrugged: a couldn't-care-less gesture. Mia ignored it, and said, 'Do you get on well with your sister, Tom?'

'He does,' said Mrs Bates. 'They're as good as gold, the pair of them.'

Mia acknowledged her interruption with a forced smile. 'Now, the loading bay at Tesco's … it's just round the corner from Argyle Street, isn't it?'

That sullen lift of the shoulder again. 'So?'

'So, that means you work very near the shop where Hannah works.'

'So?'

'What time did you finish work on Friday?'

He looked away, not bothering to answer, and started to drum his fingers on the draining-board, his impatience all too evident. Shirley Bates desperately wanted her son to create a good impression in front of the police. She knew only too well how quickly his mood could deteriorate into a full-scale strop. He was heading for one now and, in order to create a diversion, she said, 'Tom works shifts, DS Harvey. Either six till two, or two till ten.'

'What shift were you on last Friday, Tom?' When Mrs Bates took in a breath to speak, Mia held up a hand to stop her. 'I want Tom to answer, if you don't mind.'

'Come on, son,' his father cajoled. 'Let's all do the best we can for our Hannah – eh?'

Tom was intent on watching the dog strutting around the kitchen, lurching from one giant shoe to the next and bravely tapping each one with a tentative paw. And just when it seemed that his brusqueness was impenetrable he skimmed a rueful look at Mia. 'Two till ten.'

'I beg your pardon,' said Mia, being deliberately obtuse. 'I didn't hear you, Tom.'

'He said two till ten,' said Mrs Bates, trying to be helpful.

The woman's attractive features were now marred by an anxious frown. Her stress levels were rising rapidly and Mia's heart went out to her. She not only had the worry of a missing daughter to contend with, but also the repugnant ways of a son who looked and behaved like one of the living dead in the throes of a pubescent hormonal surge. She was hardly a woman to be envied.

'Mrs Bates,' said Mia, softly, 'I know you're only trying to help but I need Tom to answer our questions.'

Over by the sink Tom delivered a loud theatrical sigh and cast his disdainful gaze from Jack to Mia. 'What if I don't want to answer any more questions?'

Mia raised an eyebrow. 'Why wouldn't you, Tom? Have you got something to hide?'

He let out a huff and said, 'As if,' in a tone that brimmed with bravado. But the hand that crept to the lower part of his face, effectively hiding his mouth, told an altogether different story. Anyone who had studied body language would state that such a move was tantamount to the covering up of a lie. It would seem that young Tom Bates was holding something back. But, why?

Keeping her own body language open and unguarded, Mia said, 'It's up to you, Tom. If you don't want to answer our questions, that's fine.' She got to her feet and said to the anxious parents, 'Try not to worry. We'll be in touch the minute we have any news.' At the door she turned back, her eyes on Tom. 'And, rest assured, we will find out the truth. We always do.'

CHAPTER SIX

Over at the morgue John Lloyd had warmly welcomed Nick and Danny, promptly fixing them up with white coats and latex gloves so they'd be able to observe the post-mortem procedure in close proximity to the body without any risk of contaminating the evidence.

Entering the morgue, located in a line of single-storey laboratories at the rear of Larchborough General Hospital, was like stepping into a giant freezer. And it was with much reluctance that the two men shrugged off their heavy jackets in order to slip into the flimsy lab coats. The jovial John Lloyd – his own bulky frame well insulated by a dense layer of body fat – was oblivious to the icy temperatures, and he let rip a loud guffaw at the sight of his guests' pinched features and chattering teeth.

'I bet you a fiver,' he said, leading them towards the body, 'that you forget all about the bloody cold the minute I make my first incision. They all do.' That laugh came again, loud and hearty. Here was a man who enjoyed his work.

The room where the body lay was large and fitted out with white cupboards below stark white marble worktops littered with glass jars, metal trays holding test tubes, ominous containers of varying sizes, and countless other pieces of paraphernalia with which the pathologist reached his conclusions.

Danny's stomach rolled with a sickening fascination as his hungry gaze took in everything. And he was suddenly reminded of a long-forgotten childhood memory. He was five years old and alone with his alcoholic father on Christmas Eve because his mother had deserted them the previous week for a wealthy lover who'd whisked her away in his sporty red car to start afresh in a place where nice things happened, a place where grasping little boys and drunken, bad-mouthed husbands were forbidden to go.

Danny had been blamed for his mother's audacious behaviour and was told on that special night – by a father whose mental faculties were shrivelling as quickly as he could pour the Scotch – that there would be no Santa Claus for him. Oh, no. His father went on to relate in crisp detail a plethora of horrific facts about a species of hostile goblins that were always in search of young boy's hearts, eyes, kidneys, tongues, ears and feet – everything, in fact, needed to build a brand new race of terrifying monsters. And they'd be coming for Danny, one night when he was least prepared. Danny soon discovered, even at such a tender age, that sleep deprivation was a terrible thing.

He smiled to himself now, remembering the time with a feeling akin to fondness. It was, after all, the only childhood he'd known. And his gaze fell upon the mysterious containers. The five-year-old Danny would have imagined them full to the brim with body parts, waiting in quiet contemplation for the moment when the mad professor – John Lloyd? – prepared to build his gruesome prototype.

'Let's get started,' said Lloyd, ushering them towards the marble slab. 'You two watch from the opposite side, well away from the action. We don't want you spattered with blood.'

'Blood doesn't gush from a dead body,' said Danny.

'Well done ... well done,' said Lloyd, giggling wildly. 'You spotted the deliberate mistake. Give the man a lemon.'

The detectives exchanged a look. Neither had witnessed a post-mortem before and both were looking forward to the experience in a morbid, detached, sort of way; but they hadn't counted on the pathologist's persistent joviality which, even after a mere five minutes, was beginning to grate. For now, though, a pleasant silence ensued, and all three took a moment to assess the girl's body.

She lay stretched out, all stages of rigor mortis completed. And she had been scrubbed clean. Now that the forensic scientists had taken sufficient samples of all dirt, debris, and blood smears from the body the pathologist needed it to be in pristine condition so that even the tiniest of pinpricks would not be overlooked.

Nick noted, almost subliminally, that the girl's tan covered the whole of her body. So, she was either a naturalist, or it was indeed fake. And he committed to memory the tiny black mouse tattooed on her right side just above the hip.

John Lloyd spoke into a tape recorder, giving date, time, and names of all present. And then he conducted an intense study of the body, examining every inch from feet to head and mentioning, as he progressed, all cuts, slashes, gouges and marks for the benefit of his future report. By the time he'd finished that initial investigation Lloyd had documented a whole catalogue of injuries.

No fewer than thirty-nine cuts and slashes had been counted – the number was undoubtedly higher, but damage caused by the rats had made a final count impossible – and Lloyd concluded that these had been made by a short-bladed instrument, quite possibly a Stanley knife. The majority were less than an inch deep, and all had been inflicted while the girl was alive.

An attempt had been made to hack off the right breast – again, while the girl was alive. Either the Stanley knife had proved to be inadequate for the task, or the killer had simply lost his nerve.

The eyeballs had been poked and prodded with some force, resulting in a number of tears across the retinal areas and a leaking of fluid within them. John Lloyd – his usual grin now replaced by a scowl – confessed to the tape recorder that his all-abiding wish would be that this awful act had been committed after death, but he had no way of knowing either way.

A close examination of the mouth, vagina and anus revealed that all three orifices had been crammed full of detritus from a heavily wooded area: bits of twigs; blades of grass; a dark-brown soil rich in organic matter; a smattering of gravel....

Bruising around her neck was consistent with the positioning of large hands and long fingers, indicating that the perpetrator was most probably a man. The arrangement of the bruises – the majority being at the back of the neck – showed that the killer was facing his victim at the time of strangulation. And the fact that the bruises on the right side of the neck were darker than those on the left showed that he was right-handed.

John Lloyd was unable to ascertain, during this initial investigation, whether strangulation was indeed the cause of death. One indication – ruptured capillaries in the eyeballs – had been negated by the damage inflicted by the killer. And the second clue – congestion of the face – had effectively been hidden by the feeding frenzy of the rats. He would have to wait and see what the internal examination revealed.

At the moment of death, when the heart stops beating, all of the blood is pulled by gravity to the lowest point in the body. In Hannah's case this proved to be the backs of the shoulders, buttocks and legs. The pooling of blood in these areas told the pathologist that the body was placed on its back for a number of hours after death and then moved to its final destination at the landfill site. That small snippet did little to further the investigation, but it was a place for them to start.

With that preliminary examination completed to his satisfaction, Lloyd selected a scalpel from the orderly row of surgical instruments to his right. 'I will now start the postmortem proper by making that famous Y-shaped incision to the front of the body,' said Lloyd, wielding the scalpel dramatically.

As the sharp blade travelled easily through the dead flesh, blood bubbled weakly behind it. Nick looked towards Danny and observed with rising distaste the excitement that brought to life his usually thoughtful features. Nick was finding it hard to bond with the young officer, and knowing that he himself was to blame did nothing to quell the undercurrent of misgivings that had been his constant companion since the two of them had been thrown together.

Danny was proving to be the consummate partner: considerate, keen to pull his weight, slightly prepossessing, and prone to a touch of hero worship whenever Nick felt inclined to divulge anecdotes about past successes. He had an open, comfortable way about him and should have been easy to like, but Nick found something mildly distasteful about the eagerness with which the man approached his work. But there had been a time, not too long ago, when Nick had had that eagerness, that enthusiasm for his own career. Perhaps he disliked Danny because the man was a mirror image of the way he used to be and, therefore, a constant reminder of the past. Thoughts of that past did no good at all, for Nick knew that they brought with them a myriad of truths that he preferred to ignore.

Nick's profound love for his job died the moment he heard news of the car crash that had fatally injured his wife, Angela, and their unborn child.

Angela had been seven months pregnant when she decided to drive up to Inverness to spend time with her parents. The two-week break was meant to be a "breathing space", a time for them both to "choose what it was they wanted". The marriage was breaking down rapidly and they "needed to do what was right for the baby". Those platitudes, and many more like them, were on Angela's lips constantly, grinding him down, driving them further apart. When the day of her departure eventually arrived Nick felt nothing but relief. For two weeks he'd be able to concentrate on the job.

He'd have two whole weeks without the raging hormones and the tiny library of pregnancy books that was making his life intolerable.

Nick was in charge of the drugs squad, and his team had been keeping close surveillance on a number of Manchester's top drugs barons for the better part of two years. Now all threads of a finely tuned operation were about to be pulled together, culminating in the biggest raid in the division's long history. And all Angela could do was gripe and complain about the unsociable hours and the fact that he always put his workmates before her. So they'd agreed she should take the Scottish break.

It had always been Nick's habit, before any long journey, to give the car a complete overhaul. This time, however, with Operation Aardvark almost coming to the boil, he gave it no more than a cursory glance, even though Angela had been complaining about the sloppy brakes for more than a week.

She got as far as the Scottish border before a patch of black ice sent her skidding into a thick circle of evergreens and then oblivion. A verdict of accidental death was recorded at the Inquest. Damage to the car was too extensive for any of its workings to be checked, so Nick would never know for sure whether faulty brakes were responsible for the crash. It made no difference, anyway. He would always blame himself. The baby was a girl. And the spot that held her ashes was marked by a brass plate bearing her name. Sophie Violet Ford. His daughter.

Nick shuddered violently as an insidious coldness travelled the length of his spine, plucking him immediately from the awful depths of his reverie. He could almost taste the self-disgust, the revulsion that stuck in his throat like bitter bile. An involuntary groan escaped his lips, causing John Lloyd to throw him a quizzical glance.

'Feeling queasy, DI Ford?' The pathologist's eyes danced with devilment as he dangled a handful of bloody entrails in front of Nick's face before dropping them with little grace into the gaping hole that was the girl's abdomen. Other organs followed, and then Lloyd closed the chasm with a succession of neat little stitches.

Nick checked through his hastily scribbled notes and pocketed his notebook. DCI Wells would be well satisfied with what they'd got so far. For now, though, Nick was desperate to get out, to breathe fresh air again. Watching the post-mortem had been an interesting experience, but he hated the stark, clinical surroundings. There was something about the place that set his skin crawling. He glanced across at Danny, was about to say, 'Let's go,' and found him staring down at the body, his eyes wide like a child's. Danny must have felt Nick's piercing stare, for he looked up quickly and grinned.

'Do you know something, Nick? I reckon I was born to do this.'

Nick gave a rueful shake of the head. 'Get a life, mate ... before it's too late.'

They heard the demonstration before they actually saw it. As Mia eased a slow path along the series of sleeping policemen that was Trafalgar Road a cacophony of loud chants, drum rolls and piercing whistles approached them from the opposite direction.

'Oh, shit,' Jack muttered softly.

'What?' said Mia, frowning.

Keeping her speed to a near crawl, she turned the car into Campbell Square and pulled up sharply. About 200 yards ahead and marching purposefully towards them was a group of about fifty protesters. And from the look of it they meant trouble.

They made a diverse bunch: senior citizens sporting their sprightly defiance with pride; young world-weary mothers pushing buggies and prams, the youngsters within them looking frozen and perplexed; older kids causing havoc on the periphery with football rattles and whistles; and college types with their stripy scarves and important-looking folders tucked under their arms.

Above their heads unwieldy banners displayed a number of legends: MANOR HIGH BELONGS TO THE COMMUNITY, and, HANDS OFF OUR SCHOOL, and, JUSTICE FOR THE CHILDREN. Each protester was warmly wrapped, and many carried thermos flasks. If the powers that be had hoped the weather would keep them off the streets they could think again. Those people were clearly in it for the long haul. On the pavements, at either side of the mob, a handful of uniformed constables, blue with cold, dithered ineffectually.

Jack scanned the crowd, his anxiety evident. 'Oh, shit,' he said, again.

'What?' said Mia, looking towards the protesters for some sort of clue.

'You see that pair mouthing off to Tony Wright...?'

Her gaze followed his pointing finger and she saw a young couple shouting loudly to a police officer whose brief was obviously not to provoke. They were ordinary types, respectable, probably in their early thirties. The woman wore a green waxed jacket, khaki combat trousers, and an orange knitted bobble hat with matching scarf that clashed horribly with her red hair. The man was good looking, but too academic for Mia's liking. A date with him would probably consist of two halves of lager and a lengthy discussion about the merits of cancelling all Third World debts.

PC Wright was holding up his gloved hands in a calming gesture. Given the choice he'd rather be smashing his truncheon against the sides of their heads by now. Tony had never been on speaking terms with patience.

'Do you know them?' Mia asked Jack.

He let out a sigh. 'That's Mandy, my sister. And the twat with her is my brother-in-law, Stuart.'

'They're the ones you're staying with?'

He gave another sigh and nodded dejectedly. 'I've got to get out of there, Mia. I'll lose my mind if I don't.'

'Then talk to Michelle.' Dear God, had she actually said the name out loud? Mia closed her eyes and fell back into the seat. OK, all she could do now was pray that the mistake wouldn't lead to another boring account of the poor girl's faults and failings. 'What's your sister doing here, anyway?' she said, hurriedly trying to lead him away from the subject of his wife.

'Stuart teaches English at the Manor High School—'

'Oh, I thought he might be a teacher,' said Mia, with a grin.

'Yeah, you can tell them a mile off, can't you?' He nodded towards the demonstration. 'The Manor's likely to be merging with Larchborough Comprehensive, and everybody's having a fit about it.'

'Why?'

'It'll mean redundancies for a start, and teaching standards'll drop. And all for the sake of a building plot that'll only hold about twelve upmarket properties for those rich bastards from London.' He rolled his eyes and mimed a yawn.

Mia laughed. 'That's an argument you've heard before by the sound of it.'

'Once or twice,' he said, pulling a face. 'I'm not kidding, Mia, that's all they talk about. It's like living with a cracked record and the needle's stuck.'

It must run in the family, she thought, hiding a grin.

The protesters were slowly drawing near and Jack sank down in his seat. 'Let's get out of here before they see me,' he said, pulling up his coat collar.

'OK, hang on.'

While the crowd steadily approached Mia displayed her considerable driving skills by executing a perfect three-point turn, even though little space was available. And then she was back in Trafalgar Road, verbalizing her contempt for the traffic-calming measures laid out by a sadistic council.

They were heading for the Marshcroft remand unit. After leaving the Bates's house Jack had phoned to ask permission to interview Colin Fowler. As it was Sunday the unit was being managed by a skeleton staff so no one from the governor's offices was available. But Jack spoke to the head warden, who promised to keep free the hours between two and four o'clock.

Mia called DCI Wells and filled him in on the morning's events, giving special importance to the tiny black mouse that Hannah had tattooed on her right hip and the ruby and diamond engagement ring that she wore at all times.

Wells's tone was brooding. Nothing had come from the house-to-house enquiries so far. And the fingertip search taking place at the landfill site had yet to produce anything remotely resembling the dead girl's clothes. Wells's ears pricked up sharply at the news that Hannah's fiancé was in the remand unit.

'The unit's no more than a mile away from the landfill. Ain't that right, darling? A mile and a half at the most?'

'Oh, my God, yes, sir. I'd forgotten that.'

It was definitely food for thought. And as food was beginning to dominate Jack's thoughts, and as they still had a good hour to kill before their appointment at the unit, they decided to stop off for a quick lunch at the Prince of Bengal, where the All-You-Can-Eat buffet cost a mere £5.99, and the chicken biryani was to die for.

CHAPTER SEVEN

The Marshcroft remand unit nestled snugly between the local abattoir and a sewage works, the stench of which choked the whole of Larchborough whenever the wind was a gusting north-easterly. Its high barred windows looked out over acres of desolate scrubland that had once been a thriving agricultural venture, but which now lay barren due to a dispute over ownership. And that bleak atmosphere seemed wholly appropriate, in Mia's view, for the housing of criminal types destined for more secure accommodation.

The route to the unit was treacherous, its unadopted roads were largely ignored by a council whose budget for snowploughs and gritters was pitifully inadequate. Tightly packed snow – inches thick in places – and black ice kept Mia's speed to a careful twenty miles an hour. And it was with more than a little relief that she turned into the small car park at the rear of the imposing red-brick building.

They left the car and felt at once the full force of a bitter northerly wind that was able to whip unheeded across the flat and barren landscape. With coats pulled tight they hurried across the slippery tarmac, eager to be inside, and were almost at the security door when Mia's mobile phone buzzed from the depths of her shoulder bag.

It was Paul Wells with news that Nick had reported seeing the tattoo of a small black mouse on the body in the morgue, and that a ruby and diamond ring had been handed to him by the pathologist, along with a nine-carat gold signet ring and a gold chain holding a nine-carat gold St Christopher medal. There could be no doubt now – they were officially hunting the killer of Hannah Bates.

Mia suggested she should be the one to break the news to the girl's parents; she'd promised to be in touch when new information became available and it was only fair she should keep that promise. The DCI agreed, but strongly advised that Colin Fowler should be kept in the dark until she'd told them. And so it was with heavy hearts and much trepidation that they followed the hulking figure of the head warden to a quiet and private interview room.

At the door the warden shot them a warning look. 'Be careful with him. He plays mind games.'

The detectives exchanged glances. 'Thanks for the advice,' said Mia.

Colin Fowler was waiting for them, his sizeable bulk resting awkwardly on the moulded seat of his black plastic chair. He sat at a plain wooden table, its surface heavily stained and defaced by a multitude of past residents who'd offset their boredom by gouging out their initials, thus assuring themselves of lasting notoriety. A pack of cigarettes and a red disposable lighter lay on the table at Fowler's right hand. Two more plastic chairs waited in readiness for the detectives. Another warden stood inside the room, to the left of the door, his steady gaze focused on his charge.

The detectives took their seats while Fowler's intense blue eyes appraised them critically, his full mouth hinting at a smile. He was an attractive man with a clear complexion and lean angular features that made him appear far older than his twenty-five years. His blond hair was thick and expertly cut, its healthy sheen catching the light of the overhead fluorescent strip.

Mia delved in her shoulder bag for notebook and pen, her movements deliberately unhurried. The first impressions of any interviewee were vital. Facial expressions and body language could throw up a multitude of significant observations before even a word had been uttered. Would Colin Fowler show his true colours with the smallest of gestures? An anxious frown? The biting of a lip? The constant fumbling of nervous fingers?

She cast a surreptitious glance in his direction and found him observing her with a wry smile, his demeanour completely relaxed, forearms on the table, fingers loosely clasped. If he was at all intimidated by their presence, then he was hiding it well. The introductions were made, and he said, 'To what do I owe this pleasure?' in a clear and powerful voice, the West Midlands accent only discernible in the vowel sounds.

'We bring bad news, I'm afraid,' said Mia.

'Is there any other kind in a shit hole like this?' he said, still smiling.

'I'm afraid we're here to tell you that your fiancée, Hannah Bates, has been missing since 5.30 p.m. on Friday, and we're beginning to fear the worst. Any idea where she might be?'

Fowler's blue eyes widened in horror. 'I wasn't expecting that,' he said, his tone a breathless whisper. 'I thought....'

'You thought what?' said Mia.

'I thought you'd come to tell me I was free to go … that you'd found the bastard who'd set me up.'

'Afraid not, Mr Fowler.'

Jack said, 'Do you know where Hannah might have gone?'

Fowler shook his head. 'How would I know? I've been stuck in this hole for the past three months. How could she just disappear?'

'She was meeting somebody after work on Friday,' said Jack. 'A man. He was going to get you off, apparently. Any idea who that man might be?'

'No.' Fowler reached for his cigarettes. 'Can I smoke? Do you mind?'

'Feel free,' said Mia.

His shaking fingers fumbled with the packet and half a dozen cigarettes tumbled haphazardly on to the table. 'Shit,' he muttered, trying to put them back.

Mia said, 'We've been told Hannah visited you just over a week ago – on Saturday, the seventeenth. Did she mention the fact that somebody had offered to help with your case?'

'No.' He lit the cigarette, watched smoke rise lazily towards a ceiling already brown with nicotine.

'Think back, Mr Fowler. What did the two of you discuss?'

He shrugged. 'We talked about the wedding more than anything. My two sisters are gonna be bridesmaids. They're due to come down and be fitted for the dresses. We talked about that, about the place settings at the reception, the invitations.... It was all wedding talk. She never mentioned the court case. She knows I'm gonna get off. She knows I'm innocent.'

Jack said, 'Does she talk about anybody specific during her visits – anybody her parents might not know about?'

Fowler gave a mournful shake of the head, his cockiness all gone. 'Oh, God ... Shirley and Russell.... How're they holding up?'

'They're doing OK,' said Mia. But not for much longer. 'What exactly have you been accused of, Mr Fowler?'

Straight away he was on the defensive, stubbing out his cigarette with heavy-handed brusqueness. 'What's that got to do with anything?'

'Hannah went off with someone connected with your case, however slight that connection might be....' Her pleading eyes held his for a moment. 'Mr Fowler, surely you must see that anything you can tell us might be useful. God knows, we've got precious little to go on as yet.'

The man gave a hesitant nod. 'I've been set up – that's the truth of it. Somebody's got it in for me, and if I could find out who....'

'What have you been accused of?' Mia asked again.

Fowler sank back in his seat, his shoulders sagging. 'I've got a security firm – Securicom. I hire out minders, security guards, doormen – you name it, and my boys'll do it. I hired out three of them to oversee the opening of that new upmarket jewellery store, Compton's, in Castilian Street....'

'I know the one,' said Mia. 'They lost around two hundred thousand pounds worth of stuff in an armed robbery the night before they were due to open.'

'That's right. And the bastards left the manager and one of my boys bleeding from superficial wounds.'

'How did your name come into it?'

Fowler huffed. 'I told you, I was set up. I'd been done for theft in the past. Petty stuff … and I got off, anyway. But somebody made sure I'd be in the frame this time. They planted a cup with my prints slap bang in the middle of the crime scene.'

Jack's laugh was highly cynical. 'You sure that wasn't you, being just a touch forgetful?'

For a mere second temper showed in Fowler's eyes. 'I'd hardly shoot one of my own boys.'

Jack shrugged. 'You said yourself the wound was only superficial.'

'Oh, fuck off,' Fowler muttered. 'You're the same as all the rest.'

'OK, that's enough,' said Mia. She thought for a moment. 'Let's say you've got an enemy, somebody who wants you put away for a while. That same guy might possibly want to get at you through Hannah. Have you had a bust-up with anybody in the recent past? Have you trodden on any toes? Think, Mr Fowler, whatever you come up with might be important.'

He stared into the distance, his frown deepening. 'I've had to sack a couple of the boys. They got to like using their fists, and that's not good for business. My reputation's important to me. I like getting work from top class businesses—'

'Like Compton's,' said Jack.

'Exactly.'

Mia said, 'Have you ever been into heavy stuff? Drugs, for instance?'

Fowler sat upright, shook his head vigorously. 'No way. There's no way I'd ever get into that. I've seen too many of my mates get wasted by that shit.' He stared at Mia, his blue eyes wide and entreating. 'Listen, all I've ever wanted is to run a good business and make enough money to live the good life. It's what Hannah wants, as well. I want to be able to give my kids all the things I never had.'

Jack smirked. 'You'll have me crying in a minute.'

Fowler lunged from his seat, teeth bared. 'Fuck you,' he said.

'Enough,' said Mia. 'Pack it in.'

Jack's laughing eyes continued to goad Colin Fowler, who was on the verge of muttering another expletive when the door to the interview room burst open. Mia turned to see a huge bear of a man, dressed in prison warden's uniform. He pulled himself up fast. His face – partly concealed beneath a full covering of beard – was a mask of surprise.

'Oh … apologies,' he said, his warm voice holding the hint of a Highlands accent. 'I thought the room was vacant. I'm sorry.'

His smile was good-natured, and it caused a warm stirring in Mia's solar plexus. She smiled and held his gaze for a long moment before the door was quietly closed. When she turned back Fowler was frowning and picking at a set of initials on the tabletop. He was clearly perplexed.

'What's wrong, Mr Fowler?'

He looked at her, his eyes uncertain. 'Sorry? Oh, it's nothing….'

'Let us be the judge of that.'

That frown came again. 'It's just….' He nodded towards the door. 'Well … Chris Lennox … that's the bloke who just barged in … he's been trying to wind me up since day one.'

Now it was Mia's turn to frown. 'How do you mean?'

Fowler shrugged. 'I don't know, just little things, like making me late for meals so when I get to the canteen there's nothing left … making me exercise longer than the others … taking away my privileges for no reason. He's started flirting with Hannah in front of me, in front of everybody. It's been going on for weeks.' He flinched. 'Everybody's been taking the piss out of me something rotten, saying he was having Hannah behind my back, saying I could kiss the wedding goodbye…. I was just wondering….'

'Oh, great,' said Jack, grinning widely. 'Are you suggesting that Hannah met a prison warden after work on Friday? Oh, please….'

Fowler flashed an angry glance at Mia. 'You did ask.'

'Hold on a minute,' she said. 'What was Hannah's reaction to the flirting? Did she like it? Did it make her feel uncomfortable?'

Fowler grimaced at the memory. 'Let me put it this way – she didn't beg him to stop.' He quickly held up a hand. 'I'm not saying she's a slag or anything. My Hannah's a good girl – I wouldn't be marrying her if she wasn't. But she's … well … let's just say she's accommodating and she likes a laugh.'

'How does that make you feel?'

'I'm hardly over the moon. We argued about it. I said to her, you're making me look a right nonce in front of everybody….'

'And what did she say to that?'

He tut-tutted. 'The usual – that I've got to let her be herself, that I've got to stop trying to change her. She doesn't try to change me, so fair's fair. Like I said, the usual.'

Mia said, 'Why do you think Mr Lennox likes getting at you? Do you wind him up?'

Fowler's hands flew to his chest. 'Me? I've done nothing.'

Mia considered the man. They had seen no evidence of the 'mind games' hinted at by the head warden. So far he'd shown them the persona of a normal, genuine and trustworthy individual, but even with one eye closed she could see straight through it. Jack could, too. Why else would he be provoking Fowler at every turn?

Colin Fowler was clearly a ladies' man. Even Shirley Bates had fallen for his smooth charm, whereas her husband growled with distaste at the very mention of his name. Supposing Fowler pressed the same buttons in Chris Lennox as he was pressing in Jack – and Russell Bates, for that matter. Wouldn't Lennox be as eager to provoke as Jack obviously was? But Lennox was a warden; he had his job, his professionalism to protect. He couldn't be seen to be reacting harshly to an inmate; he would have to find more creative ways to retaliate, hence those outlined by Fowler. And if Hannah had enjoyed a little harmless flirting with the man – well, why not? Mia could understand completely if that had been the case. After just a few fleeting moments in the man's presence she'd detected an almost palpable charisma that few women would be able to resist.

She said, 'Could you give us the names of the men you had to sack, please?'

'Sure, but if you need to interview them, you'll have a long wait.'

'Why?'

'Because one of them dropped dead with an aneurysm about three months ago, and the other one's in Los Angeles, minding Jennifer Lopez – lucky bastard.'

Mia sighed inwardly. This quizzing of Colin Fowler had been necessary, if only to eliminate any friends, colleagues and acquaintances from their enquiries, but she couldn't quite quash the feeling that this whole interview had been a complete waste of valuable time.

'OK, Mr Fowler, thanks for seeing us,' she said, hastily dropping her notebook into the depths of her bag. 'If we need to speak to you again, we'll be in touch.'

They got to their feet, their chairs scraping noisily against the concrete floor. At the door she turned back to find him watching them, his face a mask of utter despair. That emotion was genuine, she was sure of it. Not even a conman as proficient as he could conjure up a look so heartrending.

Without warning, she found her dislike of him melt away a little.

'Good luck with the court case,' she said, warmly.

'Oh, never mind me. Just find Hannah. Will you? Please?'

CHAPTER EIGHT

Up in the board room DCI Wells surveyed his team and a small part of him quivered with an almost juvenile delight at the hint of cigarette smoke that hung languidly in the air above their heads. Superintendent Shakespeare had long ago declared that room a no-smoking zone. Even his grandiose friends from the lofty offices of local government had to light up their fat cigars in the corridor. And, of course, the Government had now banned smoking in the work place. Nevertheless, Wells had decided to countermand the ban. He'd been in the grips of the habit for a good many years until finally managing to quit and he knew how persistent the craving for nicotine could be, overriding all other thought processes in its quest to be salved. And he didn't want the concentration of his officers compromised for the sake of a cigarette, as long as they kept it to a moderate level.

Anyway, they deserved a smoke. Many of them had been sorting through the decaying muck on the landfill site for up to seven hours with hardly a break. It wasn't the most luxurious of introductions to CID, and Wells wondered how many of them were now wishing they'd stopped to consider the boring downside of working on a murder case before so willingly raising their hands to volunteer. Quite a few, if their morose expressions were anything to go by. They'd worked well, though, never complaining once about the bitterly cold conditions and never giving less than one hundred per cent – no easy task when, at the end of it, nothing worthwhile had been achieved.

The gentle murmur of jaded conversation was almost drowned out by an antiquated central heating system that clattered and bumped constantly, like a torrent of disembodied souls trying vainly to rouse the living. But at least the room held a warmth that, little by little, was thawing out the pinched faces of his team.

He waited while they filled coffee cups and pulled up chairs, puzzled as to why Nick Ford should choose a spot on the opposite side of the room from Mia. He'd noticed before that those two were failing to gel and it wasn't good for morale. He made a mental note to find out why, and set about bringing his notes into some semblance of order.

When they were all seated Wells banged the heel of his hand on the table. 'OK, kiddies, let's make a start.' He walked in front of the table and perched on its edge. 'You all know by now that our body is Hannah Bates. I believe the girl's parents have been given the news….' He aimed a questioning look towards Mia.

'Yes, sir. We called in on our way back from the remand unit.'

'How are the poor sods?'

'Not good, sir. They wanted to see the body but we thought that might not be a good idea, the state it's in. Trouble is, now they're left wondering how bad the damage is.' She heaved a sigh. 'I'm thinking they might be better off actually seeing her. At least, then, they can stop imagining.'

'No,' said Wells, with a definite shake of the head. 'I think they're better off not viewing.'

'OK, sir. Oh, and they asked when they could collect Hannah's jewellery. I said as soon as they liked. All right?'

'I can't see why not. Forensics have already been over it.'

He took a moment to sift through the papers on the table. 'Right, the bad news first. We've completed our search of the landfill site and come up with bugger all. And if you're wondering where our extra officers are....' He glanced at his watch. 'I'd say they're back in their own canteen, by now. The super didn't want them on our patch for a minute longer than was necessary, to keeps costs down.' His features settled into a grimace. 'What does it matter that I never had time to grill them properly – or to thank them, even.'

Nick said, 'What about door-to-door, sir?'

'Another big fat zero. Mind you, with the short days and nobody inclined to venture out much in this weather, it's hardly surprising. But on a more positive note, forensics have found that traces of soil taken from the body don't match the soil at the landfill. And that ties in with what the pathologist found. Isn't that right, Nick?'

'Yes, sir.' He flicked through his notes to the relevant page. 'Judging by the way the blood had settled in the body, Mr Lloyd confirmed that Hannah was lying on her back for some hours after death and was then moved to the landfill site where we found her in the kneeling position inside the sack.'

'So,' said Wells, 'we now know that Hannah was killed somewhere else. It's not much, but if forensics can pinpoint where the soil came from it'll give us something to work from.'

Danny Rose raised a hand. 'Can they do that, sir? Can they tell us exactly where the soil came from?'

'Within a given radius, yes.'

'Wow,' said Danny, his eyes widening in surprise.

Wells stifled a sigh. The force was desperate for enthusiastic officers like Danny, it was true, but the lad was beginning to get on his nerves. 'OK, tell us what else was found during the post-mortem.' When Danny took in a breath, ready to launch into a detailed description, Wells was quick to stop him. 'Not you, Danny ... I want Nick to tell us.'

Nick cleared his throat. 'Cause of death was definitely strangulation.'

'OK,' said Wells, writing it on the whiteboard.

'And there was no actual evidence of sexual intercourse – no semen found, anyway – but that doesn't mean it didn't occur. There was plenty of bruising, but Mr Lloyd reckons that was probably caused by some sort of implement being rammed repeatedly into the vagina, rather than by rough sex. And, interestingly, an amount of debris was found inside the vagina – twigs, moss, dirt … stuff like that. It hampered his investigation. But going back to whether sex was involved – Mr Lloyd couldn't find any trace of lubricant from a condom. Again, though, that might be down to the debris. He definitely believes the killing took place in a wooded area.'

'So,' said Wells, continuing to list the facts in large letters, 'the murder was most probably committed in the open air, and the motive was possibly not sexual. Or, rather, it's possible the killer didn't need to climax inside his victim to achieve satisfaction. That small fact might prove to be useful later on, should we need to involve a profiler. So, could he have stripped off her clothes to take away any possible fibre evidence? Carry on, Nick.'

'The dirt and what-have-you found in the vagina had also been stuffed into the mouth and anus—'

'Really?' said Wells, felt-tip pen poised in mid-air. 'This is a new one on me. Any ideas why he might have done that?'

Once again Danny Rose held up a hand. 'Perhaps she was making a noise, sir, so he filled her mouth to shut her up.'

'Nice one,' said Wells, adding it to the list of points on the board. 'And, if that's the case, it could mean the murder was committed in a place where her screams might have been heard by others. What else, Nick?'

'The body had been slashed repeatedly with a small-bladed knife – possibly a Stanley knife or something similar. And the killer had tried to slice off the left breast, but the attempt had been aborted, making Mr Lloyd wonder whether the weapon was a Stanley knife and it just wasn't up to the job.'

Nick concluded his post-mortem information with an account of the damage to the girl's eyes, then Mia related their conversation with Colin Fowler. Wells's face took on a hangdog expression when it became clear that nothing new had been gleaned. His ears did prick up, however, at the news of animosity between Fowler and the warden, Chris Lennox.

'We'll get him in,' he said, printing the man's name on the whiteboard. 'Let's see what he has to say.'

'But, sir,' said Mia, 'you don't really think a prison warden would be capable of inflicting the kind of damage done to Hannah, surely?'

Wells gave her a knowing look. 'Who'd have thought the good Doctor Shipman could have killed so many of his patients?' He threw his marker pen on the table. 'It's imperative we keep our minds open to all possibilities, kiddies. I hope to God this murder is a one-off but we can't afford to relax our vigilance for a minute. Like I said, stay open to all possibilities.'

Mia was reading through her notes, teeth biting lower lip. 'In that case, sir, I think we should get Hannah's brother, Tom, into the station. He was a bit evasive during our first visit.'

'If so, why didn't you tackle him the next time you called?'

She frowned. 'He's a typical stroppy teenager, sir, and I think we'll have more luck with him in a proper interview situation. I've an idea he's hiding something about Friday. Get him away from his adoring mother, away from home ground, and he might just open up.'

It would seem that the yobs were upping their game. They had, so far, been content with merely littering the fields beyond Janet's house with empty lager cans, cigarette packets, disgusting pages torn out of pornographic magazines. And keeping everybody awake whilst doing so.

Now and again they'd start a blaze in the neat hawthorn hedgerows that bounded the fields. After the last fire Janet had begged them to look into their hearts and find compassion for the animals and insects suffering at their hands. But they'd simply laughed in her face and complained about the cold. It was an annoying state of affairs, but hardly dangerous to human life.

Things were different now, though. During the last couple of nights Janet had felt a significant shift. She'd annoyed the boys with her constant complaints and now it was payback time. They'd started to dismantle the fence that divided her garden from the fields. She'd watched them from the safety of her bedroom as they parried with the wooden slats, wielding them heavenwards like light sabres, and laughing as they observed with satisfaction the full extent of their destruction.

Any threats of informing the police were pointless. The yobs knew as well as she did that the Larchborough force was grossly undermanned. All available officers would be concentrating on catching the killer of Hannah Bates. The local paper was full of it. They wouldn't want to waste time and precious resources on minor disturbances. The boys were outside police radar and they knew it.

Janet felt powerless, entirely at their mercy. Had she brought this on herself? And what would happen next? When the barrier between them was completely obliterated, would they converge on the house? Had she, by championing the faceless creatures that lived in the burning hedgerows, put herself at risk; worse still, had she endangered the life of her beloved mother? Edith was, after all, a sitting target. Would they show as little charity to her as they did to the rabbits and the spiders and the mice?

Janet's nerves were stretched tight and ready to snap with the slightest of nudges. And the gambling was no longer a comfort. If anything it was only adding to her feelings of desperation because she was losing heavily. Over the weekend alone £2,000 had been wasted on the hope of the ball rattling to a stop on number seventeen. It was money she didn't have. And there was little chance of borrowing it because that morning's post had included rejections from all three of the loan companies that she had approached in the past week. Janet was fast running out of options.

She'd hoped for a quiet word with Mia Harvey about the vandals; but Mia was too busy with the murder enquiry to visit her mother. She'd phoned to say as much, asking Janet to give Barbara her love and to say she'd be in as soon as possible. Janet had mumbled something appropriate into the telephone while her gaze was fixed with horror on the loan rejection slips that lay before her on the desk. As a precaution Janet had made sure all correspondence from the loan companies went to St Stephen's. It wouldn't do for Edith to find out about her secret life. Edith had enough on her plate, worrying about the future; Janet didn't want her brooding about the present as well.

She glanced at her watch. It was ten past eleven. Less than an hour to go before the lunchtime drugs round. After carefully closing the door to her office Janet pulled the Yellow Pages from the bookcase and took it to her desk. The L section was well-thumbed, containing as it did the ten and a half pages of loan companies, most of whom had already been approached.

But there must be one she hadn't tried. There must be one that would help her. Hardly daring to breathe, and with heart pounding in her chest, Janet opened the heavy book and began her search.

CHAPTER NINE

The incident room was awash with officers, all intent on being the first to puncture a hole in the vacuum of despondency that had formed itself so securely around their enquiries. Some sat with telephone receivers glued to their ears, working through long lists of members' names retrieved from the multitude of nightclubs and casinos scattered in Larchborough's town centre. The plan was to compile a database of all those who had partied and gambled away the hours between Friday night and Saturday morning. Those people would then be shown Hannah's photograph in the hope that memories would be jogged. It might be a vain hope, but one that needed to be tested.

Others liaised by telephone and e-mail with all police divisions throughout the United Kingdom, hoping to match the unusual *modus operandi* of their killer with any unsolved murders still mouldering within their files. The rest took calls generated by the many inches of newsprint that had so far been written about the murder inquiry. Past experience told them that the majority of those seemingly helpful individuals were mostly cranks and attention seekers after their fifteen minutes of fame. But all calls had to be taken in case one nugget of solid information should be loitering amongst the grains of grit.

The main members of Wells's murder squad sat huddled with the DCI around a corner of Shakespeare's precious walnut conference table, sharing tasks, discussing strategy, and taking the opportunity to enjoy a much-needed coffee before their next round of frenzied activity. Their dark moods were matched perfectly by the stagnant air that stank of stale sweat, and a strange mix of fervent expectation and hopeless resignation.

'If only we knew what the motive was,' said Wells, staring morosely into his coffee mug. 'Perhaps then we could put together a picture of our man. Why did he target Hannah specifically?'

'Maybe she reminded him of somebody from his past,' said Mia. 'Somebody he's anxious to obliterate. Only, he couldn't get rid of the real thing because … oh, I don't know … she's already dead, or killing her would be too risky, so he picked a substitute.' She spread her hands. 'It's common among serial killers.'

Nick snorted. 'In CSI – Miami, or NYPD, perhaps, but this is real life.' He turned to Jack. 'Who's she got you playing? Cagney or Lacey?'

'What's your theory, Nick?' Mia goaded. 'Or are you too thick to have one?'

DCI Wells failed to notice the underlying tension behind their supposedly innocent parrying; he was too busy downing his coffee. But, Jack was all too aware. Mia had said nothing to him about Nick's off-duty activities, but she made no secret of the fact that there was little love lost between them. Jack had no time for their childish spats. He had real worries to keep him awake at night, real dilemmas to consider. They should walk in his shoes for a day; then they'd know what real hatred felt like.

Michelle had asked him to meet her after work. She'd been coy about voicing the reason, but he guessed it had something to do with money. She always needed money – to get her tan topped up, or her nails redone, or her hair highlighted. Talk about high maintenance….

With shoulders drooping under the weight of his self-pity, Jack fiddled sullenly with his polystyrene cup and tried to keep his attention on the conversation. It wouldn't do to antagonize the DCI. There was no way he could manage on a uniformed constable's salary again, not with that bitch of a wife sucking him dry.

Danny Rose, eager to be at the heart of things, was saying, 'Our killer must be very clever, sir. He's left no clues, so far.'

Wells nodded glumly. 'So far. But as soon as forensics can tell us where those soil specimens came from we'll be able to get some momentum going. We're only stuck now because we don't know where to look.'

Danny said, 'Didn't I read somewhere, sir, that the majority of killings are committed by close relatives of the victim?'

'Spot on, mate.' Wells sank back in his chair, a deep frown creasing his forehead. 'And that's why I'm starting to worry about this one. There's not one likely suspect in her immediate family. They're all ordinary, decent people, unless you count the boyfriend – although he's hardly what you'd call a hardened criminal – and he was banged up when the murder took place. You can't get a better alibi than that.'

'We've still got Hannah's brother to go at,' said Mia. 'He's definitely got something to tell.'

'You think?' said Wells, his tone despondent. 'No, I want a go at Chris Lennox. Phone the unit, Mia. Let's get him in.'

Mia raised a dubious eyebrow. 'If you like, sir, but if you want my opinion—'

'I don't,' Wells cut in. 'Lennox has a history of antagonism with the boyfriend. It ain't much, I agree, but it's a place to start.'

Nick sniggered openly at the DCI's rebuff, and Mia shot him a disparaging look before breaking away from the group to put in a call to the remand unit on her mobile. Danny followed her and stopped at the refreshments table to top up his coffee.

Nick said, 'Shall I do the Angel Mood shop first, sir?'

Wells nodded. 'And take Danny with you.' When Nick swallowed an angry curse Wells gave him an old-fashioned look. 'Anything wrong?'

'Nothing, sir,' he said, shifting his weight in the chair. 'But I thought I might take Jack this time. You never know, a different perspective might make all the difference.'

Jack gave Nick a surprised look and opened his mouth to argue. He liked partnering Mia and had no intention of altering the arrangement.

'No,' said Wells, 'you and Danny have worked well together, so far. So have Mia and Ginger here. I see no reason to change now.'

'Sir,' said Mia. 'You'll never guess.'

'You'd better tell me then.'

She slid into her seat, pocketing her mobile. 'Chris Lennox has asked for some leave ... completely out of the blue.'

'Has he, now? Where's he gone?'

'That's the funny thing,' she said, frowning. 'He wouldn't tell anybody. I've just been on to the guy we liaised with yesterday and he said Lennox put in for two weeks' leave, to start immediately, almost as soon as we left the premises.'

'We shouldn't read anything into it,' said Wells. 'Nobody at the Unit knew Hannah was dead at that point.'

Danny leant forward eagerly. 'But Lennox would, if he'd got anything to do with the murder.'

Wells nodded. 'I take your point. Even so there's probably an innocent reason for the man to suddenly bugger off. And the fact that he kept quiet isn't really significant. Not everybody likes to have their private business known by all.'

'Especially Chris Lennox,' said Mia. 'He's a real loner, apparently. He'll pass the time of day, but he won't go out of his way to talk. And he never socializes outside working hours.'

Wells gave a snort. 'We can hardly lock the man up for not wanting to go for a drink after work.'

'But I thought you wanted to talk to him, sir?'

'I did,' Wells said, scratching the stubble on his chin. 'I do. But I'm only clutching at straws, really, on account of how close the unit is to the landfill. He's away for two weeks, you said? OK, we'll just have to wait till he gets back.' Wells let out a long breath. 'In the meantime, let's concentrate on Hannah's brother, find out if he has got something to hide. And, Nick, you get as much information as you can from the girls at the crystal shop. There'll probably be aspects of Hannah's life that the parents know nothing about. Nobody's as innocent as that pair thinks she was.' He got to his feet, signalling the end of the session. 'Right, off you go, kiddies, and bring something back for Daddy … please.'

He wandered across to the dais and started thumbing through a pile of papers, his back towards the rest of the room. Nick lounged in his seat, a smile flashing in his eyes as he looked towards Mia, intent on causing a quarrel.

Straight away, she bit. 'What are you playing at, Nick – undermining me in front of Wells?'

He grinned. 'It's so easy, I couldn't resist.'

This was the first time they'd been together for any length of time since their spat at the landfill site. Nick was clearly still itching for a fight.

Jack shot a wary glance towards Wells. 'I want no part of this,' he said. 'I'll wait for you down in reception, Mia.'

She nodded and stayed silent while he left the room, closely followed by a curious Danny Rose. 'You think you're so bloody great,' she spat. 'But I know different….' She wriggled her little finger in front of his face, implying a deficiency on his part of a sexual nature. 'You really should keep the washroom door closed after your shower, Nick. You never know who might be passing.'

'I didn't realize you made a habit of lurking around the showers,' he said, with a vicious laugh. 'But, then again, I don't suppose a fat bird like you gets any regular action. I suppose you have to get your thrills any way you can.'

'At least I don't have to pay for it. But, if I did, I wouldn't waste my money on the bit you've got.'

'One of these days ...' warned Nick, his eyes bright with hatred. He jumped to his feet, his heavy chair toppling behind him.

DC Billy Finch was talking on the phone when the chair caught him square on the shoulder. 'Hey, what the...?' Billy swivelled round to face Nick. 'What you doing?'

'Sorry,' Nick said, hands held aloft.

Up on the dais Wells became aware of the fuss and turned sharply. 'I thought I told you two to get on with your bloody work,' he bawled. 'Right, see me at the end of the shift, the pair of you. Now get out.'

A lacklustre sun shone bravely through the low-lying mist that had so far failed to clear on that cold February morning, its thin, wintry rays holding just enough warmth to turn the pavements of Argyle Street into lethal sheets of watery ice. Nick and Danny trod gingerly, hugging the shop fronts as they wove a painstaking path towards the Angel Mood shop.

Nick's own mood was deteriorating rapidly. He found Danny's constant chatter so wearing. Still, there was nothing he could do about it. He was stuck with the twat. And, what would Wells have to say tonight? If he ended up with a verbal warning because of that fat bitch....

Nick heaved a sigh. What was happening to him? He'd accused Mia of being unprofessional and yet, here he was, at the start of a murder inquiry and the job was the last thing on his mind. He couldn't stop thinking about Lisa Mackey. He needed the girl. He needed the sexual release she so skilfully orchestrated. And he hated himself for needing it. But if he gave her up – what then? Normal relationships – and the life enhancing feelings that came with them – were beyond him now. He didn't deserve to find real love again. Not after what he'd done to Angela.

Perhaps he should see a counsellor; work through the past and one day find himself a future. Those thoughts brought on a sickening adrenaline rush. No, he wasn't capable of expressing his thoughts surrounding her death. And how could he possibly find words to describe his feelings for their baby, the daughter he'd never see? He'd simply have to work through it alone. He'd dug the hole; now he had to find a way to scramble out of it. And he'd start now.

Clinging to the front of the Carphone Warehouse shop, his leather soles sliding precariously on the ice, Nick squared his shoulders and gave Danny a conciliatory look. 'If we get there without breaking any bones, Dan, I'll let you take the lead. OK?'

'OK … thanks,' said Danny, grinning.

The shop was empty, apart from two female assistants huddled together in the cramped space behind a glass-fronted counter. They were both around Hannah's age, one with blonde hair that fell in loose curls around her shoulders, and the other sporting a hennaed bob. They wore a uniform of black hipster trousers and tight black T-shirts finishing well above the navel to show a good few inches of tanned flesh. Name badges pinned to the T-shirts told that the blonde was EMILY, and the bob was CHERYL. When an old-fashioned bell signalled the detectives' arrival the girls turned tear-stained faces towards the door.

'Oh, sorry, we're closed today … for personal reasons,' said Emily, dabbing at her eyes with a sodden, scrunched-up tissue.

The detectives wandered across, their warrant cards held aloft. While Danny made the introductions, Nick took time to glance around the small space. It was crammed with crystal merchandise and talismans aimed at lifting the spirit.

Joss sticks smouldered slowly on the counter top, their thin lines of smoke drifting directly towards Nick. Quickly moving aside, his nostrils complaining about the sickly sweet vanilla scent, he waited for Danny to open up the interview. But that was easier said than done. The girls were distraught and wailed repeatedly that they'd only just read about Hannah's death.

'Catch him, won't you,' groaned Cheryl.

'We want to,' said Danny. 'And you can help us.'

'How?' asked Emily. 'We'll do anything….'

'Tell us all you can about Hannah. We need to know everything. What sort of girl was she? What made her tick? Tell us about her likes, her dislikes. Help us build up a picture of the girl, one we can work with to catch the killer.'

Danny's eagerness, his thorough wholesomeness, was inspiring the girls. They were hanging on his every word. He reminded Nick of those American evangelists, those holier-than-thou reverends who could do no wrong until they were caught with sticky fingers in the collection tin.

'Where do we start?' asked Cheryl, all fired up and ready to go.

'Friday,' said Danny, opening his notebook. 'Who was Hannah meeting after work?'

Cheryl raised her shoulders in a pathetic little shrug. 'She couldn't tell us.'

'Couldn't,' said Danny, 'or, wouldn't?'

Cheryl dabbed at her eyes and took in a monumental breath. 'When Hannah came into work on Friday she kept on about this bloke who was going to help get Colin's case thrown out by the CPS. Colin's her fiancé….'

'We know him. Carry on.'

'She said it was all pretty hush-hush and she hated keeping us in the dark but she'd tell us everything after Colin was out. We thought it was strange – didn't we, Em?'

The other girl gave an energetic nod. 'She said she was meeting this person after work and we weren't to follow or even look to see which way she went. I said it was like something out of a James Bond film. But Hannah's always been a bit of a drama queen….' A hand shot to her mouth. 'I'm not being nasty or anything. Hannah would be the first to admit she liked a bit of excitement in her life.'

'Is that why she got involved with Colin, do you think? Living on the edge of the law, like he does, must have seemed exciting.'

'Hmm,' said Emily, staring into space. 'That was part of it … to start with.' She turned back to Danny. 'It didn't last, though. It never did with Hannah. She's been bored with Colin for ages.'

'Really?' said Danny, lifting an eyebrow. 'But they were supposed to be getting married in August.'

The girls shared a glance, and then Cheryl said, 'Hannah needed Colin out of the remand centre because she wanted to break off the engagement and she couldn't do it while he was still banged up. That's why she was so happy when that bloke said he could help.'

'Had she got somebody else?'

'Nobody in particular,' said Emily, surreptitiously eyeing up Nick. 'She'd been out with a couple of blokes while Colin was inside, but nothing ever came of it.' She noticed their surprise immediately. 'You can't really blame her though. What sort of future would she have had with Colin? He only ever wanted to make money the easy way, through stealing stuff. He'd have spent most of their married life behind bars and no girl would want that.'

The indignation behind the girl's words seemed to sap her strength. With a small ethereal sigh she pulled a stool from under the counter and flopped on to it, brushing the blonde hair away from her shoulders as she aimed an unwavering glance into Nick's handsome face. 'Do you speak,' she said, 'or, are you just here for decoration?'

Nick managed a smile but ignored the remark. 'Hannah's parents weren't aware of her plans to scrap the wedding. They looked set to lose a fair bit of money. Wasn't she bothered about that?'

'Not really,' said Cheryl. 'They spoilt her rotten.'

'Where were they planning to live after the wedding – if it'd gone ahead? Were they buying somewhere together?'

'No, Hannah was going to move in with Colin. He's renting one of those new barn conversions over at Stratton Heights – not far from her parents' place, actually.'

Nick decided to change tack. 'These men she's been dating recently – did you meet any of them?'

'Oh, yes,' said Emily, suddenly animated, 'but they weren't serious boyfriends. Just blokes we met at the Apollo. Do you know the Apollo – that new nightclub over by the river?' He nodded. 'She'd lead them on, promising God knows what while they kept the drinks flowing, and then, come midnight, she'd be off ... just like Cinderella.'

'No second dates, then?' said Nick, sensing a dead end.

'No, Hannah always went for a certain type. She liked her men tall and strong and handsome.' She favoured the detectives with a huge smile. 'She'd have gone for you two, big time.'

'Thanks,' said Nick, aiming a long-suffering glance at Danny. 'OK, let's get back to this mystery man. Any ideas where she might have met him?'

Cheryl shrugged. 'No, like we said, she was keeping us in the dark till Colin got out.'

'When was the last time you all went for a night out?'

'The Saturday before last,' said Emily. 'But Hannah went to the Apollo with Gina – the other girl who works here – last Wednesday.'

'Where's Gina, now?'

'At home. She slipped on the ice coming into work on Thursday morning and broke her ankle. She was still pissed, if you ask me.'

'And you're sure we'll find her at home.'

Emily nodded, suddenly overcome with emotion. 'We saw the headlines outside the newsagents on our way in this morning ... Body Of Young Girl Found At Landfill Site. Well, of course, we rushed in for a copy of the paper, what with Hannah being missing all weekend.... Anyway, as soon as we read it was her we rang Gina and told her. She's at home all right.'

'Thanks, you've been really helpful,' said Nick, dropping his notebook on the counter. 'Would one of you like to write her address and phone number out for me, please? We'll see whether she can tell us anything.'

'I'll see you out,' said Cheryl, after hastily writing the details. 'I'll put the CLOSED sign up while I'm there.'

She followed them on to the slippery pavement, and after a quick glance back at Emily, said to Nick in a low voice. 'I can save you the trouble of going to Gina's….'

'Oh, yes' he said, his tone equally conspiratorial.

'Hannah was seeing somebody, only she didn't tell Emily – I mean, she's great and all that, but she's got a big mouth and it had to be a secret till Colin got out 'cause the bloke works at the remand centre.'

Nick's heart missed a beat. 'Do you know his name?'

'It's Chris … Chris Lennox.'

'Oh, shit,' said Jack, riffling through his pockets as he sat in Mia's passenger seat. 'I've forgotten to bring my wallet. You'll have to drive me back to Mandy's. It won't take long.'

'But, Jack—'

'Please, Mia, I'm meeting Michelle after work. She'll be wanting some money. I really need my wallet.'

'Oh, you and your bloody wife,' she muttered, manoeuvring the car into a precarious U-turn.

They were on their way to Stratton Heights to pick up Tom Bates for a formal interview at the station. With Paul Wells already hot under the collar about Mia's run-in with Nick in the board room, she was loath to anger the DCI still further by wasting time and petrol on the personal vagaries of Jack Turnbull. Fortunately, Jack's sister lived on a new housing estate about ten minutes' drive away from the Bateses, and they could go along main roads already cleared of ice by the council gritters so she could really put her foot down.

In no time at all she was pulling up outside a spacious semi-detached, identical in every respect to all the other houses on the vast estate. On the neat driveway stood a new Volvo Estate, its boot open, as was the door to the house.

'Oh, shit, they haven't gone yet,' said Jack, running irritable fingers through his unruly thatch of red hair.

'I thought your brother-in-law was a teacher,' said Mia, trying to stay calm. 'It's not half term, is it?'

Jack let out a long breath. 'The school's closed today. There's a big march planned in London. They're taking a petition to Downing Street. There's coaches being laid on and everything. I was hoping they'd already be gone.'

'Oh, well,' said Mia, unbuckling her seatbelt. 'I might as well meet them while we're here.'

They were almost at the house when a heated discussion could be heard starting in the hallway. Then, seconds later, a dishevelled woman – almost a mirror image of Jack – came storming through the open door, arms wrapped around a weighty cardboard box stuffed to the brim with A4-sized papers. She came to a staggering halt when she spied them over the top of the box.

'Oh, crikey,' she said, clearly startled. 'I didn't realize you were here. I hope you didn't hear what I just said.' She made a face. 'I don't normally swear – do I, Jack? Only Stuart will insist on leaving everything to the last minute, and time is of the essence, as they say.'

As if on cue her husband appeared on the doorstep, his languid features attempting some semblance of an irritable frown. 'Well, hello,' he said, bounding towards Mia, hand outstretched. 'I'm Stuart Wilson, Jack's brother-in-law and that's my lovely wife, Mandy. You must be Mia, Jack's illustrious partner. We've heard a lot about you.'

Stuart's handshake was like an iron vice and when he eventually released Mia's tortured hand she turned to Jack, eyebrows raised questioningly.

'Told you they were nuts,' he said.

'Ah,' said Stuart, 'that's what comes from marrying a luscious redhead. It frazzles the brain.'

'Oh, Stuart,' Mandy gushed. 'Whatever will Mia think of us? Get into that car, you naughty boy. We have grown-up business to see to today.'

Mia fixed a grin to her face. Were that pair for real? She felt as though she'd been roused from a deep sleep, only to find herself transported to the land of the Tweenies. She stood with Jack while they put the cardboard box into the boot and then scrambled into the front seats, their constant bickering adolescent but completely amiable. When the Volvo was eventually swallowed up by a diaphanous mist Mia found herself waving them off with hearty enthusiasm.

'Get out of there,' she said to Jack. 'If you have to beg Michelle to take you back, get out of there before some of it rubs off on you.'

CHAPTER TEN

It was their first major breakthrough. The soil taken from Hannah's body proved to be an exact match of that found on the southernmost banks of the River Stratton. Forensics could be so accurate because the soil's elaborate composition included a compound that was originally part of the rape seed; and enquiries made of the farmer whose fields flanked the river revealed the actual area taken over by rape the previous spring.

DCI Wells was positively euphoric when he read the contents of the interim report. Now things could really start rolling. DNA could be found – DNA that would point a finger at the most probable suspect. The girl's clothing could be retrieved, along with her mobile phone, its saved text messages pointing towards the killer....

Sadly, that scenario belonged in some form of parallel universe because in the real world, as every copper knew, the job of policing was never so simple. And that particular maxim was demonstrated most sharply to Wells as he stood on the banks of the river and considered the actual size of the area involved in their search.

The fields where the rape had grown covered approximately two acres. A perfectly manageable area, he would have said, but add to that the ferocity of the winds that had blown last spring and the picture changed dramatically. Rape seeds could be carried for miles on even the lightest of breezes. Forensics had tested samples at various intervals along eight miles of riverbank, and had come to the conclusion that the crime scene was somewhere within the middle three. Wells dug his frozen hands deeper into the pockets of his overcoat and struggled to remain positive as he gazed along the river, the magnitude of the task in front of them hitting home at last.

Its banks were choked with shrubs and heavily weeded apart from a thin path permanently worn into the terrain by the countless outdoor types who had, over the years, taken advantage of the area's hostile beauty. The water's edge was crowded with reeds and impenetrable vegetation that languished under a thick cover of ice which had formed at the water's edge rendering it immobile apart from a particularly energetic current that kept the water moving midstream.

A tall leafless hedge separated the farmland from the track. Wells's discerning eye followed its meandering path into the far distance. Could the killer have disposed of Hannah's clothes by throwing them over the hedge? That would have been easier than breaking the ice and depositing them into the water with an object heavy enough to keep them submerged. But, then again, the water might not have been frozen on the night of the murder. They would need to contact the Met Office and find out what the overnight temperatures had been during the early hours of Saturday, 23 February.

He sighed heavily, his breath fogging in the freezing air. A fingertip search amongst such dense undergrowth would take a vast number of man hours. And what if nothing was found at the end of it? They needed results now. In case the killer struck again.

Wells's team of six officers, all dressed appropriately for the search, stood patiently by the police van which stood next to his Sierra in a small makeshift car park taken over from a disused piece of council land by members of the local angling club. Wells trudged towards them, a short speech of encouragement taking shape in his mind.

'OK, kiddies, you all know what's expected of you.' He nodded back along the track. 'I'm asking a lot, I know, but when you're out there on your hands and knees, frozen to the bone and getting scratched to buggery, just think of Hannah Bates … and resolve to bring me the killer because, believe me, I want to make that bastard suffer like he never has before.'

The men yelled out affirmatives, seemingly fired up and raring to go, but Wells could see a hopelessness in their eyes at odds with their enthusiasm. That hopelessness, that despair, was in his own heart, too; he was about to buckle under its interminable weight when he was struck by a random thought. Hannah's mouth had been stuffed with debris…. Had the killer done that to stop her cries from being heard, as Danny had surmised? And, if so, who would have been out here in this wilderness to hear them?

Wells spun round on his heel, his fevered glance searching for a solitary dwelling, a cluster of houses, perhaps; indeed, any place where a girl's frightened cries might be overheard. But all he could see, in every direction, was farmland cloaked in its hostile wintry garb.

He turned back towards his men, his imagination in overdrive. 'Where's the nearest place from here?'

The officers exchanged glances, their expressions blank. Then DC Billy Finch, said, 'The town, sir, about three miles south, as the crow flies.'

'No … no …' said Wells, shaking his head impatiently. 'I mean, where's the nearest building? Is there anywhere on the river where people might gather?' He frowned. 'I can't bloody think—'

'Oh,' said Billy, realization dawning. 'There's the Apollo nightclub, sir….'

'Of course,' said Wells, turning to face due south. 'About a mile past that bend, and well within the three miles forensics claim are ripe for the crime scene.' His mouth stretched into a smile. 'That's where we'll start the search – the stretch of bank nearest the nightclub. And – who knows? – if we're lucky we might just nail the bastard before he has time to choose his next victim.'

Tom Bates was slumped in the chair, his body language arrogant. But his gaze was distinctly nervous as it engaged with those of the detectives through the thick fringe of black hair. They'd eventually made it to interview room number one. His mother had wanted to sit in, but Mia reasoned that the boy would find it harder to manipulate the husband and it was Russell who sat now at Tom's side, his expression fixed.

The room's temperature seemed to be barely above freezing. Its central heating radiator was broken and would remain so until sufficient funds could be found to mend it. An electric storage heater had been provided, but its capacity was too meagre for the job asked of it. Therefore they all kept on their outdoor coats. Tom and his father faced the detectives across a table that was empty apart from the tape-recording machine and a large stainless steel ashtray, its polished sheen obliterated by the grinding out of hundreds of cigarettes that left a strong nicotine odour permeating the air.

Mia inserted a fresh tape into the machine and proceeded to tell it the date and time of interview and the names of those present.

The father fidgeted in his seat. 'Why's he being recorded? Tom's not under arrest or anything, is he?'

'Of course not,' said Mia, her tone conciliatory. 'We just do it to cover ourselves.'

'But we're the innocent ones in all this. Why should you need to cover yourselves?'

'It's just procedure, Mr Bates. I'll turn it off, if you like.'

'No, it's OK,' he said, waving a hand. 'I was just wondering.'

'Good. Right, Tom, don't be nervous. We're all on the same side. We all want to catch Hannah's killer as quickly as possible. Yes?'

He nodded and folded his arms, stared morosely at the table top. He wasn't going to make this easy.

Mia observed the boy critically. 'When we were at your house yesterday, Tom, we had the distinct impression you were hiding something. Care to tell us what it is?'

'Don't know what you're on about,' he said, shifting his weight in the seat.

She watched him for a long moment, sensed the edginess he was trying so desperately to hide. 'Did you get on well with your sister?'

'You asked that yesterday, and I've already said ... yes.'

'There's only a couple of years between you. Did you ever go out for a drink together? Or, dancing, maybe?'

Tom let out a disgusted laugh. 'You must be joking. I wouldn't be seen dead listening to the stuff Hannah likes ... I mean ... liked.' His face puckered as though he might burst into tears, but he restrained himself and continued to stare at the table top.

'So you didn't spend time with Hannah socially?'

'She'd got her friends and I've got mine.'

'You never met her for a bite to eat or a quick drink at lunchtime? You worked only just round the corner from the Angel Mood shop. You'd have plenty of time.'

'Oh, give me a bloody break. Running round after my big sister would be so uncool. What do you think my friends would say?'

'Sorry, I should've thought. I just got the impression you two were really close.'

'You were wrong, then.'

Mia wrote *warring siblings?* in her notebook and motioned for Jack to take over. He was more than willing to do so.

'What do you think of the Walking Dead?' he asked.

Tom sat bolt upright, suddenly animated. 'They're wicked, man. I've got all their CDs. I've even got the latest – *Putrid Carcasses*.'

'How come? It's not even released, yet.'

Tom grinned. 'I'm in the fan club. We get complimentary copies.'

'Is it as good as the hype says it is?'

'You bet, man, it's fucking awesome.'

'Hey,' said Russell Bates, digging Tom in the ribs. 'What've I told you about using language like that?'

'Sorry, Dad.'

'The Apollo does Goth nights every Wednesday,' said Jack. 'Do you ever go?'

'Every week, yeah. It's brilliant.'

The boy's father lunged forward in his seat. 'What's any of this got to do with Hannah?'

Jack stiffened at the man's tone. 'Sorry, Mr Bates, I shouldn't have gone on about music but with Tom being a Goth I guessed we'd like the same stuff.'

Russell Bates heaved a tired sigh, wrapped a fatherly arm around his son's shoulder. 'No need to apologize. Actually, this is the first time I've seen him smile for ages.' He buried his face in the boy's black hair as a tide of emotion washed over him. When he eventually looked up, he said, 'They were close, you know … Hannah and Tom.'

'What happened to change that?' Mia asked, gently.

He nodded towards Jack. 'When you mentioned the Apollo it came into my mind. Hannah caught him smoking cannabis there. She told us and we grounded him for a fortnight.'

'And I missed the Walking Dead concert in Birmingham,' Tom said. 'I'd had the ticket for months. I never forgave Hannah for that.'

'Jesus … I bet you were really annoyed,' said Jack. 'I would've been.'

'Too true, I was. All my mates went.'

'How did you get your own back? Did you think up something really evil?'

Tom was about to respond, lulled into complacency as he was by the friendly conversation about his heroes. But then he was struck by a thought. 'Oh, I know what you're after. You think I've got something to do with Hannah's murder and you're trying to get me to talk. Well, you can think again, you fuckers, because I'll never talk … never.' And before anyone could stop him Tom was out of his seat and through the door.

Mia cast an impatient glance at Russell Bates. 'Your son's hiding something, sir. And sooner or later he'll have to tell us what it is.'

CHAPTER ELEVEN

The dank relentless mist that had dogged the rush-hour traffic and reduced the streets of Larchborough to lethal tracks of ice had lifted at last, bringing after it a faltering sun with a warmth that had not been felt for weeks. That significant change in temperature was a huge stroke of luck for DCI Wells and those officers employed in scouring the frozen banks of the River Stratton.

Inch by inch of frigid earth melted before the sun's rays, giving up all that had been kept hidden during the weeks of the big freeze. Indeed, as the day wore on, even the river began to flow again as its icy cover finally gave up the fight. And at precisely 12.45 p.m. a black knee-length sock was found within its murky depths. It had become entangled around a knot of tree roots just below the surface, about two feet from the bank.

As no distinguishing marks could be found it was impossible to say for sure that the sock was Hannah's. Could some unfortunate angler, misjudging the water's edge, have discarded it in a fit of furious frustration? Or had the murderer flung it into the water, believing it would sink without trace and keep his dreadful secret safe for ever amongst the silt on the riverbed?

DCI Wells had been sitting on the back seat of his Sierra, drinking coffee from a thermos flask when the sock was discovered, and he was putting his money firmly on the second option. Without wasting a moment he radioed through to the team of frogmen that Superintendent Shakespeare had so grudgingly provided and ordered them to concentrate on the area where the sock was found.

Forty-five minutes later another shout went up. DC Billy Finch had found a large number of brown spots, in a spatter pattern, on a patch of earth that was surprisingly devoid of vegetation. Had the ground been cleared deliberately? That was how it looked to Wells. Billy was instructed to bag samples of the brown matter as soon as it had been photographed. Wells wandered along the riverbank, intent on watching the bubbles that rippled the water's surface and marked the slow progress of the frogmen.

At last, things were looking up. That sock, and the brown stuff which Wells dared to believe was blood, had been found in an area of around ten square metres. It was too much of a coincidence for the sock not to be Hannah's.

As he marched back to the Sierra, hands plunged deep into his overcoat pockets, Wells's grizzled features managed a smile. The killer obviously believed he was clever – and he probably was – but he was careless, too. They'd get him. And when they did….

Another cry went up, cutting into the silence and plucking Wells from his reverie. He swivelled round to see Billy Finch waving his arms and gesticulating wildly at a frogman holding a large green object clear of the water.

'They've found them, sir,' Billy shouted, hardly able to contain his excitement. 'They've found Hannah's clothes.'

It had been a long and draining day for Janet Munroe; a day that had started with a crisis in the day room. Alzheimer's victim Herbert Staines, intent on going home to a house that had been sold over five years ago, was trying to escape through the double doors.

Only five-foot-five, with a particularly small build, Herbert was demonstrating an almost unbelievable strength that needed two male nurses to subdue it. He was wailing continually for his twin girls, Edna and Lottie. But Herbert had never married and had no children as far as Janet was aware. Was he harbouring a secret past? A past that was now causing regret?

Normally with Alzheimer's patients Janet prayed for a slow deterioration. But in Herbert's case she hoped that the disease would quickly mix up the pieces of his life – like a completed jigsaw dropped to the floor – so that regret wouldn't be an option. Regret was the Judas of all emotions. Janet should know; she had enough.

She was in her office thinking about regrets, about the pain they caused, as she finished the day's work. She thought about the yobs who were now dominating their lives. Even when they weren't there Edith worried about when they'd be back and what they planned to do next. It was no way to live.

Of course, if Janet had never started to gamble, if she'd saved her money instead, they'd be in a position to move. For years now Edith had had her heart set on a bungalow. But money from the sale of the house alone wouldn't be enough; they'd need extra cash to afford the exorbitant prices that bungalows pulled in nowadays. Janet had never thought to apply for a mortgage. How would she manage the repayments? She couldn't afford the debts she already had.

As she tidied her desk Janet imagined how wonderful it would be to go home with a handful of estate agents' particulars and throw them into Edith's lap. Instead she was having to think of ways to pacify the loan sharks who'd eagerly shoved money at her in the beginning, knowing full well she'd have no means of paying it back; loan sharks who were now claiming the moral high road and refusing – with noses wrinkled as though she were a nasty smell – to entertain the thought of parting with another penny. She just thanked God the house was still in Edith's name. At least that was safe.

As she pulled on her coat Janet brooded about the evening to come, the now familiar feeling of guilt sweeping over her. She was about to steal her mother's pride and joy: an eighteenth century walnut card-table. It had been given to Edith by her employers – the Harley-Grainger family – with whom she'd started working as a humble kitchen-maid in 1937 before rising to revered housekeeper within the space of five years.

Edith met and fell in love with Frederick Bowman in 1943. Frederick was gamekeeper to a rich lord and lived in a tied cottage some twenty miles from Edith's place of employment. So when she accepted his marriage proposal Edith had little choice but to hand in her notice and prepare to leave the house that had become her home. By that time the Harley-Graingers had fallen on hard times and were unable to pay Edith's final wages and buy a betrothal gift. Therefore a compromise was reached and the card-table was quickly plucked from its position in the library and handed across with much affection.

Neither Janet nor Edith had thought its value was anything other than sentimental … until their water pipes burst during the winter of 1995, flooding all the ground floor rooms. When the insurance company sent a man to assess the damage, his eyes widened considerably as his gaze fell upon the table. Searching out antiques and collectables was his hobby, they were told, and that little card-table – *circa* 1710, no less – was a find indeed. It was a pity, he said, that the wood had been allowed to fade in direct sunlight but, even so, given its overall condition and the concertina action of the legs they'd have no trouble selling it for anything up to £15,000. He was willing to write out a cheque for £12,000, there and then, if they'd allow him a couple of days to gather sufficient funds to cover the cheque.

Edith refused, point blank. She wouldn't part with the table for all the tea in China, she said, feeling more than a little pleased to know that the Harley-Graingers had given her something of worth.

If that table had been worth £15,000 in 1995, how much would it sell for now? Whatever the amount, it wouldn't pay off all the debts, but it would satisfy the hounds for a while. It was imperative that Janet satisfied her creditors. Better to sell the table for that end than have it carted off by bailiffs. But how could she take the table without her mother missing it? That question loomed large in Janet's mind as she closed the door of her office for the night.

'OK, kiddies, I know it's late and you want your beds, but listen up, we've got some news,' said Wells, bustling into the board room with Nick and Danny close at his heels.

Before they'd even come to a stop at the dais, Danny said, 'Hannah was seeing that prison warden, Chris Lennox, behind Fowler's back.'

Nick glared at the young officer and Danny was all too aware that he'd wanted to give the news himself. During the ride back to the station Nick had made it plain that Danny had contributed well in the crystal shop but he would take the lead from now on. Danny had looked steadily through the side window so Nick wouldn't see his smirk. He knew Nick was desperate to please the DCI and he found the continuous arse-licking so very amusing. All Nick longed for was faint praise now and again to bolster a frail ego.

Danny knew he wasn't well liked in the station but that small fact hardly touched the high esteem in which he held himself. He was used to being an outsider, viewing life from the sidelines. It all mattered little to Danny. He was a fighter who strove daily to reach his dreams, never stopping until he'd achieved them.

Nick Ford might be satisfied with the occasional pat on the back for a job shoddily done. But, he was aiming for the top. With his skills and talents he could go for chief constable and beyond. He could have it all. Oh, and the power! If appreciation was Nick's drug of choice, then power was Danny's. He wanted to show all those who had derided his abilities, scoffed at his efforts, that he was somebody. And he'd do it too. By the end of this investigation DCI Wells would know without a doubt who was the best man to head his team, and Nick Ford would be way down the list. Danny smiled inwardly as Nick quickly jumped on to the dais and faced the others.

'Like Danny said, Hannah was seeing Chris Lennox. The girls at the crystal shop said the reason Hannah was so desperate to get Fowler out of the unit was because she was planning to dump him for Lennox, and she didn't want to do it while he was still in there for obvious reasons. That's why she was so pleased when our mystery bloke came on the scene and said he could help.'

'Who else knew about this?' asked Wells.

'Nobody, sir. Only the girls at the shop. Hannah went with one of them – a Gina Allen – to the Apollo Nightclub every Wednesday night, but it was just a cover. Once there they'd split up. Gina would pair up with her bloke and Hannah would go off with Lennox. And, here's another funny twist – Gina's bloke – Johnny Preston – handles security at the Apollo. At one time he and Fowler were best mates, but Fowler got the hump when Preston took the Apollo job – he'd been trying for it himself. There's plenty of bad blood between them now.'

Wells was pouring a coffee and Mia said to him, 'Hannah's brother must have known about the affair as well, sir, because he goes to the Apollo every Wednesday for their Goth night. Hannah caught him smoking pot there one week and told their parents. Tom was grounded for a fortnight. He was really pissed off because he missed an important concert in Birmingham. I don't think they were as close as the parents are saying, sir.'

'And he never mentioned that his sister was doing the dirty on Fowler?'

'No, sir.'

'Interesting,' said Wells, taking his place on the dais while Nick returned to his desk. 'So Tom's there while his engaged sister's messing around with another man, and he doesn't say a thing. Now, that's strange, especially as you say there's no love lost between them. What else did you find out?'

Mia made a face. 'Not a lot, sir. Tom did a bunk soon after … caused his dad to run after him, worried to death.'

'Keep on at him. Do him for obstruction, if you have to, but find out what the little bugger's hiding.' He started to pace. 'OK, kiddies, you all know by now that we've found the crime scene and things have started to move. Forensics have got Hannah's clothes and they've promised to work into the small hours. And her mobile network's sending us a list of all her calls a.s.a.p.' He perched on the desk and took a sip of coffee. 'We need to find Lennox. No more waiting till he finishes his leave. We need to get him back, now.'

'If he was ever planning to come back,' said Danny.

Nick said, 'If Lennox had anything to do with the actual murder he wouldn't just ask for two weeks' leave. What would be the point?'

Danny hid a grin. 'If Lennox had just committed a murder and guessed we'd soon find out about his involvement with the victim he wouldn't just disappear – that'd show his guilt quicker than anything. He'd want everything to appear normal. He'd ask for some leave so he could get away without arousing suspicion.'

'What about when he comes back?' said Nick.

Danny laughed out loud, no longer hiding the disdain he felt for his partner. 'That's the whole point – he won't be coming back. He didn't know how long it'd take us to find out about him and Hannah – not long, as it's turned out – but he's almost had enough time to get to the other side of the world by now.'

'Fucking rubbish,' Nick muttered.

Wells said, 'Let's not be so hasty, Nick. It does make a kind of sense.' He crossed to the whiteboard and started to write. 'OK, finding Lennox takes priority over everything else. Mia, tomorrow morning I want you and Jack back at the unit to find out all you can about the man. See if you can pick up any clues about where he might have gone. And we'll need to check all airports, train stations, ferry ports et cetera.'

Mia was still far from convinced that Lennox had anything to do with Hannah's murder but she thought it best to keep her own counsel. There'd be time enough to score points when he turned out to be squeaky clean.

Billy Finch said, 'What about the blood we found, sir?'

'Forensics have got the samples, Billy, and we'll have all info a.s.a.p. Those green sacks containing Hannah's body and her clothes … I'll need one of you to find out where they were bought.' He let out a sigh. 'I hate all this bloody waiting around. Still, we've got something to keep us busy now so let's look on the bright side.'

Nick said, 'What about Gina's boyfriend, Johnny Preston? I think it might be worth having a word with him, sir. What do you think?'

'OK, mate – why not?' Wells quickly consulted his watch. 'Not now though. I'd rather you all got a decent night's sleep. Ring the Apollo when we've finished and arrange to see Preston in the morning. Danny, you go with him.' Wells delved into his briefcase and held up a large notebook. 'If any of you fancy the boring jobs talked about tonight, put your names in here. And if your energies start to flag, take a look at these photos.' Moving swiftly to the whiteboard, Wells pinned up a series of large black and white prints showing various angles of Hannah Bates as she lay in the green plastic sack on the landfill site.

He turned abruptly, his caustic gaze directed at Nick and Mia. 'Don't forget to stay behind, you two. Daddy wants a chat. OK, the rest of you can go and get a good night's sleep. I want you all ready for the off at 8.30 tomorrow.'

While most of the officers formed an orderly line at the dais, eager to volunteer, Danny approached the whiteboard for a better look at the photographs. Nick watched him closely. He knew what Danny was up to. He was trying to gain favour with Wells. But Nick could see right through that overconscientious, totally blinkered commitment to the job. And Wells would see through it too. Nobody liked a know-all, least of all Paul Wells. Danny would come unstuck. All Nick had to do was wait.

He put a brotherly arm around Danny's shoulder. 'Get yourself home now, Dan. We both need to be on the ball in the morning.'

'Sorry?' said Danny, a faraway look in his eyes. 'Oh, right. I was just reinforcing my resolve to catch the bastard who did this.' He heaved a sigh. 'Although if Chris Lennox is the killer Mia's likely to get all the glory. Shame, really.' He shrugged off Nick's arm and made for the door, a smile playing on his lips. Nick watched him go. He was right, of course. Yet again it looked as though she'd been given the prime assignment, the best of the pick.

Staring fixedly at Mia, Nick took out his mobile phone and prepared to call the Apollo nightclub. She was talking to Jack, helping him prepare for his confrontation with Michelle, when DCI Wells started to hover like an ominous black crow in the background.

Quick to take a hint Jack was out of the door like a lightning bolt, leaving them to face their nemesis. They took chairs on opposite sides of the walnut table, eyeballing each other like fighters before a bout. Wells was about to speak when the door flew open. All three turned to see a flustered uniformed constable come to a screeching halt.

'Sir,' he said, 'there's been another murder.'

Straight away Wells thought the worst and his face paled. 'Our man again?'

'No, sir. The victim's an elderly lady. The daughter's asking for you, DS Harvey.'

Mia frowned. 'Me? Why? What's the daughter's name?'

'Janet Munroe. She said she looks after your mother at St Stephen's nursing home.'

A hand shot to Mia's face, her eyes widening with disbelief. 'You're joking … Janet's mother's dead? What happened?'

'Apparently, Mrs Munroe and her mother have been getting grief from a bunch of lads for a while now. Seems like the bastards have gone that little bit too far this time.'

CHAPTER TWELVE

The officer responding to Janet's frantic 999 call had relayed back to central control that Edith's death looked like the result of a burglary gone wrong. No other details had been given, so Mia was left to imagine all sorts of horrific scenarios as she huddled in the back of Wells's Sierra, while the DCI shared theories with Nick in the front. They were heading for Janet's home, their chat about teamwork – or lack of it – temporarily on hold. The crime scene had been secured and forensics and the police doctor alerted. Everything was in place for the murder investigation to begin.

'I can't believe it,' said Mia, for the umpteenth time. 'I was planning to ring Janet at home tonight.'

'Is she a close friend?' Wells asked, gently.

'Not particularly, sir. It's just that I haven't been to see Mum since Saturday and I wanted to know how she was.'

The Sierra came to a halt at a set of traffic lights, and Wells watched Mia closely for a moment through the rear-view mirror. He said, 'You're going to be all right with this investigation, darling? It won't be too close for comfort?'

Mia strongly shrugged off the implication. 'I'll be fine, sir … I'll be fine. It's a shock, but it won't stop me doing the job.'

Nick stared into the unbroken darkness beyond the windscreen, his eyebrows raised questioningly. He'd long since believed that women had no place in the force, other than behind a computer keyboard, and he wouldn't rest until Mia Harvey was pushed out of CID. He'd directed his venom towards her at every available opportunity to achieve that end, but her own attempts at spite had always bettered his. Whoever said that women were the fairer sex clearly knew nothing about the breed.

But now as the darkness gave way to an ocean of twinkling lights that was Staples Brook, Nick wondered whether the soft touch of masculine consideration might not be the tool with which to loosen her grip on Paul Wells's respect. Perhaps he should cut her some slack, take the lion's share of the work and at the same time outline to Wells how utterly useless females were at putting the job before their so-called finer feelings. He'd start now.

Twisting round in his seat, Nick said, 'You know, if you feel like going to see your mum tonight, it's not too late. I'll assist DCI Wells, and I can bring you up to speed in the morning.'

Mia was taken aback by the softness of his tone. 'That's really nice of you, Nick, but it wouldn't be fair. I've got to pull my weight. I'll find time to see Mum before the end of the week.'

'If you're sure. I just thought seeing her might be a bit of a comfort after the shock you've had.'

He turned back to stare out of the windscreen a little too quickly, and Mia worried that he might have taken her words as a snub. All of a sudden she felt an irrational urge to reassure him. 'Nick, I'm grateful for the thought, and—'

'For bloody Christ's sake,' blustered Wells. 'I know I want you pair to get along, but could you wait till I'm out of the way before you jump into bloody bed together? Where we going again?'

Mia said, 'Fairfield Crescent, sir … number nine. The turning's coming up any time now … on the right.'

They pulled up outside Janet Munroe's semi-detached, its rendered front a dull grey in the harsh glare of a nearby streetlamp. The front garden was on a steep slope, and as DCI Wells scanned the frontage to conjure up his usual thumbnail assessment, he thought vaguely that the lawn would be awkward to mow.

News of the murder had clearly travelled fast and the crescent was alive with gossiping neighbours huddled in groups to embellish the few scant facts in their possession, despite temperatures that were fast approaching zero and a thrusting wind that cut to the bone.

A panda car stationed in front of Wells's Sierra, its blue light flashing silently, was attracting the local children as surely as a honeypot lured in the bees, their excited cries totally inappropriate given the seriousness of the situation. Wells tutted loudly as he edged through the gaggle of small bodies obstructing his path to Janet Munroe's black-and-gold metal gate. The uniformed officer at the front door nodded a quick greeting as the detectives approached.

'I want those kids off the street ... now,' Wells informed him briskly. 'No wonder we've got bloody delinquents killing old ladies. They should've been in bed hours ago.'

'I'll see to it straight away, sir,' said the officer, stepping aside for them to enter.

'Where's the body?' Wells asked.

'Front room, sir. The daughter's in the kitchen with WPC Perkins.'

'OK, mate, carry on.'

The hallway was a large oblong with a stairway to the right. Two doors led off it: one to the kitchen straight ahead, and another to the living room on the left. Wells indicated that they should follow him into the living room.

They walked into what looked like a bombsite. Everything that could be broken was now in pieces, littering the brightly coloured Axminster carpet. China ornaments, clocks, photo frames. Everything that represented a life had been reduced to jagged fragments. The television set had been smashed; the video recorder, too. Two glass-fronted cabinets were overturned, their contents little more than a heap of junk amongst the lethal shards. The three-piece suite, a heavy old-fashioned relic in burgundy leather, had been toppled.

Edith's lifeless body lay in front of the large bay window, between the settee and a nest of solid oak tables. She'd been struck on the forehead with a heavy blunt object, the force of the blow shattering her skull an inch or two above her left ear. A slight spattering of blood soiled the carpet to the side of her head.

Mia balked at the horror before her. She'd met Edith once or twice at St Stephen's, when the old lady had attended birthday parties and the like. 'I'll go and see how Janet's doing,' she said, eager to flee the scene.

She found her sitting at the kitchen table, staring blankly at the opposite wall, a glass of brandy at her side. WPC Gillian Perkins was kneeling at Janet's feet, patting her hand in a comforting gesture. The constable glanced up sharply at Mia's abrupt entrance but Janet kept her eyes on the wall, her features dark with horror and disbelief.

Mia was approaching softly, as though the smallest sound might shatter Janet's fragile nerves. She pulled up a chair and sat down. 'Janet, it's Mia Harvey. I'm here to help.'

Janet turned red-rimmed eyes her way, was about to speak, but the tenderness in Mia's voice brought on tears that fell in a tumultuous rush. Gillian Perkins quickly plucked a handful of tissues from a box on the sink and laid them on Janet's lap.

Mia said, 'I'm so sorry, Janet. I'll do everything I can to help.'

After a while the tears stopped and Janet said, 'I came home to find this, Mia, all this.'

'What time did you get home?'

'About six-thirty … I think.'

'Janet, you told one of my colleagues that some boys had been causing a nuisance…. Do you know who they are?'

She nodded. 'I don't know their names, but I'd recognise their faces.'

'And you think they're responsible for this?'

Janet's face clouded. 'They've been threatening for ages. They've almost torn down our fence out the back. I knew they were getting ready to do something, but I'd no idea they'd go this far.'

Mia got to her feet and glanced around, her practised eye searching for signs of a forced entry. 'How did they get in?'

'Through here.' WPC Perkins pointed to the kitchen door. 'It wasn't locked.'

Mia wandered across to the door, a cheap wooden type, its top half frosted glass. She pushed a hand against it. It was as she thought: the door was flimsy. If someone was intent on breaking in then that door would hardly be a deterrent, locked or not. She pulled across the net curtain shielding the glass and peered out into the darkness. 'They've wrecked the fence, you say?'

'Yes,' said Janet, calmer now. 'All the gardens back on to open farmland. The yobs have been using the fields as a meeting place ever since the youth club burned down. They've been causing a nuisance for ages. Mum….' She faltered briefly. 'Mum's life was a misery because of them.'

Mia turned to her, sighing heavily. 'I wish you'd told me. I might have been able to help.'

'I was planning to. Only you haven't been in and….' She gave a helpless shrug.

Mia leant heavily against the fridge/freezer and wondered momentarily about the capricious nature of life. If the brutal murder of Hannah Bates hadn't kept her away from St Stephen's, would Janet's mother still be alive? If the local council had used bricks to build the youth club instead of wood to save a few pounds, would Edith still be alive? The fabric of life was certainly flimsy.

Mia took out her notebook and jotted down all relevant details. 'Have they taken anything?'

'I haven't looked. I can't go back in the lounge. Not while….'

'Of course not,' said Mia, wishing she didn't have to ask such God-awful questions. 'Have you been upstairs at all?' Janet shook her head. 'Would you mind if I take a quick look?'

'No, as long as you don't want me to go with you.'

Mia took the stairs two at a time, conscious all the while of the deep rumbling of conversation coming from the living room. The landing was long and narrow, with doors leading off it to the right. Mia supposed that the first bedroom, overlooking fields at the back, was Janet's. A crowd of soft toys sat on the bed, their hand-stitched faces turned towards the door. The bedside tables were covered with long stretches of cerise satin, an obvious girly touch. Everything matched, apart from the computer and keyboard that stood out like a sore thumb on a table to the right of the door.

The second bedroom was clearly Edith's. Decorated in various shades of blue, it had framed photographs covering every available surface. Yet, despite its cluttered appearance, the room was as tidy as Janet's. A third bedroom – little more than a box – held a selection of suitcases, a treadle sewing-machine, and little else. None of the rooms showed evidence of criminal activity.

Mia hurried down the stairs with a distinct feeling of unease. It was unusual for thieves to leave the upstairs level of a house untouched – unless they were disturbed, that is. But it would seem that those responsible had had the run of the house and time enough to ransack everywhere. So why limit themselves to the living room? It didn't make sense.

Just then the sound of the doorbell cut into her thoughts. It was Philip Williams, the same police doctor who'd attended Hannah Bates at the landfill site. Mia sighed inwardly at the sight of him. He was nice enough, but his sense of humour belonged in a primary school classroom. His stupid anecdotes, uttered at the feet of a dead victim, had irritated her no end.

'She's in the living room,' Mia said, intending to keep any conversation short and sweet.

'We'll have to stop meeting like this,' he said, before singing in a toneless voice, 'People will say we're in love.'

Mia gave him a tight smile. 'Like I said, Doctor, she's in the living room. DCI Wells and DI Ford are already in there.'

Without further banter Williams disappeared into the room while Mia sat on the stairs and took out her notebook, still perplexed by the fact that the bedrooms had been left untouched. And why make such a mess of the living room? Criminals searching for valuables didn't usually take the time or trouble to smash everything they could get their hands on. And the noise must have been horrendous. Hadn't they worried about alerting the neighbours? She'd noticed on the way in that the semis had been built with the hallways together, so the living rooms were effectively detached. But, even so....

The men came into the hall. The doctor was saying, 'You do realize that the blow to the head came after death.'

'I did wonder about the small amount of blood,' said Wells. 'What did kill her, Phil? Any idea?'

The doctor pursed his lips. 'Can't say. Although it could be a heart attack.'

'You mean the shock could have killed her?'

'It's possible. She was very frail, an angina sufferer, too. Her heart wouldn't have been at its best.'

Wells raised an eyebrow. 'You could tell that from your brief examination?'

'No,' said the doctor, smiling. 'I noticed that prescription on the way in.' He nodded towards a small telephone table standing at the foot of the stairs. On it was a doctor's prescription form. 'It's made out to an Edith Bowman. That's the name of our deceased, is it not?'

'It is,' said Wells, looking suitably impressed. 'You're in the wrong game, mate. You should have been a detective.'

'I think not. I like the job I've got.' He opened the door to sounds of several vehicles pulling up at the kerb. 'Looks like our friends from forensics have arrived, Paul. Happy hunting.' And then he was gone.

DCI Wells, conscious of a cold draught, closed the door and turned to face his detectives. 'You know, kiddies, one thing's really puzzling me,' he said, stroking his chin thoughtfully.

'What's that, sir?' said Nick.

'Why crack the old woman's skull open when she's already dead?'

As luck would have it, John Lloyd – Wells's favourite pathologist – was at a loose end. He'd been due to jet off to Jamaica at five o'clock on Wednesday morning, but the flight was cancelled due to bad weather. The next available flight wasn't until 1800 hours on Friday, leaving Lloyd with more than enough time to discover the secrets of Edith Bowman's death.

It was decided that Janet should take a spare room at St Stephen's for the foreseeable future. The whole of number 9, Fairfield Crescent was effectively a crime scene and the forensics team would need undisturbed access at all times.

Mia slept fitfully that night, her mind refusing to release those dreadful images of Edith and the chaos around her. All of a sudden she was desperate to see her own mother, to be reassured that all was well with her. There was nothing like murder to sort out a person's priorities. She'd make time to visit St Stephen's today, and she'd give her mother a cuddle. What did it matter if Barbara didn't cuddle back? Mia wasn't a child any more. Barbara was the child now, and Mia would act accordingly.

With the decision made, she set off for work feeling positive and ready for anything, even the latest instalment in the saga of Jack's marriage. She found him waiting for her in the station car park, a broad grin on his face.

'Ask me what happened with Michelle last night,' he said, buckling up in Mia's car.

'What happened with Michelle last night?'

'She wants me back. She begged me to go back.'

They were on their way to the Marshcroft remand unit to investigate Chris Lennox. Easing the car on to the road, Mia said, 'You were telling me yesterday you wouldn't go back even if she did beg. What's changed?'

Jack's face flushed and Mia had to suppress a smile. 'We made up … big time … if you get my drift. It was great. Just like before we got married.'

Mia stayed silent as she settled the car into the long line of early-morning traffic, and she could see Jack regarding her suspiciously out of the corner of her eye. He said, 'Aren't you pleased?'

'You should see your face,' she said, laughing. 'Of course I am. You two were made for each other, and if you could both stop playing silly-buggers for long enough, you'd see it as well.'

'Good,' he said, breathing a sigh of relief. 'You had me worried for a minute.'

Mia quickly told him about the awful scene that had confronted them at Janet's house the previous evening. It was enough to knock the ridiculous smile from his face.

'Shit, that's terrible,' he said. 'You OK?'

She assured him she was fine. There was no need to treat her with kid gloves. Nick had tried, she said, and she'd soon put him in his place. She didn't tell him that Nick's apparent concern had touched her deeply, had in fact forced her to view him in an altogether different light. Indeed, in the small hours, while her thoughts had kept sleep at bay, she'd even dared to acknowledge a fondness for Nick that she'd so far been forced to keep hidden. Too much antagonism had passed between them for anything to come of this new development. And, anyway, a good-looking bloke like Nick would hardly give her a second glance.

Mentally shrugging off that absurd line of thought, Mia said, 'Wells is taking the lion's share of Edith's investigation – for today, at least. So let's just concentrate on Lennox.'

Jack phoned ahead to the remand unit and explained to the governor's secretary the reason for their visit. The governor was called Vincent Perry, a former Green Peace activist who had generated a good many column-inches in the 'heavy' newspapers of late because of his controversial theories regarding the rehabilitation of the thirty or so alleged criminals housed at the unit.

It was Perry's strong opinion that reformation should begin while they were awaiting trial, and not after sentence had been imposed; especially now that judges across the country were being advised by the government to banish prison sentences in favour of punishment within the community.

Mia had kept a close eye on the growing controversy and was expecting to be introduced to a small softly spoken liberal with hippy beads around his wrists and hair that touched his collar. As it turned out Vincent Perry was six-foot-two and seventeen stone of highly toned muscle; with hair as short as an army recruit's and a handshake that could crack a brazil nut.

Upon arrival they were ushered into his office with an expansive sweep of his arm. 'Do take a seat,' he said, smiling broadly. They made themselves comfortable while Perry relaxed into his chair, arms resting lightly on the desk. 'I understand you're here to discuss Chris Lennox. How can I help?'

Mia said, 'Could you tell us a bit about the man?'

'OK.' He picked up a blue folder and handed it to Mia. 'That's his file, by the way. You might find it illuminating.'

'Could we have a photocopy of this?'

'I can't see why not. You'll keep all information confidential, I assume?' Mia nodded. Perry folded his arms, his forehead creasing into a thoughtful frown. 'Basically, he's a good man. We don't always see eye to eye on matters of discipline, but his heart's in the right place.'

'Does he have a temper?'

The frown deepened. 'No, nothing like that. I have a rather progressive attitude towards offenders and Chris doesn't.'

Jack said, 'Has he ever been violent towards the inmates?'

'Good God, no,' said Perry. 'He wouldn't still be working here if he had.' He eyed the detectives with suspicion. 'What's he done?'

Mia quickly divulged all that Colin Fowler had said during their previous visit; and she told him about Lennox's alleged involvement with their murder victim.

Perry sank back in his seat, clearly stunned. 'It doesn't surprise me that Chris should go to such lengths to keep a prisoner in his place. He really does believe that bullyboy tactics work more efficiently than my kid gloves method. But to actually form an attachment with the fiancée of that prisoner.... That's a sackable offence, DS Harvey.'

'When did Mr Lennox put in his request for leave?'

'Let me check.' He took from his desk a pile of official forms held together by a large bulldog clip and passed the relevant paper to Mia, saying, 'Application approved at 17.25 hours on Sunday, twenty-fourth February – two weeks to start immediately.' He raised an inquisitive eyebrow. 'Does that help you at all?'

'I'm not sure. I'll need to photocopy this as well, Mr Perry.'

'No problem. I'll get my secretary to do it before you leave.'

Jack said, 'Do you know where he's gone?'

'No idea. Chris keeps very much to himself.' He leant forward, suddenly earnest. 'He's friendly enough. And there's no animosity between him and the other wardens. If anything, he's quite popular, especially around Christmas when the staff put on a pantomime for the inmates. Chris's very good at entertaining, and he always ends up with the star part ... even if it's Cinderella. I'd go so far as to say the shows would be quite boring without him.'

Jack frowned. 'Bit of a contradiction, don't you think? He's devious and heavy-handed with the inmates, yet he loves to entertain them at Christmas. He's a loner and doesn't mix, but he's popular with his fellow wardens.'

Mia consulted the man's file. He lived at 3, The Horseshoe, Blacksmith's Lane, Larchborough. Mia knew The Horseshoe well. It was just a few streets away from the police station. The building had recently been converted into three two-bedroom town houses. They'd need a look inside.

Watching Perry, an eyebrow raised hopefully, she said, 'Where do your employees keep their personal belongings while on duty?'

'Under lock and key in the rest room. They've each got a numbered locker. Why?'

'Mr Perry, bearing in mind that a girl has been murdered, and given that Chris Lennox was having a relationship with the dead girl … would it be possible for us to see inside his locker?'

'Of course,' he said, easily. 'As long as you've got a search warrant in your bag.'

Mia shrugged. 'We don't have a warrant.'

'Then you can't see inside the locker.' Perry spread his hands. 'You know the rules as well as I do, DS Harvey, and I'm not the sort to deviate an inch.'

'I thought not,' said Mia, heaving a sigh. 'Still, these are special circumstances. Can't you bend the rules a bit?'

He shook his head. 'Chris could sue us for every penny we've got.'

'He'd never know. Nothing we found in that locker could be used in a court of law. The defence team would be screaming inadmissible evidence the moment they found out we'd searched without a warrant. And they would find out.'

'I know,' Perry said, nodding sagely, 'I'd tell them myself.'

'Then where's the problem?'

Vincent Perry thought for a moment. 'All right, you can have a quick look. But, you must assure me I won't be thrown to the wolves over this.'

'You have my word,' said Mia.

A large metal safe stood behind Perry's chair. From this he retrieved a heavy key ring and invited the detectives to accompany him to the locker room. At the secretary's desk Mia handed across the papers to be photocopied and then all three marched purposefully along a series of depressing corridors, the walls of which were painted a grim khaki colour.

In the room two wardens were preparing for their shifts, their conversation animated. But as soon as the detectives entered all conversation ceased and both men appeared to find something of huge interest inside their lockers.

'Ken … Sammy …' said Perry. 'Are you starting or just finishing?'

'Starting,' said Ken. 'We'll be out of your way, sir.'

As soon as the door closed Perry ushered the detectives to the far side of the room. 'This is Chris's locker … number 144.'

He selected the appropriate key and the flimsy metal door swung open to reveal a mishmash of belongings heaped into an untidy pile. Mia put on her leather gloves and pulled out a white cotton shirt and a pair of black polyester trousers – standard issue for all wardens. Next came aftershave, deodorant sprays, a comb, a mouldy Satsuma.

At the back of the locker was a large scrapbook; the majority of its pages covered with newspaper and magazine articles about kidnappings and ransom demands, rapes and murders. Mia took the scrapbook to a nearby table and laid it out for the others to see. Page upon page showed pictures of torture equipment, guns of every description, bomb-making paraphernalia.… Lennox seemed to be obsessed with the idea of holding a woman prisoner, and the book included stories from around the world of girls who'd been held captive for years. Alongside the narratives were grainy pictures of the small hovels and confined spaces in which the victims had been found.

'I'm beginning to wish we'd come with that warrant,' said Mia. 'This is explosive stuff.'

'And you won't be able to use any of it,' Perry pointed out.

'What if we came back later with a warrant? Who's to know we've already seen inside?'

'Ken and Sammy, for a start,' Perry said.

Mia shrugged. 'They didn't see us searching a locker. Anyway, how would they know we hadn't already got the warrant?'

'OK, you win,' said Perry, after a moment's hesitation. 'Go and get your warrant, but make it quick. I like my job. I don't want to lose it.'

Jack turned to Mia, his face grim. 'I've an awful feeling we've been viewing Lennox from the wrong angle. What if he hasn't done a runner? What if he's taking time out to select his next victim?'

Perry let out a wary laugh. 'This is ridiculous. Chris isn't a killer. He's got his faults – we all have – but basically he's a very charming man.'

'Lots of killers are charming,' said Mia. 'Mr Lennox certainly had me fooled.' She picked up the scrapbook and rifled through its pages. 'This changes everything, Jack.'

'So, what's next?'

'We get the warrant. And then we get Lennox. Come on.'

CHAPTER THIRTEEN

A large hoarding stood before the Apollo nightclub, its message declaring to all that WEDNESDAY NIGHT WAS GOTH NIGHT.

'Bloody freaks,' Nick muttered.

He'd woken that morning with a pounding headache and it was only getting worse. If he didn't get to see Lisa soon, something would have to give.

He'd found Danny in the board room, peering closely at the pictures of Hannah Bates with all the exuberance of a pervert regarding his prey. The very sight of the young DC's face, alive as it was with the eagerness he always brought to the job, had Nick longing to aim a fist between his smiling eyes. But instead he'd put a hand on his shoulder, saying warmly, 'All right, Dan? Ready to get the bastards?'

In the car, with Danny expounding his many theories about the case, Nick's nerves were pulled so taut it would almost have been a relief to smash the car's bonnet into the central reservation. He'd stayed on the road, of course, nodding his agreement and making the odd comment where necessary. But by the time they reached the Apollo he was ready to give somebody grief. And security manager Johnny Preston would do just fine.

They found him in a tiny office – no bigger than a large cupboard – directly behind the DJ's platform at the rear of the main dance floor. From a distance Preston appeared to have an athletic build; as they approached Nick saw a formidable opponent and decided to tone down the aggressive interrogation he'd had in mind. But up close he could see the man was going to seed. The start of a beer belly showed above his skin-tight jeans; and his biceps, bulging in a T-shirt at least two sizes too small, were more fatty tissue than muscle. Johnny Preston would be no match for Nick. Not today.

'Hello, sir,' he said, holding out a hand. 'I'm DI Ford, and this is DC Rose. We'd like to ask you a few questions.'

'Can I see some identification, please? You can't be too careful nowadays.'

They showed him their warrant cards. 'We're investigating the murder of Hannah Bates, Mr Preston.'

'Gina told me.' Preston gave a shrug. 'Bloody shame, ain't it?'

'You knew Hannah Bates?'

Preston considered the detectives. 'Shall we cut the crap? Gina's told me everything. You know Hannah met Chris every Wednesday, and you know me and Gina acted as a cover. Shall we take it from there?'

'Fine by me, sir. The sooner I'm out of this rat hole the better. I get claustrophobic in confined spaces.'

Sensing tension, Danny cut in. 'How well did you know Chris Lennox, sir?'

'Not that well. We'd have a drink sometimes. Not often. They didn't want me and Gina around. He was friendly enough, though.'

'How long had he been seeing Hannah?'

Preston pondered the question. 'A couple of months, I guess.'

Nick said, 'Did they always stay in the club or did they go off somewhere?'

'It depended on the group that was playing. They have poxy heavy metal groups here on a Wednesday. Chris liked some of them. He's into heavy metal 'cause his cousin's one of the Walking Dead. Anyway, if he fancied the look of the group they'd hang around. If not they'd piss off.'

'And what about the nights they went off?' said Nick. 'Where did they go?'

'How should I know?' said Preston. 'They never told me.'

'OK, what can you tell us about Colin Fowler – Hannah's fiancé?'

'Nothing any more,' said Preston, with a couldn't-care-less shrug. 'Me and Colin go way back, but we had a falling out, as Gina no doubt told you.' He couldn't resist a grin. 'Poor sod, banged up while his girl makes out with somebody else. Bloody shame, ain't it?'

'What about Hannah's brother, Tom? Do you know him?'

The man huffed. 'Oh, yes.'

Nick raised a questioning eyebrow. 'You said that as though you wished you didn't, Mr Preston. Does Tom Bates give you grief?'

'No,' said Preston, laughing. 'Tom's just feeling his feet, that's all. He's harmless enough. Chris used to get pissed off with him, though.'

'Really?' said Nick, ears pricking. 'Tom knows Chris Lennox? Your girlfriend said you two were the only ones who knew about Hannah's affair with Lennox.'

'Little brothers don't count, do they? Anyway Tom kept well away to begin with. But once he found out Chris was related to Walking Dead's lead singer … let's just say hero worship doesn't come anywhere near it.'

'He wouldn't leave them alone?'

'Followed them round like a little puppy dog.'

'How did Lennox react to that?' asked Nick. 'It must have been annoying, bumping into Hannah's little brother every time he turned round.'

'Suppose. He was patient with the little bastard though.' Preston pulled a face. 'Even so, I think he was glad to get rid of him after the bust-up.'

'What bust-up?'

'Chris caught Tom smoking cannabis one night. He'd been using it for a while. Hannah knew but he was old enough to please himself, so….' He shrugged. 'Chris's real anti-drugs, though. He can't bear the stuff. Anyway he threatened to finish with Hannah unless she told Mummy and Daddy so she'd got no choice.'

Nick stayed silent while he noted everything down. Presently, resting notebook and pen in his lap, he considered Preston's physique with an appraising eye. 'You look as though you'd know your way round a boxing-ring, Mr Preston.'

'I like to keep myself in reasonable shape,' Preston said, puffing out his chest.

'Is Lennox handy with his fists?'

'What?' said Preston, laughing again. 'Chris's a big teddy bear.' Suddenly his laughter faded. 'What's he making of all this?'

'We don't know where he is. We were hoping you could give us a few pointers.'

'Me?' Preston sounded surprised. 'Haven't got a clue.'

Nick sighed inwardly. There was nothing to be unearthed here. 'OK, thanks, Mr Preston. Sorry to have wasted your time.'

They crossed a dance floor still littered with last night's debris, thankful to be out of the stale atmosphere of the so-called security office.

Danny was hurrying to match Nick's determined strides. He said, 'Lennox doesn't sound like much of a threat. What do you think?'

'I'm not sure,' Nick replied, frowning. 'Nobody's ever just black and white, are they?' At the car he activated the central locking device and stood at the driver's door, pondering. 'I'd like to have a go at Tom Bates.'

Danny gave a dismissive huff. 'Mia's already had two bites of that cherry. She should have got something out of him by now.'

'That fat cow? She's fucking useless.' Nick got into the driver's seat, a smile spreading across his face. 'Yes, I'll have a go at young Tom and I'll get him to spill his guts – you just see if I don't.'

Danny had to swallow a laugh; it was such fun fuelling the flames of Nick's paranoia. 'You do that,' he said, eyes twinkling with mischief. 'You show DCI Wells who's the best copper in this team.'

'I will, Dan. I will.' Nick started the engine and released the handbrake with an aggressive jerk. 'And I'll tell you one thing – I'll have both balls cut off before I let Mia beat us to the finishing line on this one.'

To an untrained eye it would seem that Mia was already way ahead in the race to catch the killer.

After leaving the remand unit she phoned Paul Wells for permission to apply for two search warrants: one for Lennox's locker, the other for his house. The DCI eagerly agreed after hearing of their find. Then their arrival at the magistrates' court just happened to coincide with a break in the morning session, so Mia was able to get the warrants signed with the minimum of fuss.

Everything was going incredibly smoothly and in no time at all they were pulling up outside The Horseshoe with the contents of Lennox's locker safely installed in the car boot. They sat for a while surveying the impressive building while each slipped on a pair of latex gloves.

They gave the front door a miss. It was a solid oak structure and would be difficult to break into. The backs of the houses faced a ten-foot brick wall that separated the communal patio area from the forecourt of a one-storey retail unit supplying agricultural equipment to the local farming community.

'Brilliant,' said Mia. 'It's not overlooked at all.'

'And see the back door?' said Jack, already selecting a credit card from his wallet. 'I'll be able to get into that, no problem.'

Mia gave her partner a dubious look as he slipped the door's catch with the minimum of effort. 'You're too good at that.'

He grinned and pushed open the door, stepping aside for her to enter. 'After you, madam,' he said, bowing graciously.

The kitchen told them that Chris Lennox was a tidy man with an almost obsessive desire for cleanliness. Everything gleamed: the stainless steel mixer tap, the bone-handled cutlery, the rows of stainless steel containers lining the breakfast bar; even the terracotta floor-tiles looked as though they'd been scrubbed with a vengeance.

The living area was equally tidy. Lennox had gone for the minimalist look. Anything that might be guilty of harbouring dust was banned from this austere space. The overall colour scheme was mocha and beige with splashes of red supplied by a set of three large modern prints lining the far wall.

'Not very homely, is it?' said Jack. 'Can't see him sprawled on the settee, watching the footie.'

'We're not here to admire the furnishings. We'll start in his bedroom and work down.'

They found nothing in the main bedroom apart from a stash of mild pornography and an assortment of flavoured condoms. The spare bedroom was little more than an office housing a computer terminal and printer. There was, however, a tall steel cabinet with three deep drawers – all locked.

'Why would he keep it locked?' said Mia. 'We'll get uniformed to collect it. We'll need to see what's on the computer anyway, so they can get the lot.'

They examined the bathroom next and were intrigued to find a number of brown spots on the black-and-white-checked linoleum between the end of the bath and the washbasin. The rest of the flooring was immaculate and the spots were only found when Mia picked up a large midnight-blue bath towel that had fallen from its hook.

Jack got down on all fours for a closer look. 'Blood. And it's been there for a long time.'

'Strange. Everywhere's so clean … How did he miss that?'

'Everywhere's too clean. The whole place feels wrong to me.'

'But we've already found the murder scene on the riverbank.'

'We've found Hannah's murder scene, Mia. He could've damaged some other poor sod here and washed away the evidence. This place is too clean, especially for a bloke with a bloody great beard.'

Mia laughed. 'What?'

'It's been researched. Men with bushy beards aren't meticulous when it comes to cleaning their homes. Those who are don't go for facial hair. They like their bodies to be as clean as their living areas.'

Mia was far from convinced and a good-natured banter began between them, a banter loud enough to cover the sound of hesitant footsteps that sounded on the uncarpeted staircase. Suddenly a low growl came from the landing and the detectives swivelled round to face a very large and extremely angry German Shepherd bitch. The dog was pulling at her leash and salivating profusely at the idea of sampling young police officer for lunch.

Mia recoiled, her jaw dropped in mortal terror, as the dog inched ever nearer to her tasty shins. She hid behind Jack, hands firmly gripping his hips to keep him from fleeing. Then a wizened hand – thankfully attached to the other end of the leash – appeared around the doorjamb; and they were looking at an elderly woman, her snow-white hair pulled tightly into a neat bun on top of her head. She was tiny – no more than four-foot-ten – with not an ounce of surplus fat on her sprightly frame. The dog would have found more meat on a discarded lamb bone after the head of the house had picked it clean. The woman was wielding a baseball bat with a fair amount of menace; Mia didn't doubt for a moment that she'd use it should events turn nasty.

'What's going on here?' she said, her voice surprisingly low for one so slight.

'We're the police,' said Jack, reaching for his warrant card.

Both cards were proffered at arms' length. 'If you could … sort of … restrain the dog …' said Mia, still hiding behind Jack.

'When you've explained what you're up to and not before,' the elderly lady said.

'We're investigating the recent murder of Hannah Bates. You might have read about it in the papers—'

'I have. What's it got to do with this property?'

'We have reason to believe,' said Jack, 'that the owner of this property – Mr Chris Lennox – knew the dead girl and we'd like to interview him, only he seems to have disappeared, so….' His words faltered and he lamely waved an arm, as if that were explanation enough for their breaking and entering. 'We do have a search warrant,' he added swiftly. 'We'll show you if you promise to keep hold of the dog.'

'All right.' She scrutinized minutely the piece of paper that was held out by an eager-to-please Jack. At last she said, 'Thank you, that seems to be in order.' Then, stooping to talk to the dog, her voice soft, she said, 'I do believe we can stop the charades now, sweety.'

Her more gentle tone caused the dog, as if by magic, to change instantly from a ferocious killing-machine into an oversized lapdog, nuzzling its mistress's stomach and sniffing the pockets of her fleecy cardigan for titbits.

Mia let out a long breath. 'That's better. Now, Mrs…?'

'Miss … Miss Joyce Leadbetter. If we frightened you, Fluffy and I, then please accept our apologies. Only it's rather disconcerting to find the kitchen door wide open, especially as I've got the only spare key.'

Jack said, 'Would you mind answering a few questions, Miss Leadbetter?'

'It all depends on what those questions are.'

'Could you tell us where Mr Lennox is?'

'No, I haven't the faintest idea.'

'Pity,' said Jack. 'Any idea when he's due back?'

'No.'

'When did you last see Mr Lennox?'

'Last Sunday evening. He came round and played our little tune on my doorbell. He always does that when it's dark so I'll know it's him. He's such a considerate man.'

'You two sound very close,' said Jack, with a suggestive wink. 'Come on, Miss Leadbetter, tell us more. We're very discreet.'

She let out a hearty laugh and the dog took to padding excitedly about her feet. 'Ladies don't tell,' she said, her tone skittish. 'And, anyway, DC Turnbull, there's nothing to tell … unfortunately.'

'He's a good neighbour then?'

'Oh, yes. I live alone and I'm not what you'd call fainthearted, but it's nice to know that Chris's next door should I ever need him.' She gave a tiny sigh. 'I'll be glad when he gets back.'

Mia said, 'What did he want on Sunday?'

'He said he needed to go away for a while and could I keep an eye on the house till he gets back. I agreed, of course, I'd do anything for Chris.'

'He sounds like a nice man to have next door,' said Mia, her frown a picture of puzzlement.

'Chris's the perfect neighbour.' She gave an indulgent tut-tut. 'He does have his television volume up too loud sometimes, but that's just a small fault.' She laughed. 'Goodness knows what he was watching recently – it sounded as though somebody was being tortured. I mentioned it the next day and he was so distressed to know I'd been disturbed. He went as white as a sheet, poor thing. He said he'd no idea the walls were so thin. It won't happen again, Joyce, he said, his lovely strong arm around my shoulders. He's gorgeous.'

Mia glanced at Jack. 'Does Mr Lennox ever bring his lady friends home?'

The old woman looked appalled. 'Chris doesn't have any lady friends. At least, he's never brought any back here. He's a very private person.'

Clearly unhappy with the line of questioning, the old woman abruptly turned her attention to Fluffy. The dog, clearly bored, was nudging her arm with such force that she almost lost her footing. She undid the leash and allowed the dog to roam freely. It found its way to Mia and sat on its haunches, looking up at her with huge doleful eyes the colour of ancient amber.

A thin keening sound started at the back of its throat. 'Fluffy wants you to fondle her, DS Harvey. Go on, don't be shy.'

Oh, shit, thought Mia, bending down to stroke the dog. Its hot breath smelt of rotten meat and wave upon wave of it assaulted her nostrils. After several moments she broke away. 'I could play with her all day, Miss Leadbetter, but we really need to get on.'

'Is that it?' said Miss Leadbetter, sounding almost disappointed.

Mia was moving towards the door, keen to get away from the dog. 'We'll be off now. And we're going to need Mr Lennox's keys, if you wouldn't mind handing them over.'

'I don't know about that.' The old lady frowned. 'Chris gave them to me for safekeeping. Why do you need them?'

'Our enquiries have only just begun, I'm afraid. Some of our uniformed colleagues will be here later in the day.' Mia nodded towards the dog. 'Perhaps you should put the lead back on. I'd hate Fluffy to get out of the door and be run over by an articulated lorry.'

The old woman attached the lead and handed over the keys. 'Do you want Chris's mobile phone number?'

Jack's eyes widened. 'You've got his mobile number?'

'Of course. How else would I get hold of him in an emergency?'

'Great. Would you write it down please?' Jack hastily handed across his notebook and pen. 'And we must ask you not to contact Mr Lennox for the time being.'

She tapped the side of her nose. 'You don't want me tipping him off that the police are on his trail.' She gave a high-pitched laugh. 'Only joking … Chris's incapable of committing a crime.'

In the car they sat in silence, quite unable to believe their luck. Then Jack nudged Mia. 'We've only got his bloody mobile phone number.'

'I only hope his number one fan doesn't ring him first.' Mia frowned. 'He doesn't sound much like a killer though. What if we're wrong?'

'Are you kidding? We've found blood on the bathroom floor…. His neighbour's heard sounds of torture…. Mia, he's had a girl in that house and they weren't playing footsie.'

CHAPTER FOURTEEN

If Mia had harboured hopes of getting her relationship with Nick on to a less hostile footing, they were cruelly dashed the moment she set foot inside the board room. Nick was helping himself to coffee. As soon as he saw her he started up a slow clapping that resounded with bitter derision, causing all in the room to look her way.

He said loudly, 'Here she comes … Larchborough's answer to Miss Marple. How does it feel, Mia, having Wells slavering after your fat fanny?'

Mia wandered across, a frown creasing her forehead. She'd planned to use this debriefing session as an opportunity to build bridges. 'What's up now?' she said, a placatory smile hiding her disappointment.

He fixed her with a hostile glare. 'I wanted to have a go at Tom Bates but, oh no, it wouldn't do for me to override all your good work.' He snorted. 'It doesn't matter that you've had all this time to break him and you've got fuck all to show for it.'

Mia recoiled from the sheer hatred in his voice. 'If you're unhappy with your duties then take it up with the DCI. It's got nothing to do with me.'

131

'I'm the senior officer here,' he said. 'I should have the pick of the jobs. But time and again he favours you. It makes me sick.'

Mia sidled up beside him. 'Maybe he can see my mind's on the job, whereas yours is always in your bloody Y-fronts.' She raised her eyebrows as though struck by a sudden thought. 'By the way, Nick, had your leg over yet? It is Wednesday, your day to scare the pants off Lisa. Come to think of it, that's the only way you'd get them off. That girl's got taste.'

She started to walk away but Nick gripped her tightly by the arm, his face so close she could feel his warm breath on her ear. But before he could release his next volley of abuse the door flew open and in breezed DCI Wells, holding up a number of folders for all to see.

'We're making progress, kiddies,' he said, shrugging off his overcoat on the dais. 'Forensics found a pubic hair on Hannah's clothing and it doesn't match hers. So now we've got a DNA sample.'

'What a prat,' said Danny. 'He's almost making it too easy.'

The DCI huffed. 'It can never be too easy, mate. And we've still got to find him, don't forget.'

Mia said, 'Sir, there's good news about Lennox's house as well.' Ignoring Nick's quiet snort she launched into a hurried account of the blood found in the bathroom and the information naïvely offered by Miss Leadbetter. 'And we've got his mobile phone number, sir.'

'Brilliant. We'll have him in a.s.a.p. In the meantime we'll get DNA samples from all male residents in the immediate area just to be on the safe side.' He pointed towards the back of the room. 'I want two volunteers after this session and we'll set up a room.' He selected one of the folders from his desk. 'Now, the green sacks containing Hannah's body and her clothes are sold at all Tesco stores, so we'll need to know whether Mr Lennox uses our local branch.'

'Something else pointing to Tom Bates,' said Nick. 'He works at the Tesco store in town.'

132

'Good point, mate, but it's hardly one we should be worrying about at present.'

'Why not?' said Nick, hotly. 'Surely we should be covering all bases till we know for sure that Lennox is our man.'

'Thanks for telling me how to do my job, Nick. And, I know you're disappointed because I won't let you have a crack at the lad but for now I've got more pressing work for you to do.'

'Oh, yes?' The words were uttered with precious little respect.

Wells shot Nick a look of rage. 'Yes, I want you and Danny to round up the lads implicated in the Edith Bowman murder … if you've no objections. Uniformed have managed to get a list of names and addresses. I'll hand it over when we've finished.'

Wells paused to riffle through another of the folders. They watched while he scratched his head and frowned thoughtfully. 'Actually, that case is bothering me. According to the post-mortem results time of death was no earlier than eight o'clock. But we've been told that the daughter found her mother dead around half past six or thereabouts. John Lloyd reckons the woman's age and low body weight could have had an effect on rigor mortis, but not enough to account for such a large discrepancy. He also states that cause of death was not heart failure but asphyxiation brought about by an object being held over the woman's face. A number of blue fibres were found around her nostrils.' Again he scratched his head. 'There's more to this case than meets the eye and we need to find out what it is.'

Mia put up a hand. 'Sir, I was planning to visit my mother at St Stephen's after work tonight. Shall I have a word with Janet while I'm there?'

'You do that, darling. Actually, go after we've finished here. I'll get hold of Mr Lennox.' He glared at Nick. 'As long as that's OK with you, mate. I'd hate to put your nose out of joint.' Nick squirmed in his seat, aware that all eyes were on him.

'Right,' said Wells, gathering up the folders. 'We get Lennox safely into custody. We get forensics over to his house. As soon as they've finished we get his computer and filing cabinet brought back here. With a bit of luck we'll have this case wrapped up in no time.'

Jack said, 'What about me, sir?'

'You can help sort out the DNA tests for the time being, Jack. It won't need two of you going to the nursing home.' Wells clapped his hands. 'All right, kiddies, let's look lively. And make Daddy proud – yes?'

Mia and Nick approached the dais: Mia to hand over Lennox's mobile phone number; Nick to collect the list of youths to be brought in. Neither acknowledged the other. That bridge between them, far from being rebuilt, had been fitted with incendiary devices and blown out of all existence. And Mia was glad. He wasn't worth the effort.

Jack was surreptitiously reading a sexually explicit text message from Michelle when he noticed that Danny was still slumped in his chair, his face a sickly grey. 'You OK, mate? You don't look too good.'

'Last night's beer must have been off.' He clutched his stomach and winced. 'Bog for me, I think. Tell Nick where I am.'

'Poor sod,' Jack murmured, as he watched Danny disappear through the door. Now that all was well in his own world Jack could afford to be magnanimous towards others. Even so, he thought Danny Rose was a weird bloke. He'd never before encountered anybody so fired up with ambition. The job seemed to be the sole reason for the bloke's existence. Fighting to get on was all very well, just so long as you kept it a clean fight. But, Danny didn't. Jack had watched him playing Mia off against Nick more than once and that wasn't on. They were a team and they should be watching each other's backs, not sticking the knife in at every opportunity.

But why should he worry? He was Mia's partner, thank Christ. Without wasting another thought on Danny and his dubious methods of getting ahead Jack turned his mobile back on and read again Michelle's account of all the erotic pleasures she had planned for him after work.

*

Money. Was it the route to all evil? Or the root of all evil? Janet wasn't sure. But of one thing she was certain: money – or the lack of it – was the reason she'd spent the morning besmirching her poor mother's memory while her body lay in a refrigerated box at the local mortuary.

On the desk before her was an HSBC cheque to the value of £20,000. Feeling sick to her stomach Janet reached forward and picked it up. For one terrible moment she felt tempted to tear the cheque into tiny pieces. But what would be the point of that? If she didn't make use of the money then selling Edith's pride and joy would have been for nothing.

They'd offered a paltry £10,000 for the table – Messrs Thackeray & Jones, Purveyors of Fine Antiques. Pilferers of fine antiques more like. But she'd stood her ground until the offer was increased. And increased. And increased again. Then, content with the final amount, Janet had left the premises with the cheque safely ensconced in her purse.

She should be relieved – a terrible disaster had been averted – but all she felt was a hollow emptiness. Her mother, her best friend, was gone. Janet had always been a strong believer in life after death, of an existence where loved ones kept watch and waited for the time when she would join them. A happy reunion. All she had to look forward to now was a trial of retribution where her mother would harangue her for her sins. She was dwelling on that unsavoury thought when a faint knock sounded and the door was opened by Sylvia Bruce, her second in command.

'Mia Harvey's outside,' she said. 'She'd like to see you, if you're feeling up to it.'

Adrenalin surged through Janet's system at the mere mention of Mia's name. 'Show her in.'

She barely had time to thrust the cheque into her desk drawer before Mia was ushered into the office, a large bunch of yellow chrysanthemums in her hands.

'I thought you might like these,' said Mia, the words spoken haltingly.

'They're lovely,' said Janet, taking the flowers and placing them on a side table. 'I'll put them in water the minute you're gone.'

She returned to her seat and indicated that Mia should sit opposite. There was an awkwardness between them that Mia had never sensed before. Was Janet, after all these years, finding it difficult to separate the police officer from the friend?

'I've just been to see Mum,' said Mia.

Janet recoiled sharply. Those words hurt. But, why? This was a nursing home for the elderly. Mia had every right to see her mother. Of course Janet would never see hers again.... She took in a long breath.

'Barbara's doing well. Don't you think?'

Mia nodded. 'Are you OK?'

Janet shrugged. 'They won't give me a death certificate.'

Mia's gaze dropped to the desktop. 'We've found a few discrepancies. They're slowing things up a bit.'

'What discrepancies?' Mia hesitated and Janet's heart constricted in her chest. 'Tell me.'

Mia hesitated again for the briefest of moments and then the words tumbled out. 'The truth is, Janet, we're having problems with the cause of death.'

'But we know what killed Mum,' Janet said, her eyes widening in disbelief. 'Those bloody yobs battered her with God knows what and left her to bleed to death.'

'No, they didn't,' Mia said, her tone apologetic. 'The blow to your mother's head came after death. It's a fact and it's causing us problems.'

Janet's jaw sagged. 'How do you think they killed her, then?'

'Oh Janet, this is so difficult.' Mia gave a troubled sigh. 'The pathologist states your mother was suffocated. Something was put over her face until … until she died.'

'So they hit Mum just for the fun of it,' Janet said, her heart seeming to plunge in her chest. 'But why should this delay anything? Surely you can still charge them.'

'The *time* of death's all wrong as well, Janet.'

The woman gasped, clutched at her throat. 'Oh, this is too much….'

'I know,' said Mia, hating to put her through this. 'But the pathologist states time of death was nearer eight o'clock. Is there any chance you might have been wrong about the time you found her?'

'Have you any idea what it's like to come home and find your mother in a pool of blood?' Janet said, tears stinging her eyes. 'Funnily enough I wasn't too bothered about the time. What if I did leave work later? What does it matter?'

'You left at five o'clock, Janet, just like you told us,' Mia said quickly. 'I asked Sylvia to confirm it.'

Janet's face reddened with astonishment. 'You spoke to Sylvia about me?'

'What's the problem?' said Mia, taken aback.

'You've been checking up on me?'

Mia was perplexed. 'I was hardly checking up on you. I was just doing my job.'

Janet sprang to her feet. 'You're supposed to be my friend and yet you sneak around, asking others to confirm my story. Were you hoping to catch me out in a lie?'

'No, of course not.'

Janet hurried across to the flowers and picked them up. 'Get out, Mia. Get out and take these with you.' With a look of sheer hatred she threw the flowers and they landed at Mia's feet, a tangle of broken stems and scattered petals.

Mia stared down at the mess. 'You're very upset,' she said, with deliberate slowness, 'so I'll make allowances. And I'm so sorry I was the one to upset you. Please don't make

my mother's life a misery because you're angry with me.'
Then she left.

Janet looked from the door to the flowers and then to the drawer holding the cheque. Suddenly she was overwhelmed by an aching tiredness. With heavy steps she returned to her seat.

Mia had asked her not to take her feelings out on Barbara. Did Mia really think her capable of such irresponsible conduct? Her job was to make life better for the poor souls in her care, not subject them to bitter abuse because life wasn't going her way. And then she thought of her beloved Edith. The one person she should have protected.

At last tears started to fall; hot, violent tears. And what a relief they were.

'Excuse me, sir, could I have a quick word?'

Danny was shouldering his way through the double doors to police reception when he saw DCI Wells about to enter the lift. Hearing Danny's eager call, Wells let the lift doors close and wandered across to the reception desk, an impatient frown on his already fretful features.

'What do you want, Danny? Make it quick.'

Danny's own expression was regretful. 'I'm afraid we've lost our suspects in the Edith Bowman case, sir.'

'What do you mean, we've lost them?' said Wells, as though he were speaking to a disobedient child.

'They've all got cast-iron alibis for yesterday, sir. From early morning till just before midnight.'

'All of them?'

'Afraid so, sir. They were all in London taking part in a march on Downing Street.'

'You're joking,' Wells huffed.

'They're pupils at the Manor High School and it's due to be closed down to make way for a load of houses. The teachers arranged a petition to be handed in to Number Ten. A load of them went down, sir … teachers, parents, pupils … a whole fleet of coaches apparently.'

'I heard about that. And our gang was amongst them? Huh, very public-spirited of them, I must say.'

Danny shrugged. 'They obviously saw it as a free trip to London, sir. Anyway, they were definitely there.'

'Where's Nick?' said Wells, his mood darkening by the second.

'Parking the car, sir.'

As if on cue Nick came bustling through the doors, his face falling when he saw Danny with the DCI. 'You've told him, then?'

'Yes, mate, he's told me. And doesn't that just bugger things up nicely….'

Nick said, 'What now then, sir?'

'Your guess is as good as mine. I suppose we'll just have to wait for forensics. And let's hope Mia gets something useful from the daughter.'

Stan Smith, the duty sergeant, chose that moment to emerge from a door behind reception, his portly frame straining the buttons of his uniform. He was carrying a black box file with a steaming mug of coffee and half a dozen chocolate digestive biscuits balanced precariously on top. With barely three weeks to go before retirement Stan's cavalier attitude showed he was already in training for a more leisurely lifestyle. Even Wells's stony expression failed to penetrate his *joie de vivre*. He placed his load on the counter, spilling his coffee as he did so. 'Careful, Paul, if the wind changes you'll stick like it.'

'Sorry?'

'Your face…. For all you know it might never happen.'

'That's what's worrying me.'

'Anything I can do?' said Stan, carefully dunking one of the biscuits.

Wells leant an elbow on the reception desk, his temper softening before the sergeant's infectious cheerfulness. 'We've got two unconnected murders, Stan. If you could solve them, preferably within the next twenty-four hours, I'll be forever in your debt.'

Stan chuckled, his large belly wobbling with the effort. 'Leave it with me. I always did want to retire in a blaze of glory.'

'Don't we all.' Wells motioned to his officers. 'Upstairs, kiddies, we've got work to do.'

As they waited for the lift, Danny said, 'Have you spoken to Lennox yet, sir?'

Wells let out a long breath. 'I just keep getting voicemail. I'm hardly going to leave a message, am I?'

Danny suddenly clutched his stomach and grimaced. He took to pacing about. 'I wish that lift would hurry up. I need the bog.' Wells raised a questioning eyebrow. 'Bad beer, sir. I'll be fine.'

'Serves you right, mate. You should be getting early nights, conserving your energy, not enjoying yourself in the pub.'

The lift pinged and the door slid open. Wells ushered his men in and was about to step forward when Stan shouted, 'Paul … call for you.'

'Who is it?'

'A bloke called Chris Lennox. He wants CID, said it's urgent.'

Wells shot a look at his detectives. 'You two carry on up.' He hurried across to the desk and grabbed the receiver. 'Mr Lennox? Mr Chris Lennox?'

'Aye. Who are you?' The Highlands accent was clipped, the tone extremely cautious.

'DCI Paul Wells, sir, Larchborough CID. I'm glad you've phoned. I've been trying to get hold of you all morning.'

'Why? Because your men have been crawling all over my house? Don't bother to deny it. My neighbour's already tipped me off.'

'We have searched your home, sir, and we can show you the warrant allowing us to do so.'

'Can I ask why, or is the reason confidential?' was Lennox's abrasive reply.

'It's to do with Hannah Bates, sir.'

A telling pause. 'What about her?'

'We need to talk about your relationship with Miss Bates.'

Another pause, longer this time. 'Why?'

Wells considered his answer for a moment. It was imperative that he worded it correctly. If he blundered in heavy-handed then Lennox could cut off the call and disappear. 'We need your help, sir. You might be able to give us the information needed to further our enquiries.'

'What enquiries?'

Wells stifled a sigh. He'd expected the man to be guarded, but Lennox was offering nothing. 'The enquiries we're pursuing with regard to Hannah's murder, sir.'

Lennox suddenly gave a long harrowing groan and started to weep, long agonizing sobs that brought a frown to Wells's face.

'So, it's true? Hannah really is dead?'

'I'm afraid so, sir.'

Wells cast a puzzled glance at Stan. The man's grief sounded genuine and Wells was on the brink of offering his condolences when he remembered the scrapbook taken from Lennox's locker, the blood found in his over-scrubbed home.

Injecting his voice with more than a modicum of sympathy, Wells said, 'I apologize for my tactless approach, sir. I didn't realize you hadn't heard about the murder.'

'My neighbour said your officers had been round my house. She was blathering on about a murdered girl. She said Hannah's name. I couldn't believe it, so I decided to call. I thought you'd tell me it was all a terrible mistake.'

Before Lennox could lapse into another round of sobbing, Wells said, 'I'm afraid not, sir. We searched your house because you were close to Hannah and we have to start somewhere. But we've hit a brick wall. We need help. Would you come along to the station, Mr Lennox, and give us that help?'

'Aye, of course I will. I'll do anything I can.'

'Good. When can we expect you?'

'It'll be a good few hours yet. I'm in the Lake District.'

'Are you? Well, you just drive carefully, Mr Lennox.' The line went dead and Wells grinned at Stan as he replaced the receiver. 'That's a turn up for the book. It's not every day we get the killer offering to help with our enquiries.'

Stan picked up the last of the biscuits and took a bite. 'I'll get a nice warm cell ready for him. He'll need a rest after such a long journey.'

CHAPTER FIFTEEN

It was late evening and Mia was in the board room nursing a cup of cold coffee and the first stirrings of a sickening migraine. Janet's irrational outburst that morning had affected her badly and she'd spent the rest of the day trying to shake off a dreadful feeling of foreboding that only seemed to increase the more she focused her thoughts on St Stephen's and her mother. For hours now she'd been trying to analyse those unsettling feelings and perhaps put Janet's reaction into some sort of perspective. But it was all a waste of time: she was in no mood for psychological profiling.

She longed to get out of the police station. If only she could go home for a long soak followed by eight hours of dreamless sleep under a down-filled duvet. But instead she was to pussyfoot around Chris Lennox in the hope that he might somehow put his head in the noose by unwittingly letting slip details of Hannah's death known only to the killer. And she was to do this with Nick bloody Ford at her side. Jack was still smoothing out final details of the DNA marathon. Danny was on his way home after Wells had only half-jokingly declared that Superintendent Shakespeare's amenities budget would collapse under the bashing he was giving the station's loo roll supply.

Mia was surrounded by a bustle of activity: ringing telephones, juddering fax machines, the clicking of computer keys, snatched words from a medley of conversations. Sitting at the heart of the tumult, yet alone with her thoughts, she was unaware of the hurried entrance of Paul Wells with an agitated Nick bringing up the rear.

Wells said, 'We've got Lennox waiting in interview room number one, darling, and he's not in the best of moods.'

Mia said, 'How do you want us to play this, sir?'

'Tread carefully until we get the forensic report or something relevant turns up on his computer. Let him think he's here to help bring the killer to justice. He's tired and he might trip himself up. Let's bloody hope so anyway.'

She looked at him askance. 'So we're not to mention the scrapbook or the blood?'

'Not yet. Just keep him sweet.'

Nick said, 'What about his DNA sample, sir? Do we ask for it outright?'

'Yes,' said Wells, rubbing at his jowls. 'If he doesn't agree then be creative – offer him a coffee and make sure he actually drinks from the cup.' He waved an impatient hand. 'You two know what to do.'

Mia walked with Nick through a labyrinth of corridors, the silence between them almost tangible. At the door to the interview room Nick gave her a hostile stare. 'Wells said to keep him sweet, remember, so you'd better leave the talking to me.'

'In your dreams, little boy,' she muttered, following him in.

Police Constable David Corcoran was stationed to the left of the door, his bored expression clear for all to see. Lennox was slumped in his seat, elbows on the table, head in his hands. He looked up as they entered and Mia was shocked by his ragged appearance. That day in the remand unit she'd witnessed a man who took pride in his appearance; but now his clothes were dishevelled, the collar of his sweatshirt only partly tucked into his crew-neck sweater as though he'd dressed in a hurry. The skin above his thick brown beard was ashen; and his eyes held a haunted look as he watched the detectives take their seats.

'What happened to Hannah?' he said, thumping the tabletop with his fist. 'Nobody's telling me anything and I need to know.'

They were to divulge as few details as possible about the actual crime. Lennox could hardly incriminate himself if he was handed the cause of death on a plate.

'You'll be told in due course,' said Nick. 'Would you be kind enough to supply a DNA sample, Mr Lennox?'

The man scoured their guarded expressions and then sat back, all aggression spent. 'Aye, if you like.'

Nick quickly collected the sample and handed it to PC Corcoran with whispered instructions for it to be delivered to DCI Wells straight away. The ease with which Lennox had agreed to the procedure caused a flutter of anxiety in Mia's stomach. If the man had had anything to do with the crime surely he'd be less than willing to allow a test on his bodily fluids. Perhaps, though, DCI Wells was right. Perhaps the man was so certain he'd left no incriminating evidence that he saw no harm in submitting to the test. Mia's initial impression of the man had been entirely favourable. Could she have been wrong? Could he really be a cold-blooded killer? Only time would tell.

'Right,' said Nick, returning to his seat, 'would you mind telling us where you've been for the past three days?'

'You should be answering my questions,' Lennox said, the words heavy with suspicion.

'This is the way we work,' said Nick, keeping his voice light. 'We sort out the background stuff first and then get down to the details.'

Lennox attempted to relax. 'OK. I was at a creative writing course put on by the Writers' Foundation at Headingley Hall in the Lake District. You can check, if you like.'

'We will,' said Nick, writing down the details. 'You took off quite suddenly. Why was that?'

'The courses are popular. Places are hard to get. When they rang me on Sunday with a cancellation I had to grab it quick. There would've been plenty of aspiring writers only too willing to take the place.'

Nick considered the man. 'So you're an aspiring writer?'

'Aye.' He lifted a shoulder. 'My job at Marshcroft pays the bills, but it's hardly what you'd call aesthetically pleasing – do you hear what I'm saying?'

'Oh, I do,' said Nick, unable to hide a smirk. 'Pardon me for saying, Mr Lennox, but you don't look like the type who'd enjoy scribbling away about nothing until the early hours—'

Lennox sat upright, his hackles rising. 'What's that supposed to mean?'

'I didn't mean to offend, sir, it's just … you'd look more at home in a weight-lifting tournament. You're a big man, powerfully built—'

'And I suppose you think all writers are limp-wristed pansy boys,' Lennox growled.

'Something like that.'

Throughout this short exchange Nick had kept his tone pleasant, but there was no mistaking the revulsion he felt for the man; it underlined his every word and showed all too clearly on his face. So this was his idea of keeping the man sweet, Mia thought. She decided to step in before they came to blows.

'What sort of things do you write, Mr Lennox? Poetry? Short stories?'

'Short stories, stage plays….' he said, dragging his venomous gaze away from Nick. 'But more than anything I'm into novels … crime novels.'

'I'm impressed,' she said swiftly, hoping to keep this fragile link between them intact. 'It must take a lot of single-minded determination to write all those words.' He shrugged. 'Did Hannah know about your ambitions?'

His eyes clouded at the mention of her name. 'Aye, she was really supportive.'

The door opened and PC Corcoran crept back into his role of sentinel, an apologetic grimace on his face. Mia acknowledged him and then continued. 'How long were you and Hannah together, Mr Lennox?'

He heaved a sigh. 'Only a couple of months, but she was the one for me. I knew it the first time I set eyes on her.'

'Across a crowded visitors' room,' Nick mumbled with a mocking grin.

Lennox made to leave his seat, hands bunched into fists. 'I don't have to put up with this. I'm here to *help*, for pity's sake, and this obnoxious prick keeps having a go.'

'I apologise for my colleague's unfortunate manner,' Mia said, glaring at Nick. 'Let me assure you, though, he's an obnoxious prick with everybody so there's no need to take it personally.'

Nick rounded on her, nostrils flaring. 'What right have you to apologize for me?'

'A word, Nick … outside … now,' she said, already on her feet. She nodded to PC Corcoran to keep an eye on Lennox and stormed into the corridor.

'Do you want to be thrown off this case?' she said, the moment they were alone. 'Because that's what's going to happen when I tell Paul Wells about your behaviour in there.'

Nick snorted. 'You'd take that bastard's side? Just shows what a nasty little arse-licker you really are.' He grabbed her shoulders and pushed her roughly against the wall. 'You saw Hannah's body in that sack. He did that, that psychopath in there. And all you can do is chat about fucking novels.'

Shaking him off Mia moved to the opposite side of the corridor, her breath coming in shallow gasps. 'But how can you be so sure he did it, Nick? What evidence have you got?'

'None yet—'

'Precisely, we've got nothing, and Wells says we're not to antagonize him. So what do you do? You get him all riled up. Well done … brilliant job.'

'He's as guilty as hell. I can smell his fucking guilt. But we're never going to get anything out of him playing Mr Nice Guy.'

'Wells says we've got to.'

'Wells is wrong then. We need to get him riled so he'll make a slip.'

Mia pulled in a breath, attempted to compose herself. 'All right, we'll play it your way. But another scene like that one, Nick, and I'll be squealing to the DCI quicker than you can turn my stomach. And that's pretty quick, believe me.'

They went back in and took their seats, a furious Lennox watching their every move.

'Apologies, Mr Lennox, I was out of line,' said Nick, the words sticking in his craw. 'That's what comes from viewing pretty young women after a lunatic's had his way with them.'

Lennox regarded him with suspicion. Then, seeming to come to a decision, he said, 'Apology accepted.'

'Good.' Nick found a fresh page in his notebook and sat back to consider the man. 'You like your girls young, don't you, Chris? And tiny as well. I suppose the smaller they are, the easier it is to subdue them.'

Lennox let out a bitter laugh. 'I know what you're trying to do, but I'll not rise to the bait.'

'Don't you have fantasies, Chris? You'd be the only bloke living who doesn't't.' Nick grinned. 'Personally, I prefer the four-in-a-bed scenario. I've always been a gregarious soul.' His grin slipped. 'But you, Chris … you like to fuck in secret. You like the idea of keeping a slave. Somebody small and willing. Somebody who can be easily subdued—'

'What's all this about subduing wee girls?' said Lennox, clearly agitated.

Nick feigned surprise. 'But I thought the whole concept intrigued you, Chris. Didn't we find a whole load of papers on the subject in your locker at work?' Mia swung round in her seat, horror on her face. They were supposed to keep quiet about their find. When she opened her mouth to stop him Nick held up a hand, his expression a dire warning. He stared at Lennox, his eyes narrowed. 'You like the idea of keeping a girl prisoner in some filthy little hutch of a cell, don't you, Chris? Does the filth add to the thrill? Does your dick get harder the more dust and dirt there is? Is that why you raped Hannah outside in the mud … so the rats could sniff around while you forced it in?'

'You've been busy,' said Lennox. His voice was loud with bravado; but the way he shifted in his seat, his gaze darting towards the door, showed desperation.

Nick fell silent and tapped his pen against the tabletop while he studied the man. 'What was all that shit doing in your locker if you weren't obsessed with keeping a girl prisoner so you could fuck her whenever you liked?'

Lennox let out a sigh, his hostile gaze never leaving Nick's face. 'Those were research papers in my locker … research for my play, *The Needless Quest For Vengeance.*'

'Oh, here he goes again,' Nick said to Mia. He aimed a disbelieving look at Lennox. 'Research? Like those notes on your computer that just happened to match the MO in Hannah's murder?' he lied.

Lennox's eyes widened. 'You've looked on my computer?' He swallowed a curse. 'As far as I'm concerned you've worked hard to make that information fit Hannah's injuries. In any case, every bit of it was taken from a variety of police profiles on the most famous serial killers in British history. It's all on the True Crime shelves at any library. Anybody could have access to it.'

Nick thought for a moment. 'That play of yours … what's it about?'

'A humanitarian aid worker who's imprisoned abroad by hostile forces. Why?'

'Where's it set?'

'Iraq.'

'Would you say all perverts are the same, whether they come from Birmingham or Baghdad?'

Lennox considered the question. 'I'd say the basic deviations in their characters would probably be the same, but their motives and methods might differ. Somebody growing up in Birmingham would have a different mindset from a native of Baghdad.'

Nick's grin was triumphant. 'So what good would those research papers be for your play? The abductions all took place over here.'

Lennox skimmed him an impatient look. 'If you're going to steal my stuff, at least have the good grace to look through it properly. My research covered abductions from all over the world. It also included the making of bombs, torture equipment, the sorts of guns used on an everyday basis – all information I needed for my script.'

Nick decided to change course, keep the man on his toes. 'You knew Hannah was engaged to Colin Fowler … how did that make you feel?'

Lennox dropped his gaze and began picking at a cigarette burn on the tabletop. 'I wasn't happy about it. I felt bad about seeing his woman behind his back. But we had to keep it quiet. I was breaking the rules. I'd have lost my job if they'd found out.'

'Hannah was going to give Fowler the elbow as soon as he was released – is that right?'

'Aye, with Colin no longer in the unit there'd be nothing to stop us going public and that's what we were planning to do.'

'Do you get on all right with Fowler?'

'We're not great pals, if that's what you mean. He keeps on pushing the boundaries – they all do – and I have to keep pushing back. It's all part of the job.'

'How come you ended up working at the remand unit?'

'It's a job, and it pays well.'

'How long have you lived in Larchborough?'

'About three years.'

'What made you move from Scotland?'

'I met a Larchborough girl and moved down here to be with her, but we hit the rocks a good twelve months ago.'

Mia cut in then. 'I'd like to talk about the Apollo nightclub, Mr Lennox. You met Hannah there every Wednesday night, I believe?'

'Aye. We were into heavy metal and the Apollo has some good groups.'

'Did you meet Hannah at any other time?'

'No, we had to be careful. Like I said I could've lost my job.'

Mia smiled. 'Were you always phoning each other, sending romantic text messages?'

Lennox nodded, tried to hold back the tears. He certainly didn't look like a man who'd committed the ultimate sin. His emotions looked real enough to Mia. But if she'd learned one thing during her years in the force it was that killers were great manipulators. It was those calculating skills that helped trap the victim in the first place. And later, after their deadly lust had been satisfied, those same tactics were used to throw the police off course. Was Lennox doing that now; playing the grieving boyfriend to distract them?

Mia looked pensive. 'What's bothering me, Mr Lennox, is why you didn't bother getting in touch with Hannah over the weekend. Especially on the Sunday when you knew you'd be going away for a fortnight.'

'Who said I didn't try to get in touch?' he countered. 'The last time we spoke was Thursday, around midnight. We always liked to talk before we went to sleep. Friday was a busy day for me. I didn't have the time. I sent her some texts though, and I got replies back. But when I called later that evening – around ten o'clock – her phone was dead. I just thought her mobile network was down.' He started to fidget, picking again at the tabletop. 'On the Saturday, when I still couldn't get her, I started to worry. So I phoned her brother and asked him to get Hannah to call me. He said he'd give her the message and I left it at that.'

'Hold on,' said Mia. 'You phoned Tom Bates?'

'Aye.'

'On the Saturday?'

'That's what I said.'

'And he said he'd give her the message?'

'Aye.'

Mia glanced at Nick, her thoughts racing. This was a development she hadn't seen coming. Was Chris Lennox telling porkies in the hope of leading them to the wrong conclusions? Or was Tom more involved in this murder than any of them had ever thought possible? Tom Bates couldn't possibly have given his sister a message on Saturday because Hannah was already dead by then.

Mia said, 'What did you think when Hannah didn't call, Mr Lennox?'

'That Tom hadn't given her the message,' he said, shrugging.

'Did you expect him to give her the message?'

Lennox made a face. 'Let's just say I wasn't surprised when she didn't phone. I wasn't exactly in Tom's good books.'

'Because of the cannabis episode at the Apollo?' said Nick.

'Oh, you know about that.' Lennox looked at Nick, a question in his eyes. 'Did you know Tom wrote to Colin telling him about Hannah and me?'

'No,' they said in unison.

'What was Fowler's reaction to the letter?' said Mia.

'He never saw it. All letters to inmates are opened and read. You'd be surprised what people try to smuggle in through the post. I was on duty the day Tom's letter arrived and I destroyed it.'

'Did you tell Tom you'd destroyed it?'

'No.'

'Why do you think he wrote the letter?'

'To get back at me.'

'Did Tom ever visit Colin in the unit?'

'No, Hannah either went on her own or with her mother. Tom never went. Neither did Mr Bates.'

Nick said, 'Hannah's workmates reckon she was planning to meet a man after work on Friday. This man was going to help get Fowler out of Marshcroft. Any ideas who he might be?'

Lennox raised his shoulders in a lengthy shrug: he was about to speak when the door flew open and DCI Wells lunged in, his features ablaze with triumph.

'Chris Lennox,' he said, stopping short of the table, 'I'm arresting you on suspicion of the abduction and murder of Hannah Bates. You do not have to say anything, but it may harm your defence….'

While Wells continued to read the man his rights Mia looked at Nick and, for once, their puzzled expressions were in total agreement.

The murder team was instructed to meet up in the canteen for a celebratory snack of strong coffee and sandwiches. While they all filled their plates Wells found himself a vacant seat and devoured his supper with vigour. Mia sat next to him and said, 'Lennox is our killer then, sir. I must say I'm surprised. He doesn't seem the type.'

'If killers were that easy to spot, darling, we'd get them before they had a chance to kill.'

'I suppose so.'

I *know* so,' Wells said, wiping his mouth with a gleaming white handkerchief. He reached into his briefcase for a bundle of papers, then jumped to his feet. 'Listen up everybody. This is the interim report from forensics and it makes interesting reading. The blood found in Lennox's bathroom is type 'O'. Hannah Bates's blood was type 'O'. Now, I realize that's a common type but it's too much of a coincidence to ignore. Of course, Lennox could be type 'O' as well but, hopefully, we'll be eliminating him the minute we get his DNA results back.'

When Wells paused to sip his coffee, Mia said, 'Is that all we've got, sir? It's pretty flimsy evidence to warrant a murder charge.'

'There's more,' Wells said, grinning. 'We've had our computer whizz kids probing around Lennox's computer files and it seems he's fond of making lists. Lists of murder weapons, torture methods, ways of causing death…. He's a very dark fellow is our Mr Lennox.'

'Does anything on the computer match our killer's methods?' asked Nick.

'A Stanley knife was mentioned. Destroying the eyeballs was also there. Strangulation, restraining the hands and filling the mouth with dirt….' Wells shrugged. 'So much of it tied in with Hannah's murder that it'd be foolhardy *not* to charge him.'

Mia said, 'What was locked in those metal drawers, sir?'

'A selection of grisly reading matter. There were dozens of books on criminology, pathology, forensic science … you name it, Lennox has a book about it.' Wells smirked. 'He must know his way around a crime scene pretty well after reading that lot but he still slipped up big time.

'Now, the house had been thoroughly scrubbed but, as we all know, it's extremely difficult to eradicate all evidence from a crime scene. Forensics found a number of hairs, fibres, fingerprints…. We'll obviously be comparing any DNA and prints with Hannah's.'

Mia was finding it difficult to suppress her niggling doubts. With great caution, she said, 'It sounds a lot, sir, but none of it's solid. We've got nothing to hold up in court.'

Wells had the decency to look shamefaced. 'The fact is … I've led the super to believe Lennox's DNA sample matched the one found on Hannah's body and that's the main reason he allowed me to charge the man.' There were a few sharp intakes of breath from various parts of the room and the DCI quickly added, 'Come on, this isn't the first time we've bent the rules to get our man safely into custody. None of the evidence is valid yet, I'll admit, but it all points to Lennox being our killer. I need time for us to prove that, and to keep Lennox off the streets while we do it. What's wrong with that?' He pointed a warning finger. 'None of this goes beyond these four walls. OK? If it gets out we've made a pre-emptive arrest then the big-mouth had better watch out because I *will* find out who blabbed and I'll have him for breakfast. Now finish your sarnies and get a good night's sleep. We've got a busy day ahead of us tomorrow.'

While the majority hastened to make a fast exit Mia remained in her seat. The day had taken its toll. She felt bruised, her control of the investigations seemed to be slipping away. Paul Wells was quick to pick up her negative vibes. After returning the report to his briefcase he pulled up a chair and considered her closely.

'What's wrong, darling?'

'It's Janet Munroe,' she said, tears pricking her eyes. 'Our chat this morning didn't quite go according to plan. When I pointed out the inconsistencies thrown up by the post-mortem she sort of lost it, sir. She accused me of being out to get her. It wasn't pleasant.'

'In that case you won't be pleased to know that more conflicting evidence has come to light.' It was Mia's turn to look at him questioningly. 'I was planning to go over it with you earlier, only this investigation gathered momentum and there wasn't time. I won't go into details now, but let's just say another talk with Mrs Munroe is definitely called for.'

'And you want me to see her?'

'Is that a problem?'

'No, sir, it's just … I'm worried about my mother. Janet already thinks I'm hounding her. If things get worse I'm frightened she'll take it out on Mum just to spite me.'

'Do you think she's capable of that? She comes across as a very caring person.'

'You didn't see her this morning.'

Wells rested a hand on her shoulder, his touch reassuring. 'We'll talk to her together then. How's that?'

'Thank you,' said Mia, relief coursing through her.

'And don't worry, darling, if my assumptions are right your mum'll be quite safe.'

CHAPTER SIXTEEN

Weathermen had been predicting the arrival of a warm front for days now. And during the early hours of Thursday morning it finally arrived, bringing with it a vigorous thaw. Slowly but surely it cleared the last coverings of snow that had stubbornly clung to the lower reaches of Larchborough's countryside, causing chaos for the rush hour traffic. The borough was located in a valley, its town centre the lowest point, and all roads leading out of it were little more than heaving rivers of muddy water and debris by the time Mia buckled herself into the passenger seat of Wells's Sierra.

Their conversation was sporadic as with grim persistence Wells negotiated a slow path through the murky rapids *en route* to St Stephen's nursing home, the solemn faces of all those they passed mirroring Mia's own portentous misgivings.

The car park was empty apart from a delivery van and two cars, one of which was Janet's red Fiat. Mia's stomach gave an unpleasant lurch when she spotted it. She'd been dreading this encounter throughout the night, had hardly slept because of it. And as she trudged behind Wells, feeling decidedly overdressed for the unfamiliar warmth, she wanted nothing more than to see her mother. A mere glimpse would be enough to ease her worries. Then she could bring to the interview a renewed determination and an easy mind. But she dared not ask the DCI for permission; it would be unprofessional. He needed to know she was ready for anything, not pining after her mother's apron strings.

They found Janet in the kitchen, supervising breakfast. She flinched when they entered; it was a subtle movement, but one that failed to escape Wells's inscrutable gaze. Their opening pleasantries were subdued and conducted on the move as Janet propelled them almost forcibly towards her private office.

'Do sit down,' she said, taking her own seat. 'What a change in the weather. I can almost believe spring is just round the corner.'

'Quite,' said Wells, rummaging in his briefcase for the relevant papers.

For some indefinable reason Mia felt the need to speak. Holding Janet's stare, she said, 'How are you today? Better, I hope.' Then as soon as the words were out she flushed violently for they sounded so full of bravado, as though they'd only been uttered because of the DCI's guarding presence.

'I'm as well as can be expected in the circumstances,' Janet replied, her tone flat. She turned to Wells. 'Why did you want to see me, Chief Inspector? Have you found the evidence you need?'

Wells held up the papers. 'We've had the report from our forensic scientists. But first, that group of boys you accused of killing your mother … They couldn't have done it, Mrs Munroe, because they were in London all day on Monday and didn't get home till just before midnight. They went on a school trip.'

'What? I'm … I'm shocked,' said Janet, suddenly deflated. 'I was convinced they were the guilty ones. They've been making our lives a misery for so long. It seemed a perfectly reasonable assumption.'

'But the wrong assumption, I'm afraid. Still, it's better to get them out of the picture from the beginning. That way we don't waste valuable time chasing up the wrong alleyways.'

'What's next then?' Janet said, lifting a trembling hand to fiddle with the gold crucifix hanging around her neck. 'Does the report point you in any other direction?'

'It's put us in a quandary, Mrs Munroe.'

'Oh, dear,' she said, skimming a look at Mia.

'The timing's all wrong, you see. The sequence of events just doesn't fit into the time frame provided by you.'

'Oh, dear,' she said again, the fingers now clutching her throat.

Wells scanned the report. 'I'll just tell you what was found, shall I? And, hopefully, you can put my mind at rest.'

'I'll certainly try.'

'Mrs Munroe, your mother's stomach contents told the pathologist that she'd eaten a hearty meal of shepherd's pie and vegetables less than an hour before her death. And as the pathologist states your mother died around 7.30 to 9 p.m. that would mean she ate the meal at some time between 6.30 and 8 o'clock. Agreed?'

'No,' said Janet, hastily. 'I've already told you mother was dead when I got home from work. As for the shepherd's pie, I left it in the microwave for her to heat up at lunchtime. She normally ate lunch at midday which would bring her time of death to one o'clock. Is that any help, Chief Inspector?'

Wells scratched his head as he pondered over the report. 'The pathologist could be wrong, I suppose. But when our officers searched through the pedal-bin in your kitchen they found onion skins, potato peelings, carrot peelings, a polystyrene container that had contained minced beef … in fact everything you'd expect to find in a bin after the preparation of just such a meal. When did you make the pie, Mrs Munroe?'

'The night before … Sunday,' she said with confidence. 'How awful of me to leave the bits in the bin. I do usually empty it every day. There must have been something good on the telly and I forgot.'

'I bet that's it,' said Wells, with a gracious smile. But then he frowned. 'The only trouble is, my officers found those peelings on Wednesday and they looked too fresh to have been there since Sunday. Can you explain that?'

She gave an impatient shrug. 'Perhaps the peelings looked fresh because my kitchen was very cold and the low temperature would have kept them fresh for longer.'

'What a good theory,' he said, clearly impressed. 'And it would hold up too, if it weren't for the fact that your kitchen has a large double radiator that works very well.' He fixed her with a quizzical stare. 'Had you forgotten about the radiator, Mrs Munroe? You hang your damp tea towels over it. And did you realize you'd left the heating running on constant after your mother's death? So any rubbish that'd been in your pedal-bin for a couple of days would've been well on its way to being rotten by the time my officers started to rummage around.'

'And your point is?' she said, her tone quite hostile.

'I wish I knew,' he said, spreading his hands. 'As I said, the time frame doesn't fit.' He took to scratching his head again. 'I'm flummoxed, Mrs Munroe. To all intents and purposes it looks as though that meal was prepared on Monday evening and yet it couldn't have been.'

Janet let out a sigh. 'Why are you focusing so much energy on my pedal-bin? Shouldn't you be looking for fingerprints or shoeprints or whatever you do look for to help you find the killer?'

'That's exactly what we are doing, but the facts as they stand at the moment are confusing us. You see, immediately prior to death your mother vomited into a bucket we found in the bathroom….'

Amazement showed clearly on Janet's features. 'I must say your men conduct a very thorough search. But I shouldn't let that small discovery confuse you. Mother was always vomiting. She suffered badly from angina and the attacks made her very sick. Those traces you found in that bucket must have been days old … nothing at all to do with the murder.'

'If only that were true, Mrs Munroe. If we could only disregard those traces of vomit our job would be a lot easier.'

'Then forget about the bucket,' Janet said, her composure slipping. 'I've told you, it's got nothing at all to do with the murder.'

'I'm afraid we can't,' said Wells, gently. 'You see, we took the bucket to our pathologist for analysis and he told us the vomit matched exactly the contents of your mother's stomach. They matched exactly, Mrs Munroe.'

Janet swallowed loudly. 'Mother must have been sick just before she died then.'

'That seems to be the case,' said Wells. 'And of course it would mean that whoever killed your mother was kind enough to first of all provide a bucket for her to be sick in. It doesn't make sense, does it?'

'I see what you're getting at,' she said, holding his gaze. 'So where do you go from here?'

Wells shrugged. 'God knows, Mrs Munroe. Those fingerprints and footprints you mentioned earlier ... they simply don't exist. We've been all over the house and can find nothing to suggest an alien presence.'

Wells had purposefully maintained eye contact with Janet throughout the whole of this exchange. Breaking it now he stuffed the forensic report into his briefcase and struggled to his feet. 'We'll just have to start from scratch, I suppose. Back to the drawing board, as they say.'

'That's right,' said Janet, leaving her seat. 'Look at it from a different angle, Chief Inspector.'

He gave her a pointed look. 'Before we go we'll pop along to see DS Harvey's mother, just to make sure she's all right. You don't mind, I hope?'

'Of course not,' she said, glaring at Mia. 'You'll find Barbara brimming with health. Our residents get only the very best of care at St Stephen's.'

A short while later they emerged into bright sunlight that held a fair amount of heat. As Mia unravelled her scarf, she said, 'You think Janet's hiding something, don't you, sir?'

'More than that, darling, I believe she killed her mother,' he said, activating his car's central locking system. 'All we've got to do now is prove it.'

On the dais, his back towards his team, Wells brought a handkerchief from his pocket and dabbed at the perspiration on his upper lip. That tell-tale moisture had nothing to do with the room's temperature, but it had everything to do with his lack of self-worth.

Why had he lied to Shakespeare about Lennox's DNA sample? It was foolhardy. As a rule Wells strayed not an inch from the book, only charging a suspect when all gathered evidence was rock solid and irreversible. He was panicking and that was a dangerous state of affairs.

He looked at his watch. It was 11.45 a.m. He was expecting Lennox's DNA result within the next couple of hours. It had to be a match, because if it wasn't … Mia was right: all their evidence so far was circumstantial. None of it would hold up in court. And what if Lennox hadn't killed Hannah Bates? By focusing all their energies on him, were they giving the real murderer the time and the freedom to kill again? No, that was unthinkable.

His assumptions, as far as Janet Munroe was concerned, were on firmer ground. He knew she'd killed her mother. He simply didn't know why yet. He'd been surprised at the depth of her reticence earlier today. He'd expected her to cave in easily under the weight of his subtle probing. That meal had definitely been cooked just before the old woman's death. If it had been prepared the day before, as Mrs Munroe had claimed, then all manner of rubbish would have been thrown on top of the peelings, and yet they'd found not one solitary teabag. But how could he get her to confess?

Just then Billy Finch caught his attention. 'Sir, there was a big storm last night in the vicinity of Headingley Hall and the telephone lines are all down. So I've e-mailed Windermere's local station and asked for somebody to suss out Lennox's alibi. I'm still waiting to hear back, sir. Oh, and his DNA result's been held up. They'll get it across a.s.a.p.'

Wells lifted a weary shoulder. 'We wait, then. And Lennox remains our chief suspect until those enquiries tell us otherwise.'

There was a brisk knock on the door and Paul Devine, a fresh-faced uniformed constable came strutting into the room, stopping just short of the dais. He held out two sheets of paper. 'Thought you might like these straight away, sir.'

Wells grabbed the papers. 'Why? What are they?'

'Witness forms, sir.'

'I can see that, Constable, but why would I need to see them straight away?'

'I've been doing house-to-house enquiries in the Edith Bowman murder case, sir, and that statement is from Mrs Phyllis Bletchley, one of the immediate neighbours. Mrs Bletchley states she was in Mrs Bowman's house on the day of the murder from lunchtime till about four-thirty. No food was cooked or heated up during that time, and the only food consumed by Mrs Bowman was a round of ham-and-tomato sandwiches at twelve noon.'

'Well done, mate, that's welcome news.' Wells struggled into his overcoat, his mouth a determined line. 'Mia, come with me, darling. It's time to nick Janet Munroe.'

CHAPTER SEVENTEEN

Over at the nursing home Janet Munroe was trying desperately to maintain the aura of grief so expected by everyone. And she *was* grieving. Janet wasn't so hard that she could simply disregard her mother's death. It was just that more pressing matters needed to be given precedence.

Janet had contacted Bignalls estate agents that very morning, barely two days after Edith's death. She realized that such haste might be viewed as crass but she was in no position to pander to the finer feelings of others. If anyone dared to mention the swiftness of her actions she simply said that living in the house would be impossible now, the horrors she'd witnessed there were too great. Of course the house was still a crime scene, but the agent had promised to view it as soon as was legally possible.

Getting rid of it would be a huge relief, and not simply from a financial viewpoint. Janet's stomach rolled horribly every time her thoughts returned to Edith's stricken body. Life had become a nightmare of monstrous proportions and Janet was beginning to buckle under its weight.

She was supervising the lunchtime drugs round when all at once she needed to get out, to be alone in her office. Without a word she lurched through the double doors …

straight into the path of DCI Wells and Mia Harvey. As soon as she saw them Janet's spirits sank.

'Not again,' she muttered.

'Afraid so,' said Wells. 'Shall we go to your office?'

Not another word was spoken until they were all settled in chairs around Janet's desk. 'Shall I call out for a pot of tea?' she said.

Wells shook his head. 'This isn't a social visit, I'm afraid. Our house-to-house enquiries have turned up some surprising information.' He motioned for Mia to hand him the grey plastic folder that lay on her lap. 'It would seem that your immediate neighbour, Mrs Phyllis Bletchley, called in to see your mother on the day of her death between the hours of twelve noon and four-thirty.'

Janet hid a sigh. 'Phyllis popped in to see mother most days.' She shrugged but said nothing more.

Wells quickly scanned the witness statement. 'According to Mrs Bletchley your mother had a ham-and-tomato sandwich for lunch. According to her nothing was cooked or warmed up either in the microwave or the oven.'

'We're back to the shepherd's pie, are we?' said Janet, failing to hide her annoyance. 'I'd say that Phyllis was mistaken, Chief Inspector. I'd say she'd better watch that memory of hers. Forgetfulness is the first sign of dementia and that nasty little disease plays havoc with a person's credibility.'

Wells smiled. 'I shouldn't worry about Mrs Bletchley's credibility. My officer said she's as bright as a pin. She even remembered seeing a carton of minced beef thawing out on the kitchen worktop. She said your mother told her you were having shepherd's pie for dinner.'

The corners of Janet's mouth turned down in a sneer. 'I do wish you'd get to the point.'

'OK, Mrs Munroe, I'm sure none of us has any time to waste.' He leant forward in his chair. 'Janet Munroe, I am arresting you on suspicion of the murder of your mother, Mrs Edith Bowman, on Monday….'

The room swam before Janet's eyes as she listened to the words, his voice seeming to travel further into the distance with every loud beat of her heart. She thought back to that awful night, to her all-consuming need for that card table.

Edith did suffer an angina attack soon after dinner. But the attack was fast progressing into a full-blown cardiac arrest. Edith's grip on life was becoming unsustainable. She was slipping away. Janet needed to act quickly, but blind panic kept her professional competence at bay. Her mind was a swirling cesspit of final demands, bailiffs, the monstrous disgrace should her predicament ever become known.

And suddenly she envisaged a way out of the mess. If Edith were to die then she could take the table and do with it as she saw fit. She could even sell the house; and in no time at all her nightmare would be over. A sudden calmness enveloped her. It was as if Janet was standing apart, watching herself place the pillow over her mother's face instead of making that vital call to the paramedics.

DCI Wells was calling her name, dragging her back to the present. She focused on his face, tried to stem the trembling that was overtaking her body like an ague. Who would have thought that a few potato peelings in a bin could have caused her downfall? She needed to think quickly. Surely she could outwit this poor excuse for a man.

Mia watched her closely, saw the undiluted horror in her face. But why did she look so wretched? Because she'd been accused of such a wicked act? Or because she'd been caught out? Could Janet actually have brought about the old woman's death? No. Mia mentally shook her head, refusing to believe that Janet's love for her mother had been contrived.

Sitting in the stuffy office Mia felt her resolve strengthening. Of course … this had been a mercy killing and not a murder. This was the result of a fatal pact entered into by a desperate mother and her devoted daughter. Edith Bowman had suffered chronic pain for years. Would she have the strength to watch her own mother suffering so much?

'Where's your proof?' Janet suddenly asked. 'Where's your solid evidence that can be put before a jury?'

Wells raised an eyebrow. 'You're not denying it, then? That's the normal reaction of an innocent person.'

'Stop....' said Mia, her hand on the DCI's arm. 'She helped her mother to die, sir. Isn't that right, Janet? Your mum asked to be released from her pain and you helped her.'

Janet's gaze moved slowly to Mia, an uncontrollable urge to laugh causing her to bite down hard on her lower lip. Well, this was a turn-up for the book: an upholder of the law offering her a way out. DCI Wells looked fit to burst. He turned in his seat and glared at Mia.

Janet transformed the threatening laughter into a shuddering sigh. 'That's exactly what happened, Mia. God help me.'

A heavy silence took hold and all that could be heard was the faint ticking of a wall clock. After a long moment Wells turned again to Janet, his teeth bared with undisguised anger.

He said, 'Mrs Munroe, are you admitting to assisting in a suicide? Is that what you're saying?'

She gave a faint nod, sat forward in the seat. 'It was mother's idea. She couldn't take any more. She'd had enough. She'd been begging me for months to help her find a way out but I kept resisting.' Janet's fingers went to her crucifix, her eyes shining with unshed tears. 'I loved her so much. I couldn't imagine life without her.' She fell back and took in a shuddering breath. 'But on Monday I stopped resisting. After dinner – that bloody shepherd's pie – mother suffered a vicious angina attack and was throwing up for ages. You'll know that, of course, you found traces of vomit in that bucket. Anyway I suddenly saw the awful existence she had, the prison she inhabited day in and day out, and I knew I had to fulfil her wish ... even if it meant that I, too, would be imprisoned for the rest of my own life.'

Wells snorted. 'Oh, you're good ... you're very good.'

Mia said, 'But, sir—'

'Shut up, you've said enough already.' He aimed his venomous glare at Janet. 'What I don't understand, Mrs Munroe, is why your mother's toxicology report came back negative, apart from her usual medication.'

She gave him a superior look. 'Which means?'

'I'll admit I don't have much experience of this sort of crime, but in every case I know of, the deceased had taken a large quantity of pills – paracetamol … sleeping pills … tranquillizers – washed down with alcohol before being smothered to death. The pills and booze help to minimize the horror of those final minutes, or so I've been told. And yet your mother allowed you to restrict her breathing while she was fully awake.' He gave a rueful shake of the head. 'To be honest I doubt I'd have the guts to go through with it. Your mother must have been a very extraordinary woman.'

Janet's lips moved wordlessly while her thoughts floundered. 'It all happened so quickly. One minute mother was heaving into the bucket, and the next I was helping to release her from the pain. There wasn't time for her to swallow a load of pills. She was frightened I might change my mind at any minute. Besides, the attack had left her very weak and barely conscious….' Her eyes shifted from the DCI to Mia. 'She didn't suffer. You know how much I loved her.'

With a furious huff Wells got to his feet, the chair almost toppling behind him. 'Assisting a suicide is still an indictable offence, Mrs Munroe, so if you'd kindly accompany us to the station….'

'Of course,' she said, her movements subdued. 'And I can only hope the jury will be sympathetic to the reasons behind my actions. But then, according to the papers, they normally are in this sort of case, aren't they?'

'Not if I can help it,' growled Wells. 'You're getting life, Mrs Munroe. If it's the last thing I do, I'll make sure of that.'

*

The station car park was practically deserted by the time Mia finished for the night. Temperatures had turned bitterly cold and the Tarmac under foot was covered by a thin sheet of ice, making her attempt to walk at speed highly precarious. So, although desperate to get as far away from Wells as possible – his lambasting at her interference in the Janet Munroe affair had subsided only with the ending of her shift – she was edging slowly around the perimeter walls like an injured rat in a sewer when the main doors of reception were flung open and Nick slithered down the steps, calling her name.

She stopped in the pale glow from a nearby streetlamp and waited for him to approach, her truculent scowl almost as frosty as the weather.

'Come to gloat, Nick?'

'What? No.' He sighed loudly, his warm breath fogging the air between them. 'If you must know, I want to say well done for standing up to that old bastard.'

'Oh, yes?' she said, pulling a face.

'I mean it. The DCI was well out of order, going on at you like that. If you think Janet Munroe's innocent of the murder charge then you'd be compromising your integrity if you didn't say so.' In the dim lamplight Mia's eyes widened with astonishment. 'I wanted to tell Wells as much. Only the least said the better when he's going off on one. Right?'

She smiled. 'Yes ... well, thanks.'

'What are you going to do now?'

'If I've still got a job in the morning, you mean?' She gave a shrug. 'I'm not going to do anything. What can I do? You know Wells – he's convinced Janet's guilty and he'll pull out all the stops to prove it.'

'But, Mia, what if you're right? What if she was just helping her mother to die? She's your friend. You can't let an innocent woman spend the rest of her life inside. It'd be a travesty. Stand up to him. Show him you've got dignity. Show him you'll always be there for a friend in need.'

She thought for a moment. 'Nick, do you think I'm right?'

He held up his hands. 'God, I don't know. I've had nothing to do with the investigation.' He rested his hands on her shoulders and pulled her round to face him. 'But I do know you, Mia, and I know you'd never make such bald statements if you didn't believe them.'

Mia swallowed hard, a solitary tear glistening in the corner of her eye. 'Thanks, Nick, I really appreciate this.'

'So, you'll carry on?' he said, his hands still on her shoulders. 'You'll show Wells you've got the guts to stand up to him?'

Mia grinned. 'Yes. Janet deserves to have somebody in her corner and, after all, I know her better than Wells ever will. She's not capable of murdering anybody, especially her mother. For God's sake, she worshipped the woman.'

'Good,' said Nick, rubbing his gloved hands together briskly. 'Now, let's both get home before we freeze to death.'

'Thanks, Nick, you've helped a lot.'

'Any time.' Without another word Nick jumped into his car and turned on the ignition, the lights from the dashboard illuminating his cruel grin. *A battle between Wells and that fat cow…now this I want to see.* He chuckled. *I know who my money's on, and it sure as hell ain't Mia fucking Harvey.*

CHAPTER EIGHTEEN

MURDER IN LARCHBOROUGH.

The very thought had Superintendent Shakespeare's heart palpitating wildly. Striding with half-hearted confidence along the corridors of the police station Shakespeare dug deep into his pocket for a handkerchief and wiped it urgently across his perspiring forehead. There would be press releases to see to – his every word poured over by the fearful residents of Larchborough – television interviews to endure, important decisions to be made … quickly.

This wasn't how he'd imagined his remaining years in the force. He should be mingling with the great and good at the nineteenth hole, a generous gin and tonic in hand, negotiating the transfer of much-needed resources for his division. He was in effect the flagship of Larchborough police division. He shouldn't be required to dirty his hands at the stark coalface of today's uncharitable and crime-ridden society. He was the brains behind those intricate deals that were struck with such delicate handling in the cosy confines of his board room. That was where he belonged: in the board room.

Shakespeare sighed and gave a rueful shake of the head. Not too long ago thoughts of the chaos in his beloved board room would have had him hyperventilating. But not now. Who cared that its furniture – until recently so beautiful – would now be refused by even the most needy of charity shops? What did it matter that the carpet was filthy from too many muddy shoes, and matted with food deliberately discarded by officers whose disgusting eating habits made the orang-utans at London Zoo look positively immaculate?

Hadn't those self-same officers been committed to finding and apprehending the killer of Hannah Bates? And hadn't Chief Inspector Wells assured him that they had their man safely in the cells? Shakespeare's frown deepened. But why was he still in the cells? If Lennox was their killer then he should be in the remand unit by now.

The door to the board room flew open on to an atmosphere so dense it could have been sliced. All heads were down, all mouths firmly closed. Only DCI Wells showed any signs of animation as he sat at his desk on the dais, muttering urgently into the telephone mouthpiece.

As soon as Shakespeare made his tentative entrance Wells's ragged features settled into a scowl. This was all he needed. Without the slightest acknowledgement Wells turned his back and continued his frenzied monologue into the telephone receiver, leaving the superintendent to pace irritably before the dais.

It was soon obvious that Shakespeare was intending to wait and, hoping to court the DCI's favour, Nick pounced instantly.

'Anything I can help you with, Superintendent?'

'No, thank you, Ford, I need a word with the chief inspector.'

Nick pulled a face. 'You could have a long wait, sir. DCI Wells is on an important call. It could take a while. Why don't I get him to ring you when he's finished?'

The superintendent was clearly battling with a dilemma. He so wanted to have it out with the DCI but was loath to spend any more time in that desecrated room than was necessary.

'No, Ford, get him to run over to my office the minute he's free. There are certain points I need to discuss with him, not least the fact that Chris Lennox is still on the premises. Why is that, Ford? Are you able to enlighten me?'

'I really think DCI Wells should explain, sir. It's a bit complicated.'

'Very well. As long as there's a valid explanation, I'll be quite happy. If not....' The superintendent's dissatisfaction hung over them like a rain-cloud about to shed its load. His patience had, at last, come to an end and heads were going to roll.

When the door slammed noisily on his exit Wells cut short his call and replaced the receiver with equal force. He jumped from the dais.

'OK, kiddies, listen to me. We're urgently in need of inspiration here. Shakespeare's not going to be fobbed off any longer, by the looks of it, so we need to pull out all the stops. I've just been on to Cumbrian Division and the news isn't good. Lennox was telling the truth. He did drive to the Lake District to attend a writing course at Headingley Hall.'

Jack said, 'But, sir, that doesn't mean he's innocent of the murder charge. Hannah was already dead by the time he left for Windermere, so he could still be our man.'

'True, but I was hoping he'd been lying. That would've helped justify our ... *my* decision to hold him here.' Wells let out a long breath. 'We really need his DNA result. If we can prove that pubic hair was his, then we've got him. Billy, when did they say that machine would be up and running again?'

'They didn't, sir. They just said they'd get the result to us as soon as they could.'

'That's not bloody good enough,' Wells muttered. 'Let's see what excuse they give this time.'

With one long gangling stride he was back at his desk and grabbing the telephone receiver. Chris Lennox had to be their man. The alternative didn't bear thinking about. Granted, Lennox hadn't provided an alibi for the actual time of the murder, but if he was seen to be telling the truth regarding his whereabouts from Sunday night onwards, and it turned out his DNA differed from that found on Hannah's body, then they'd have to let him go.

The thought of starting from scratch brought Wells out in a cold sweat. Police work was hardly a precise science. But what did the public care about that? A young girl had been found dead and they wanted the perpetrator off the streets. And, who could blame them?

They were in a no-win situation as far as Paul Wells was concerned. If they managed a swift result then they were simply doing their jobs. Should a murder investigation drag on, however, the circumstances being intricate and the killer sly, then woe betides all those involved. And Superintendent Shakespeare was more guilty than most for expecting miraculously quick results. It was almost as though he'd erased from his memory those early foot-pounding years of his career.

Wells tapped out the number of the crime laboratory and prepared to do battle. He needed that DNA result. But all he got was the engaged tone. Tutting loudly, he slammed down the receiver and faced his team. 'You know, kiddies, sometimes I get the feeling our own lot are deliberately trying to sabotage our chances of a result.'

'No luck with the crime lab, sir?' said Billy Finch.

'They're engaged.'

'I'll keep trying, sir.'

Wells ran an impatient hand through his hair. 'Thanks, mate.'

Mia watched the DCI and her heart ached. Throughout the morning she'd kept out of his way for fear of antagonizing him further. Her declaration to Nick – that she would stand beside Janet Munroe, no matter what – had been heartfelt. But now, in the cold light of day, she had to admit there were discrepancies in Janet's relaying of events on that fateful night.

They had been told there was no time for Edith to swallow any pills because she was frightened that Janet might change her mind. And yet, according to Janet, her mother was very weak and almost unconscious straight after the angina attack. How could the old woman be scared and almost comatose at the same time? It didn't add up. And, looking back, Janet had been too keen to embrace the *I helped my mother to die* scenario. It wasn't the sort of thing most normal people would brag about; yet Janet had seemed positively evangelical about it, declaring loudly all the way to the station that the jury would see she'd done nothing wrong, but had simply spared her mother even more years of endless pain and suffering.

Mia had battled with her conscience for most of the night and was now of the opinion that she'd been too hasty in opposing Wells. She'd viewed the whole sorry scene with the misguided logic of a daughter steeped in gratitude for the faultless care of her own mother, instead of employing the cool professionalism of a detective sergeant in Larchborough's police force.

She was desperate to return to that old easy relationship she'd enjoyed with Wells. Only that was impossible now because she'd planted the 'assisted suicide' seed in Janet's mind and effectively robbed him of a badly needed result. She wouldn't be let back into the fold without a struggle.

Just then the door to the board room swung open and Danny Rose hurried up to the dais. 'I'm back, sir, and this time I'm here to stay.'

'Are you sure?' said Wells, giving him an old-fashioned look. 'I'd hate to raise my hopes only to have them dashed again.'

Missing the irony in his words, Danny said, 'Imodium tablets … brilliant invention.' He pulled from his jacket pocket a long brown envelope and handed it to the DCI. 'The duty sergeant asked me to give you this, sir.'

All eyes were on Wells as he read the contents, his long face draining of all colour. 'Lennox's DNA result. It doesn't match the sample taken from Hannah's body.' He looked up. 'Right, it seems we've no choice, we'll just have to let the man go. Shit.'

So much for keeping a low profile. She'd rather be bollocked up hill and down dale than be side-lined. Now, instead of hunting for Hannah's killer Mia was having to find proof that Janet Munroe really did murder her mother.

She'd just spent a miserable two hours at St Stephen's attempting to garner information about Janet's personal life from individuals who – one and all – had made it perfectly clear from the outset that they would rather eat horse shit than utter one word against their divine manager.

The details surrounding Edith's death had spread faster than an Australian bush fire; in their eyes that heroic act had propelled Janet even nearer to sainthood. Indeed, Janet Munroe was no longer a mere angel; she was now a martyr for the Christian cause, a prophet of goodness. And Mia was the enemy – the Pontius Pilate of the piece.

Effectively ostracized from the main group Mia had shut herself away in Janet's office and proceeded to turn out every drawer and cupboard of her large desk. Pretty soon she had before her a substantial pile of final demands for payment, bailiff's letters, half-filled-in applications for finance....

Mia had stared down at the papers as though they were rare artefacts retrieved from an ancient tomb, her mind racing. What could it all mean? How could Janet have got herself into such a mess? Those bills amounted to thousands and thousands of pounds. If nothing else, it at least explained Janet's rush to sell the family home. That house would be worth – what? – £200,000? Probably. Enough to pay off the debts and have a little left to live on.

Suddenly a chill crept along her spine as an unwanted thought entered Mia's consciousness. Almost from the beginning of time the need for money had proved to be a strong motive for murder. Was DCI Wells right, after all? Had Edith's death been a conscious and premeditated act? Did Janet actually murder her poor mother for hard cash?

A subsequent visit to Lloyds TSB bank and a quick flash of her warrant card had given Mia further ammunition to aim at the duplicitous Janet Munroe. Both the woman's cheque and savings accounts had been frozen months ago after countless requests for her to pay an amount in for a change and reduce the size of her overdraft had gone unheard.

It was never pleasant to be proved wrong. Therefore it was with hesitant steps and a brooding expression that she entered the board room, mentally rehearsing her apology for Paul Wells. And her gloomy mood was only aggravated further by the buzz of positive activity that emanated from the rest of the team.

Feeling almost as isolated amongst her colleagues as she had at St Stephen's, Mia made her way to the dais where Wells was scribbling furiously on the whiteboard.

'Sir....' She pulled Janet's damning correspondence from her shoulder bag and held it out for him. 'I need a word about the Edith Bowman case.'

'What?' He turned to her, distracted. 'I haven't time. Whatever it is can wait till later.'

Mia wandered across to her desk. She was locking Janet's papers in its top drawer when DCI Wells, replacing his telephone receiver, called for silence from the dais.

'It would seem,' he said, 'that Tom Bates wants to unburden himself to Mia, but only in the privacy of his home. Let's hope that whatever he wants to say will prove useful.' He turned to Mia, his anger unrelenting. 'You'd better take Jack with you.'

'Yes, sir.'

'Oh, and Mia ... try to keep to the script this time.'

The 15.30 train from London to Liverpool was thundering across the viaduct as Mia stood with Jack before the pink facade of number 45 Larchwood Lane. Jack rapped the knocker and a small commotion could be heard almost immediately from within. They exchanged a worried glance and were relieved when the door eventually opened on to an anxious Shirley Bates.

She ushered them into the narrow hallway with an urgency that spoke of quiet desperation. 'He's in the lounge. Russell's had to go into work – an urgent crisis.'

The room was exactly as Mia had remembered it: a riotous nightmare in pink. And at its centre sat Tom, incongruous in black. He was hunched over on the settee, the tiny Candy on his lap. He failed to look up when they entered; choosing instead to focus on the dog. Her tiny paws were pounding the air in ecstasy as Tom traced a path around her nipples with the slightest touch of his fingertips.

Mia and Jack settled into the armchairs while Shirley Bates sat beside her son, an encouraging hand on his knee.

Mia said, 'You wanted to see me, Tom.' The boy remained tight-lipped. 'You remember Jack…?'

He looked up, his eyes red-rimmed and puffy behind the black curtain of fringe. But still he said nothing.

In order to kick-start the conversation, Mia said, 'We know about the letter you wrote to Colin Fowler in the remand unit.'

'You what…?' he said, eyes wide.

'That letter you wrote, telling him about Hannah's relationship with Chris Lennox.'

'Was Hannah really seeing that man?' Mrs Bates suddenly asked. Mia nodded and cast her a sorrowful look. 'I can't believe it. That wedding was costing us a fortune.'

'Who said I'd written a letter?' Tom blustered.

Mia lifted a shoulder. 'Chris, of course. Did you really think he wouldn't find out?'

Tom's haunted gaze darted around the room as though he were a fugitive searching for a suitable place to hide. 'How did he take it?' he said.

Mia grimaced. 'Let's just say you didn't do him any favours. There's tension in that place at the best of times, but after your letter….' She let out a low whistle. 'The phrase "pistols at dawn" comes to mind.'

Those words, that notion, had a dramatic effect on the boy, and Mia watched as the colour drained from his face. It was like witnessing the God-given life force taking its leave of a host body. The boy started to snivel and gently eased the dog on to the carpet at his feet. Candy sat on her haunches and regarded him quizzically, her head cocked to one side.

Mia could only watch as his mother wrapped her arms around the boy. 'I killed her,' he sobbed into his mother's breast. 'I killed Hannah....'

Mrs Bates's expression was guarded as she exchanged a look with the detectives. Taking a strong hold of her son, keeping him at arm's length, she forced him to look into her face. 'Don't be silly, Tom, you didn't kill Hannah.'

He wriggled from her grip and tossed back his hair with angry defiance. 'I might as well have done.'

Mia leant forward. Was this the moment she'd been waiting for? God knows there were plenty of hatchets to be buried as far as her professional relationship with Paul Wells was concerned. What better way to reclaim his trust than to unearth Tom's secret?

'Why are you so frightened?' she said. 'Do you think your letter might have had something to do with Hannah's death?'

He hung his head in shame, mumbled a wretched, 'Yes.'

Mia offered up a silent prayer of thanks and let out a relieved breath. The revelation was about to come. In words that gushed from him as forcefully as projected vomit, Tom told of his blind hatred for Hannah after missing the Walking Dead concert. He told of the letter that was sent out of sheer spite. And he concluded by speaking of the fears that had haunted him ever since the night of his sister's brutal death. 'If I hadn't sent that stupid fucking letter, Hannah would still be alive.'

Mia said, 'Why do you say that?'

He spread his hands. 'It's obvious … Colin got somebody to kill her because she was doing the dirty on him. He got somebody to meet her after work, and….' He faltered and put his head in his hands.

Mia shook her head. 'Colin didn't know, Tom.'

'But I *saw* them,' he yelled. 'I saw them with my own eyes.'

Mia stared at Jack, momentarily speechless.

Jack said, 'Who did you see? When?'

Tom started to cry again, a relentless sobbing that took his breath away. Even so, with hesitant words, he said to Jack, 'It was about half five on the Friday … I was coming back from the underground car park. I'd carried a load of bags to a customer's car and I was keeping to the side streets because the pavements along the main road were like sheets of ice. I was coming along Argyle Street, on the opposite side from Hannah's shop, and I saw her meet up with a guy at the top of the street.'

'What did you do?' said Jack, suddenly hopeful.

'Nothing,' he said, shrugging. 'The guy looked like Chris. I just thought they were meeting up to go out somewhere. I was a bit surprised, though. They'd never been out on a Friday before.'

'Are you certain it was Lennox – certain enough to swear in a court of law?'

The boy shook his head. 'I just assumed it was Chris, but he wouldn't have killed Hannah. He loved her.'

'The man definitely looked like Lennox?'

The boy watched Candy playing with Jack's shoelaces while he considered the question. 'I'm not sure now. He was in a black uniform, like Chris's – only he wasn't wearing the peaked cap. And his hair was dark like Chris's, but I couldn't see his face – he'd got his back to me – so I couldn't see if he'd got a beard or not.'

Mia said, 'Tom, is there the slightest possibility that this man was Chris Lennox?'

'I suppose. He was as tall as Chris – he towered over Hannah. But, like I said, I couldn't see his face.'

'How did Hannah look? At ease? Apprehensive?'

Tom shrugged. 'Just normal. I mean, they weren't holding hands or anything, but she seemed comfortable with him. They were laughing.' He let out a low groan. 'If I'd known she was about to be killed, I'd have taken more notice. I'd have run up there and battered his fucking head in. I'd have....'

'What did you do?'

He snatched a quick glance at his mother, his expression morose. 'Nothing ... I didn't do anything. I just walked back to work and left my sister to die.'

CHAPTER NINETEEN

'Tom could have killed Hannah,' said Mia, once they were in the car. 'I reckon he's got an anger management problem. And he was definitely angry enough after missing the rock concert.'

They were heading back to the station, Jack gazing intently out of the side window.

'No, that's rubbish.'

'But, why, Jack? What makes you so sure?'

'The dog,' he said, dragging his gaze away from the rolling fields. 'We've seen rats on the landfill bigger than that little runt….'

'So?'

'So it wouldn't take much to snuff the life out of little Candy, would it? She'd end up at the vets if you breathed on her too hard, but Tom treats her like she's made out of glass. Did you notice the way he handled her while she was on his lap? No, if Tom had an anger management problem that little scrap would have been gone years ago.'

'OK then, do you think Lennox did meet Hannah on that Friday?'

'Now, that's a possibility. I reckon Lennox is still our man.'

'I'm not so sure.'

'A tenner says you're wrong,' said Jack, with a grin.

*

'We'll just have to go right back to the beginning,' scowled DCI Wells, his words sounding terribly loud in the quiet of the board room.

He felt like a mouse trapped in an exercise wheel: running blind, expending a barrel-load of energy and getting nowhere fast. Chris Lennox was the killer of Hannah Bates; of that he was certain. In Wells's opinion Lennox was a raving psychopath. He had motive. He had opportunity. But unless they were careful he'd wriggle through a hole in the net. What were they missing? Was it staring them in the face?

What a relief it would be to throw open the door to Shakespeare's office and declare with a satisfied grin that the investigation had finally come to an end. He imagined the television announcements, his exhausted face showing the strain but his smile triumphant nonetheless; the heat of the spotlight as he wallowed in the glory; the inevitable celebration in the pub afterwards, with all and sundry slapping his back and buying him pints.

Wells needed a result so badly that he lay awake at night praying for the one piece of evidence needed to nail the bastard. Actually praying. When had he ever needed divine intervention to crack a case? He was losing it. And in those quiet moments, when all eyes were elsewhere, he'd feel a hot bead of sweat travel the length of his spine and he'd panic.

But he needed to quell the panic. He needed to stay calm and sift through the evidence again and again until that missing link, that vital clue, decided to show itself. They were hardly short of evidence incriminating Lennox. Indeed, it had now come to light that Tom Bates had actually seen his sister with a man strongly resembling the Scotsman at the fateful hour. His computer files and his work locker were stuffed to the gills with information relevant to the case. So why couldn't they nail him?

'We go back to the beginning, and this time we do a proper bloody job,' Wells said again, leaning over his desk, palms flat on its surface, head lolling as his gaze flicked across the sea of pensive faces.

Over by the coffee machine Mia stood rigid, fearful of catching his attention with the merest flex of a knuckle. She was still banished to the outer reaches of his circle, despite the momentous details she'd gleaned from Tom Bates. Indeed, those very details were the spark that had ignited the touch paper of his wrath. She was incompetent. She was a fool. All those times she'd questioned the boy, and never once had she managed to wheedle such important information out of his mouth. And now they were back to square one. A whole week wasted, and it was all her fault. Was she *satisfied*? Was she *pleased with herself*?

Nick had to turn away and hide his grateful smile. How many times had he made it known to Wells that he would be the better interrogator of Tom Bates? How many times had he asked to be allowed a few minutes with the boy? But Wells had always stayed faithful to his DS. Now he could see that his faith was misplaced; and Nick was loving every second of Mia's discomfort.

He said, 'Perhaps I should revisit the Angel Mood shop, sir, now we've got this new information.'

Wells nodded briskly and gave Mia a scathing glance. 'Good idea, mate. And this time you can take Mia with you … show her how it's bloody done.'

'You're enjoying this, aren't you, Nick?'

'Me?' he said, hands flat on his chest, eyes wide. He gave a wolfish grin. 'I'm fucking loving it.'

'Nasty bastard,' she muttered, striding ahead.

They were making their way to the Angel Mood shop in Argyle Street, ten minutes away from the police station. Up until now the walk had been conducted in silence, the atmosphere between them as tangible as a living presence. But Mia hated silence. Anything was preferable to that; even a no-holds-barred fistfight. Physical pain she could endure. But to be ignored, to be given the silent treatment, that was anathema to her. Any conversation with Nick Ford was, to Mia's mind, a rather dubious pleasure. But it was certainly better than having to endure the sight of that tight-lipped superior expression he always adopted whenever she caught the sharp edge of Wells's tongue.

'Hey, it's not my fault you're spineless,' Nick taunted to her retreating back.

Mia stopped abruptly and swung round to face him. 'That's bloody rich coming from you ... macho man. At least I don't have to beat up vulnerable young girls to stop myself feeling worthless.'

He bristled, his eyes darting towards the shoppers bustling around them. 'Keep your fucking voice down,' he muttered.

'Why? Are you frightened these good people might see you for what you really are – a nasty bully?' She carried on towards the crystal shop, throwing over her shoulder, 'I saw through you ages ago, Nick, and I'm as thick as shit.'

'You said it,' he said, falling in with her steps.

Again she stopped and turned to him. 'What did I ever do to you?' Without waiting for a reply she took advantage of a break in the traffic and hurried across the road to the shop, dodging the multitude of potholes that had become mini-lakes in the wake of the recent thaw. And while Nick floundered on the opposite pavement, she entered the crystal shop to the tinkle of the old-fashioned bell.

'Hi-ya,' said a tall blonde from behind the counter. 'Have a good look round. I'll not be breathing down your neck.'

Mia took out her warrant card and wandered past the angel paraphernalia. 'DS Harvey ... Larchborough police. I'm here to talk about Hannah Bates.'

'Oh,' said the girl, her smile slipping rapidly.

'So, you're Emily,' said Mia, catching sight of her name badge. 'Is your colleague around?'

'Cheryl? No, but she won't be long. She's only gone to Tesco's for the sandwiches.'

Mia took a moment to remove her gloves and unravel her scarf. She smiled warmly. 'I just want to ask a few questions in light of some new information we have. My colleague, DI Ford, should be here soon.' At that moment, the doorbell tinkled aggressively. 'Ah … talk of the devil.'

Nick marched towards them, his expression stony, and Emily's full lips melted into a smile at the sight of his handsome face. 'Oh, I remember you. Where's your friend from last time? Cheryl will be gutted he's not here.'

'If we could just concentrate on your dead friend,' Mia said, rather harshly.

'Oh, sorry,' said Emily, her huge eyes suddenly filled with an unfathomable sadness. 'You said you'd got some new information. Does that mean you know who did it?'

'Not quite, but we're getting there,' said Nick, pushing past Mia to rest his notebook on the counter. Those bloody joss sticks were there again. What was the point of them? They *stank*. He pushed them towards the far end of the counter, the movement swift and irritable, then quickly read through the notes from their last conversation.

'You said Hannah asked you not to look which way she went on that Friday afternoon when she left the shop. You said she didn't want you seeing who she met up with.'

'That's right,' said Emily, fiddling with a beaded necklace as though it were a rosary.

Nick frowned. 'And you really didn't look to see what the bloke was like?'

'No.'

'You didn't take the tiniest peek? You must have been dying to know who he was.'

The girl shrugged. 'Well … obviously.' She lowered her eyes. 'If you must know we did look. But we'd got customers when she left, and by the time they'd gone Hannah was nowhere in sight.'

'I see.' Nick ran a hand around his chin as he tried to glean some inspiration from his notes. Sadly, there was none to be had. He let out a long breath. 'An eyewitness stated that Hannah met a man in uniform on that Friday … a black uniform. Does that ring any bells?'

She slowly shook her head. 'No … no, I'm afraid not.'

'Hannah was seeing a man called Chris Lennox, a warden at the Marshcroft remand unit….'

Emily's eyes widened. 'Really? That's new to me.'

'You never met Mr Lennox?'

'Never.' She pursed her lips and blew out a noiseless whistle. 'Fancy that.'

'Have you remembered anything since the last time we spoke?' The girl shook her head. 'Are you sure?'

Tears welled in Emily's eyes and she fought bravely to hold them back. 'I've told you everything. There's nothing more to tell.' She turned to Mia, her big eyes begging for understanding. 'We don't notice stuff as a rule, do we? I mean, so much passes us by day by day and we just don't see it.'

Mia said, 'Actually, we take in more than we realize. If we were to get you in a relaxed setting, with a professional giving you just the right prompts, you'd be amazed how much comes back to you.'

Emily heaved a dejected sigh, her face crumpling. 'So, why can't I remember anything *now*?' She rapped a finger against the side of her head. 'If it's all in here, why won't it come out?'

Mia leant across the counter and rested a hand on the girl's arm. 'Don't get yourself in a state. It'll only be counterproductive. Just relax and think back to that Friday. No … try to remember the whole week. What stands out in your memory? Did anything unusual happen? Try to think.'

The girl gazed into space and chewed on her thumbnail, her other hand still holding the necklace beads. Presently, she shook her head. 'No … sorry … nothing's coming back. The only unusual thing I can remember is next door's break-in.'

Nick jumped in immediately. 'What break-in?'

'The bike shop next door. They had a break-in on the Wednesday night. They lost about ten thousand pounds worth of stock.'

'Why didn't you mention it before?' asked Nick, clearly agitated.

The girl raised a petulant shoulder and pouted. 'I didn't think it was important.'

Nick gave her an incredulous look. 'A crime was committed next door, just hours before a girl goes missing, and you didn't think it was important?'

'Don't *shout* at me,' she said, a hand going swiftly to her face. 'And anyway I thought you'd have known about it.'

'Believe it or not, I don't know about every crime that's committed on my patch.'

'Don't blame me, then. It's not my fault your friend kept it to himself.'

'What friend?'

'That nice-looking policeman who came with you last time.'

Nick frowned. 'Why would DC Rose know about the break-in?'

Emily rolled her eyes and spoke clearly, as though he were slow-witted. 'Because he was one of the officers who came to investigate after Geoff reported the burglary, of course.'

'Are you absolutely sure about this?'

'Of course I am. I didn't actually speak to him myself, but Hannah was all over him like the proverbial rash.'

'Tut, tut, Nick. How come you missed that little gem first time round? Were the girls too busy gazing into your pretty face?' Mia feigned a heartfelt sigh. 'Oh, never mind … perhaps Wells won't be too pissed. Let's hope not, anyway.'

Argyle Street had become crowded with the lunchtime trade during the twenty minutes or so they'd spent in the shop, and the congestion was thwarting Nick's repeated attempts to stride off in a huff. As a result, his anger was rising rapidly.

'Fuck off,' he muttered, still trying to dodge the shoppers.

But Mia stayed close by his side, her grin almost maniacal. 'It just goes to show … if you gloat over somebody's misfortune you'll soon end up in the shit yourself.'

He peered down at her, his eyes dark with rage, and seemed set to fire off a volley of expletives before thinking better of it and hurrying forward, straight into the path of an elderly woman pulling a heavy shopping trolley. The woman gave a startled cry and the trolley toppled, but Nick ignored her and carried on, all the while pushing indignant pedestrians from his path.

Mia was left to confront the old woman, a Mrs Pearson from Staples Brook, and rescue her groceries – mostly tinned goods, luckily – from the dirty puddles that littered the pavement. Mrs Pearson refused to believe that Nick was a police officer, hot on the heels of a thief. In the good old days, when she was a girl, coppers were courteous and kind. They were there to serve and believed that the public – their benefactors – deserved the very best in the way of protection, even if they *were* chasing a purse-snatcher. Mia could only apologize and offer to buy her a reviving cup of tea. Five minutes later she was able to leave the ruffled Mrs Pearson in a nearby café with a steaming pot and an egg-and-cress sandwich.

Mia returned to the station, eager to witness the ear-bashing Nick would surely receive from the vitriolic Paul Wells, and was rather annoyed to find Tom Bates waiting in reception with his mother. He'd been invited to make a formal statement, but she hadn't expected him quite so soon.

'Hi, Tom … Mrs Bates,' she said, planting a solicitous smile on her lips. 'It's really good of you to come so promptly.'

Mrs Bates turned tired eyes her way. 'We thought we'd better get it over with.'

Mia shrugged off her coat and scarf, and was about to usher mother and son towards the interview rooms when she caught sight of Danny emerging through a door into reception. He was heading for the lift.

'Hey, Danny, hang on a sec.' She turned to Mrs Bates, a hand on her shoulder. 'Would you two mind waiting here for a minute? I need a quick word with my colleague.'

The lift had arrived and he was keeping the doors open with his foot. He shot Mia an impatient look. 'What do you want? I'm in a hurry.'

She repeated what Emily had told them in the crystal shop. 'Why did you keep quiet about it, Danny?'

He bristled. 'I didn't *keep quiet* about anything. I filled out my crime report and handed it in. I didn't think it was relevant to our case so I didn't mention it.' He let out a long breath. 'Listen, Mia, I'll let you into a secret. And I don't want it all over the station, so promise you'll keep it to yourself.' He waited, but she simply stood there. 'Go on, promise.'

'I've got to know what the secret is first, Danny.' She snorted. 'I mean, if you're about to tell me you're the killer then I'll be duty bound to mention it to Wells.'

'Fair enough,' he said, laughing. He released the door of the lift and pulled her close, his gaze darting towards the sergeant behind the desk. 'The fact is I'm halfway through an Open University course in criminal psychology. I'm heading for the top job, Mia, and that degree will get me there a lot quicker.'

They were so close that Mia could smell his cheap deodorant, and she pulled away swiftly to create a gap between them. There was something about Danny that Mia didn't like, something unsavoury. She could imagine him using the toilet and not washing his hands afterwards, or failing to brush his teeth from one day to the next.

'So?' she said, eyebrows arched.

'So, I've learnt that the type of criminal who goes in for breaking and entering – the opportunist thief – is totally different from the sort of psychopath who commits cold-blooded murder to satisfy his warped sexual urges.' He shrugged, hands on hips. 'Nothing would have been achieved by me mentioning the break-in – apart from Nick wasting time going after the wrong bloke. You know how blinkered he is when he thinks he's on the right path. And anyway the gang that did the bike shop was soon picked up. They couldn't even get rid of a load of bikes without getting caught, so I shouldn't think they'd be clever enough to kill a girl and cover their tracks.'

Mia nodded. 'You're right, Danny. Nick would've tied the two crimes together and gone off in completely the wrong direction.' She looked at him, her expression kindly. 'Wells is going to be so pissed though. You'd better get ready for fireworks.'

Danny gave her an easy smile. 'I can handle Wells,' he said. He crossed to the lift and pushed the button. The doors slid smoothly apart and Danny stepped inside. He turned to her. 'Anyway, it'll make a change for somebody other than you to be in the firing line. Ever thought of getting a few more qualifications yourself? Your performance is pretty piss-poor at the moment.'

The doors closed abruptly on Danny's mocking grin. 'Bloody cheek,' she muttered, heading back to Tom and his mother.

The boy was sitting bolt upright on the bench. He seemed strangely traumatized, his eyes behind that lank fringe staring blankly into the middle distance while Mrs Bates gently brushed the hair from his face.

Mia picked up her things. 'Ready for this, Tom?' The boy failed to reply, simply continued to stare into space. 'Tom? Ready to give your statement?'

He acknowledged her for the first time. 'As ready as I'll ever be.'

The filling in of the statement forms was a mere formality and, once installed in interview room number two, Tom quickly dictated as Mia covered three pages with her neat hand. Afterwards, with the pages duly signed, Mia escorted them to the car park and then made her way up to the board room, annoyed that she'd missed the floorshow but happy that Nick would be sharing her space in the doghouse. Silently she berated herself. When had she become so hard, so vindictive? The animosity she sometimes felt towards Nick was totally alien to her otherwise kindly nature. And the bickering, the continuous conflict they shared, was so knackering. But what was the alternative? Lie down and let him walk all over her? No: she was a good copper – regardless of what Danny Rose might think – and she wouldn't be undermined by the likes of Nick Ford.

Fully expecting a strained atmosphere Mia pushed open the door to the board room, and was met instead by a babble of relaxed conversation. DCI Wells was clearly elsewhere.

'Where's the boss?' she asked Billy Finch.

'With old Shakespeare – getting a bollocking, I reckon.'

Mia poured herself a black coffee then settled into her chair and took grateful sips of the hot liquid. She glanced around the room. Nick wasn't at his desk. And Danny was absent, too. Were they holed up somewhere, exchanging verbal punches? Jack was busily drawing cartoon characters on the whiteboard to the amusement of officers gathered around him. Mia smiled fondly. Nothing much fazed Jack, least of all the DCI's irascible temper. She'd enjoy the peace while she could. Wells would be back soon enough. But all too soon her phone rang.

'DS Harvey….'

It was Nick. 'Get down to reception. And hurry … please.'

Mia made a face at the receiver. Whatever it was must be serious. He was almost begging. 'What's wrong?'

'Just come.'

Mia hurried down to reception, her imagination throwing up one ridiculous scenario after another. Had Nick mortally wounded Danny in his anger about the bike shop break-in? Had Wells expressed his consternation about the break-in too strongly, causing Nick to retaliate with his fists?

The lift pinged to a halt and its doors slid apart to reveal a totally surreal tableau. There in front of her, not ten feet away, was Nick, half-sitting and half-lying across the bench with a bloodied, barely conscious Lisa Mackey in his arms, the sides of his overcoat pulled tight around her so that his body heat could keep her warm.

'Oh, my God,' said Mia, rushing towards them. 'What's happened to her?'

'I don't know. I was talking to Stan at the desk when she just opened the doors and sort of … *fell in.*'

'There was nobody with her?'

'Nobody. I ran out to the car park, but it was empty.' Nick pulled the girl close, the movement so full of affection that Mia felt strangely in the way. 'She must have staggered in off the street.' He shook his head, his voice little more than a whisper. 'I'll kill the fucker who did this. I'll kill him.'

Mia hovered on the spot, feeling totally useless. She said, 'We'll need an ambulance.'

'Stan's already phoned for one. He's gone to get the first-aid box to clean her up a bit.'

Mia stared into Lisa's battered face, grimacing every time she grimaced. 'Lay her down on the floor, Nick. She'll be more comfortable.'

'No,' he said, pulling her closer. 'I want to hold her.'

Mia sighed loudly. 'Don't be a fool. Lay her on the floor. You don't know what damage you're doing, holding her like that. She might have broken bones. She might have concussion….'

'You think?' he said, staring at her like a little boy lost. 'Oh, fuck.'

Nick laid her on the floor, his movements slow and careful as though she were a priceless antique that might shatter from the slightest harsh touch. And his tears fell freely, mingling with the blood spatters that marred the prettiness of her flimsy cotton top.

'Pull yourself together,' Mia said harshly, almost dragging him away from the girl. 'What's Stan going to think if he comes back to find you like this?'

'I don't care,' Nick said, on his feet now and pulling a sleeve across his swollen eyes like a petulant schoolboy.

'You'll care well enough when Paul Wells finds out about the two of you and you're booted out of CID.'

'Fuck Wells,' Nick muttered, his anguished gaze still fixed on Lisa's heavily bruised face. 'I'll get her to hospital. I'm not leaving her.'

'Talk sense. I'll go with her. I'll keep you up to date.'

The door behind reception squealed on its hinges, the sound jarring Mia's teeth in the quietness of their surroundings. They both looked to where Stan Smith was pulling up the flap in the reception desk and heaving his heavy bulk through the small space, a white-and-red first-aid box hugged tightly to his chest.

'I won't be able to do much,' he said, falling clumsily to his knees by Lisa's side. 'Not with a few plasters and a bottle of surgical spirit, I won't. But the ambulance shouldn't be too long now.'

Mia said, 'I'm going with her. See if I can get a statement.' She shot Nick a warning look. 'Nick can tell the DCI where I am.'

'OK,' he said, backing towards the lift, eyes still glued to the girl. 'I'll tell him.'

When he'd gone and Stan was busy dabbing at the blood around Lisa's closed eyes Mia sank on to the bench and thought for a while, her mind buzzing with questions. She looked down at the girl, took in the cotton top, the mini skirt, the strappy sandals. What was she doing out on the streets without a coat, without proper shoes or boots? The temperature had lifted now, the thaw had well and truly set in, but the weather could still be raw should a strong breeze suddenly whip up. And what was she doing on the streets, anyway? Lisa didn't pound the pavements like the majority of Larchborough's prostitutes. She preferred to work from home. She thought it was safer, thought she had more control in her own surroundings. Obviously not.

Her flat was – what? – a fifteen- twenty-minute walk away? And that was on a quiet day with hardly anybody about. Having to constantly weave through the crowds, dodging the window-shoppers who suddenly – annoyingly – stopped dead in their tracks whenever something caught their eye, could easily add another ten minutes to the journey. Could she really have staggered for twenty-five minutes through crowded streets, dressed in a skimpy outfit and dripping with blood, without one single person offering to help?

But how else could she have arrived at the station? Had she been driven there by her attacker and dumped a short but safe distance away? Of course there was a third alternative. Mia's skin crawled at the thought. Could Lisa's injuries have been inflicted by the killer they were looking for? Could she have been lucky enough to escape his grip and run for her life? Every criminal makes a mistake eventually: one vital error that leads the police straight to their door. Maybe their man wasn't so clever after all.

As Lisa was clothed Mia was unable to see whether her body had been repeatedly cut. Her legs were badly scratched; and large bruises were developing fast around her inner thighs so some sort of sexual activity had taken place, but no actual cuts were discernible. The very fact that Lisa was still dressed should have dispelled any possibility that the killer had tried to strike again. Nevertheless, nothing should be ruled out until Lisa was able to speak for herself. Whenever that might be.

As they watched over her, their ears straining for the shrill wail of an ambulance, Lisa lost consciousness. It was a blessing, really, and a help to the paramedics when they eventually arrived, for they'd be able to get her into the ambulance and start their procedures without having to worry about her comfort.

When the ambulance made off for the hospital, Mia followed behind in her car, arriving at the Accident &

Emergency reception in time to see Lisa's supine body being wheeled through a pair of rubber doors into a critical cubicle beyond.

After two long hours and numerous pleas from Mia for information, a doctor pushed his way through the doors. He wore blue scrubs, and his eyes were tired but kindly above the white cotton mask still covering his nose and mouth. Pulling the mask away to reveal a grim smile the doctor sat beside Mia, the faint scent of antiseptic soap wafting across as he did so.

'Detective Sergeant Harvey?' Mia nodded. 'Apologies for the wait. We had to operate. Your Miss Mackey was in a pretty poor condition by the time she got to us. She's in the recovery room now, though. She should be fine.'

'Why the need to operate?' Mia said, horrified. 'What did he do to her?'

'Quite a lot,' the doctor said, his tone heavy with contempt. 'The major damage was to her spleen. We had to remove it before the internal bleeding killed her.' He frowned, the gesture adding years to his face. 'There's a bruise you'll no doubt find interesting on her abdomen – it's in the shape of a shoe, so it's quite possible she was jumped on or stamped on. Several ribs were broken, too. In fact, she's lucky her lungs weren't punctured.'

Mia thought quickly. 'Did you see any cuts on her body, Doctor? Was there any evidence of rape?'

He shook his head. 'No cuts. And our job was to put right the damage caused by her attacker, not look for evidence so you could build a case against him. We saw no evidence of rape because we didn't look for any. We shall, however, be happy to conduct an examination when Miss Mackey regains consciousness. If she agrees, of course.'

Mia had taken out her notebook and was listing all the information given by the doctor. 'I don't suppose she woke up before the operation? I don't suppose she said anything?'

'She did, actually,' he said with a frown. 'She came to just as we were preparing her for surgery. She put up quite a fight for such a small girl. We had to administer a pre-med. She was very agitated ... obviously in a state of shock. She was trying to fight me off as though I was the attacker. She was mumbling something like ... Nick ... Nick.... Don't take my word for it though. By then the injection was starting to work and she was very sleepy.'

'When will I be able to see her, doctor?'

'Come back in the morning. She might be more awake by then.'

Mia sat in her car for a long time, looking through the windscreen but seeing nothing, her mind in turmoil. The truth about Lisa's attack – or truth as she saw it – was obvious now. But she was loath to admit that truth; for to do so would mean incriminating a fellow officer. In order to acknowledge the facts that were staring her in the face Mia would have to put Nick slap bang in the middle of the frame. Could she do that? She hated the bastard, certainly, but could she risk ruining his career for what amounted to little more than a hunch?

What if she were right, though? Nick couldn't have headed back to the station after storming off in Argyle Street. If he had, his overcoat would have been discarded in the board room ages ago and yet he was still wearing it when Lisa fell into reception. So where did he go? Straight over to her place? Julie Franklin, Lisa's friend and Mia's eyes and ears on the street, had reported more than once that Nick had turned up at Lisa's place – his mood low after a bad night without sleep or a bollocking from Wells – and used her as a punch bag. Should she confront him with the facts as she saw them?

'Oh, sod it,' she muttered, starting the car. 'A quiet word wouldn't hurt.'

'And where the bloody hell have you been?' roared Wells.

All eyes were on Mia as she tried unsuccessfully to tiptoe to her desk. 'Didn't Nick say, sir?'

'He gave me some cock-and-bull story about a prostitute suddenly appearing out of nowhere at the reception desk and you whisking her off to the hospital like a modern-day version of bloody Wonder Woman.'

Those last words were bellowed out, the spittle flying from his thin lips. 'When are you ever going to learn?'

Mia's temper suddenly flared. 'Learn what, sir? The art of compassion? I think I've already got that. Lisa Mackey might only be a prostitute, but she's a member of the public, a citizen of this town, and she has a right to expect – no, she *deserves* – to be protected by us.'

Wells looked up slowly, his eyes showing … what? A grudging respect? 'Does she indeed?'

'Lisa was in trouble and she needed help. I was there, sir, so I provided that help. I'm not going to apologize for doing my best.'

Wells pushed himself away from the desk and folded his arms. 'What about our dead girl? Doesn't she deserve our compassion? Or doesn't she matter now she's dead?'

'Of course she does,' said Mia, annoyed. 'I'm surprised you even had to ask, sir.'

'But you keep going off at a tangent. You keep following your own agenda.' He lurched to the front of the dais, his finger stabbing the air as he pointed to each and every officer in the room. 'We're a team, and a team pulls together.'

Mia huffed. 'I'm well aware of that, sir.'

'But *are* you? *Are* you?' Wells let out a loud sigh and wandered back to his desk. Easing himself into his chair, he said, 'Get out of my sight. I've had enough of you for one day.'

The room was as silent as a grave. Mia glanced around at her mates – all of them with eyes averted – then grabbed her bag and rushed out of the board room. She was halfway along the corridor, horrified at the tears coursing down her cheeks, when she heard Nick calling for her to stop. Hurriedly dabbing a tissue at her eyes she turned to face him.

'He's still pissed about letting Lennox go. Any one of us could have got it. It just happened to be you.'

'Aren't I the lucky one,' she said with a loud sniff.

Nick caught her arm, turned her to face the double doors at the end of the corridor. 'Come on, let me buy you a coffee.'

She tut-tutted. 'Do you think you should? Start following your own agenda and Wells'll do his nut.'

'I'm on my way to the canteen anyway. He wants a sandwich so he can carry on working. If I'm a bit late getting back I'll just say there was a queue.' He took in a sharp breath and lowered his voice. 'I need to know how she is, Mia. You said you'd phone….'

'I know … sorry, I couldn't. I had to switch my mobile off. You know how it is. I'll fill you in when we're sitting down.' She gave him a sideways glance. 'What did Wells say about the break-in at the bike shop?'

'He doesn't know.'

She stopped in her tracks. 'What? You didn't tell him? You coward.'

He turned away and reached for the door. 'Would you have told him, the mood he's in?'

All the way to the canteen Mia considered him surreptitiously. Missing the fact that the bike shop had been broken into might soon be the least of Nick's worries. If her assumptions were correct – and she had no reason at this point to believe otherwise – then he might soon be languishing in a cell, stripped of his warrant card and reputation.

'Fancy something to eat?' Nick called from the counter.

'Just coffee, thanks.'

She had chosen a table in the corner, well away from the few personnel taking advantage of the early-evening lull. Nick placed the coffee before her and sat in the opposite chair, Wells's sandwiches creating a small barrier between them.

'How's Lisa?' he said, an edge to his voice.

Mia searched his face for any signs of guilt. 'Pretty bad. They had to operate.'

'What?'

'They had to remove her spleen. She had bad internal bleeding. If they hadn't taken it out, she would've died.'

'Fuck.' Nick sank back, a trembling hand over his mouth. 'Anything else?'

Mia made a face. 'Let's see … a few broken ribs, various scratches and lacerations….' She gave him a pointed glance. 'Did you do it, Nick?'

He looked at her for a moment, totally askance. 'Me? Are you fucking crazy?'

'I don't think so. You were in a lousy mood when we left that crystal shop. Who's to say you didn't go straight round to Lisa's and take it out on her?' He said nothing, jaw slack and eyes staring. 'You've hit her before, Nick. You can't say you haven't.'

His hands flew high into the air, a definite act of surrender. 'Yes, I've hit her. I can't dispute it. But I didn't do this. I didn't nearly kill her.'

Mia sipped her coffee, regarding him coolly over the rim of the cup. 'Where did you go when we left the crystal shop, Nick?'

He frowned. 'Back here. Where do you think?'

'No, you didn't. You'd still got your coat on when I came down and found you with Lisa. That was a good hour and a half after you pissed off and left me nursing that old lady you nearly knocked down in Argyle Street.'

'For fuck's sake….' He surprised her with a grin. 'Carry on like this, Mia, and you'll make a good detective yet.'

'Get lost,' she said, scowling.

'OK, you're right, I didn't come straight back here. I went to Pickwick's for some lunch. No law against it, is there?'

'What did you have?'

She saw his fists clench on the tabletop but when he spoke the words came out in an even tone. 'I had thinly sliced pork with smooth apple sauce and a crunchy sage and onion stuffing on thick-sliced wholemeal bread. And I had a steaming-hot cappuccino. It was expensive, but well worth the money.'

'Did you get a receipt?'

'No,' he said, hitting the table with the flat of his hand. 'And I didn't know anybody in there, so there are no witnesses either.'

Ignoring his irony, Mia said, 'You've got blood on your shirt cuffs, and there's some on your tie. How do you explain that?'

'I was holding her, for fuck's sake.' He leant across and grabbed her hand. 'Please stop this, Mia, you're being ridiculous.'

'Am I?' she said, pulling her hand away. 'Then why was Lisa struggling against the surgeon as though he was attacking her and shouting, "No, Nick, no," at the top of her bloody voice?'

'That attack had nothing to do with me.' He got to his feet, pocketing the sandwiches. 'What are you going to do?'

'I'll go and see Lisa tomorrow, talk to her when she is properly awake. I'll make up my mind then.'

Nick turned to go, his face a mask of hate. 'It you want a war, Mia … you've got one.'

CHAPTER TWENTY

These were trying times for the Larchborough police, and for DCI Wells in particular, whose job it was to pacify the baying newshounds whilst juggling the balls of an investigation that had gone spectacularly stale since the release of his number one suspect. Therefore, the majority of his Saturday morning was spent in Shakespeare's spacious office, head to head with the superintendent. And it was while they brainstormed that Mia felt able to visit Lisa Mackey in the hospital without being missed.

She found her alone in a side ward on the first floor, its only window overlooking a series of drab prefabricated buildings and the lone chimney of an incinerator belching out huge plumes of highly suspect grey smoke. She was attached to a couple of drips. An oxygen mask lay discarded on the starched pillow by the side of her bruised and swollen face. Mia thought she looked scrawny under the faded hospital blankets, scrawny and vulnerable.

Those at the nurses' station told Mia not to expect animated conversation from the patient. It had been necessary during the long night to administer morphine and although at times she'd regained consciousness, she was very rarely coherent.

Mia pulled a chair to the side of the bed and, careful to avoid the drip's needle lodged into a plump vein on the back of Lisa's hand, she very gently grasped the girl's fingers. They felt stone cold, yet clammy to the touch. She bent nearer to the girl's face. 'Lisa? Lisa, can you hear me? It's Mia Harvey….'

Nothing.

Mia gave her fingers another squeeze. 'Lisa, it's Mia Harvey. I'm a DS at Larchborough police station. I work with Nick Ford.'

'Nick?' Lisa said, through lips so swollen they could scarcely move. 'Nick…?'

Mia leant closer to the girl, brushed a few stray hairs away from her forehead. 'Lisa,' she said, glancing towards the closed door. 'Did Nick do this to you? Was it Nick?'

'Nick … oh, God …' the girl breathed, her head tossing from side to side on the mountain of pillows.

She had suddenly become agitated, and Mia worried that the drips might become dislodged. She got to her feet, held the girl's shoulders in a firm grip. 'It's OK, Lisa, you're safe now. You're in hospital. He can't get to you in here.'

'She's been calling for Nick all night,' said a voice at the door. Mia turned to see one of the nurses striding purposefully towards the foot of the bed. Retrieving Lisa's file and opening it up, the nurse said, 'Is he a boyfriend, do you think? She doesn't seem to have any family in the area. None that we can trace, at any rate.'

Mia returned to her chair, pushed it several feet away from the bed, giving the nurse ample room to complete her checks. She said, 'I'm not getting anything from her. Is she likely to come round pretty soon?'

'Hard to tell,' said the nurse, completing a column of ticks in Lisa's file. 'If I were you, though, I'd come back tonight. She's bound to be awake by then. You're wasting your time at the moment.'

'Aren't I just?' Mia stood up and gazed at Lisa's face, willing her to open her eyes. But they remained closed and she was quiet once more; even the thrashing had stopped. Mia made for the door. 'I think you're right. I'll come back tonight. Look after her, won't you?'

Then, for the second time in as many days, Mia sat motionless at the steering wheel, oblivious to the frantic bustle of the hospital car park, her thoughts wholly on Nick and his undeniable temper.

And then her mobile phone rang. 'Hi … DS Harvey….'

Silence for a moment, and then, 'It's me … Tom Bates.'

Still smarting after the DCI's mammoth blow-up Mia could feel her hackles rising, but she kept her tone easy. 'Hi, Tom. What can I do for you?'

'Mum said I should phone you.'

'Why?'

'Because … because I think I saw the bloke who met Hannah on Friday.'

Mia's heart lurched inside her chest. She quickly caught her breath. 'Where, Tom? Who is he?'

His ragged sigh filled her ear. 'Trouble is, you're not going to believe me.'

'Just tell me. Who is he? Where did you see him?'

A pause. 'At the police station, yesterday.'

Mia frowned at the tiny black phone. 'Hold on, let's get this straight. You saw Hannah's mystery man at the station yesterday? Why didn't you say something?' Questions were falling over themselves in her mind. Who was he? *Where* was he? Damn it, he could be miles away by now. 'For God's sake, Tom, why didn't you say something?'

'I didn't think you'd believe me,' was his breathless reply.

'Think carefully, Tom – was the man brought in by another officer? Was he put in the cells?'

'No.'

'Did he have a complaint, then? Did he come in off the street to complain to the duty sergeant?' She held her breath, forever hopeful. If that were the case, there would be some record at the desk.

'No, he was waiting for the lift. You left me and Mum to go and talk to him.'

Mia thought back, her blood running cold. Danny had been waiting for the lift. She had left them to have a word with Danny. But it couldn't be him?

'That man was one of my colleagues, Tom. I think you've made a mistake.'

She heard him let out a disgruntled huff. 'I told Mum you wouldn't believe me. I said you wouldn't.'

'You said yourself you didn't get a proper look at the man, so how can you be so sure?'

'I just am … OK? When I saw him yesterday, it all came back … his hair … the way he stands … his cocky walk. He's the man. I'd swear to it in court. He's the man who killed my sister.'

'Carol….' Mia whispered into the phone at her desk in the board room. '… you remember when I managed to get you off with Neil Doherty, and you said you owed me one…?'

Carol Clark, a long-time friend of Mia's, worked in the station's personnel department. One of her jobs was to calculate the number of hours worked each week by the uniformed officers, and the amount of overtime they'd accumulated. Mia knew from old that she was completely reliable and capable of keeping her mouth shut. At that moment, as she caught the subtle pleading in Mia's voice, Carol was highly dubious, too.

'Oh, my God,' she said, mock horror in every syllable. 'What's coming next, I wonder?'

'Nothing too awful, and it'll earn you a double gin next time we go out.' Mia paused to scan the room. Good, they were all going about their business, effectively rendering her invisible, and Danny was nowhere in sight. Keeping her voice low, she said, 'Carol, I need to know Danny Rose's shift pattern for the twenty-second of February – that was a week yesterday. Will you find out for me?'

'You know I will. Any chance of you telling me why you want it?'

'It's best you don't know. OK?'

'Sure. Give me a minute and I'll phone you back.'

Mia replaced the receiver and frowned. How could she tell Paul Wells that Danny had been accused of murder? It would be professional suicide, especially as the DCI already saw her as a liability to his team. But – strange as the scenario might sound – it did fit in with the facts as they knew them. Although Danny was now part of CID and therefore wearing plain clothes, he would have been in uniform on the Friday of Hannah's disappearance. Perhaps they'd all been focusing too strongly on the black warden's outfit of Chris Lennox instead of considering all the other professionals who also dressed in black.

Plus: Danny had already met Hannah the day before her death. And yet he'd kept quiet about it. Why was that? They'd been told that Hannah was a friendly girl, completely without guile. Had she told Danny her troubles, opened her heart, only to have him spin her a fictitious line that he could somehow get Colin Fowler's charges dropped so she'd agree to meet him on that Friday? It wasn't beyond the realms of possibility that she could have fallen for such a line. Many ordinary citizens were of the belief that police officers held some amount of power. How wrong could they be? Maybe that belief had been true during her father's time on the force, but it certainly wasn't nowadays.

So far, so good, then. But why would Danny have wanted to kill Hannah Bates? What could his motive have possibly been? Try as she might Mia couldn't find one, and that was where the theory came unstuck. Without a motive there could be no reason for murder; that maxim was one of the fundamental touchstones of a police officer's initial training.

But Tom was adamant that Danny was the man he had seen with Hannah at the top of Argyle Street on that Friday afternoon. And he was willing to swear to it in court. The motive, though … what was the motive?

Mia's telephone buzzed. It was Carol. 'Danny was on early shift – six till two – for the whole of that week. And he was booked to do an additional four hours every day, making a total of twenty hours overtime for the week. But I've only got nineteen hours down on computer, so I checked. He'd got a late dental appointment on that Friday, so he finished at five. Is that any good for you?'

'It's perfect. Carol, you're a star. Keep it to yourself, though – eh?' Mia cut off the call and made for the drinks table. She needed a coffee. She also needed someone to talk her through this awful dilemma. But, who? Jack would have been her first choice, only he was nowhere to be seen.

On returning to her desk, she set down her mug and glanced around the board room. Wells was off conspiring with the superintendent behind closed doors. But he was out of the question anyway. What about Nick? She looked to where he was conducting a whispered conversation on his mobile; no doubt phoning the hospital yet again to ask about Lisa. Would he be willing to help? Nick couldn't stand Danny. Trouble was he disliked her even more. All the other guys lounging around and generally littering the board room were Danny's colleagues from uniformed division. They were nice enough. But could she trust them to keep their mouths shut? She wasn't sure.

Nick it was then. She drained her coffee and wandered across to his desk. 'Could you spare a minute, Nick? I've got a bit of a problem.'

He pocketed his mobile, his grin malicious. 'Can't … sorry,' he said, his chair nearly toppling in his hurry to stand up. 'I've just been on to the hospital. Lisa's awake and she's asking for me. She wants to make a statement … to me.' He leant towards her, his teeth bared. 'Now, would she even want to see me if I'd been the one who'd beaten her up? I don't think so somehow.' He grabbed his overcoat. 'I'll be back before the DCI.'

Feeling deflated and in a total quandary Mia returned to her desk and flopped into the chair. Right, she'd sort this through on her own. She'd list the pros and cons of Danny's alleged involvement in Hannah's murder and she'd come to a rational conclusion.

She pulled her notebook from her jacket pocket and cursed silently as it fell from her fingers. It landed on the desk, open at the page listing all DNA evidence found so far in Hannah's murder case. The good old DNA code. It was foolproof; and that was its beauty.

'Hold on a minute….' Mia said, a smile playing on her lips. She sat bolt upright in her chair. A thought had occurred to her, a thought as bright as a light bulb illuminating the dark recesses of her tiny brain. If Danny was Hannah's killer then his DNA would match that of the stray pubic hair found on her body. There'd be no room for doubt.

She hadn't the patience to wait for an actual result to come through, so she'd call his bluff. She'd make him believe she'd matched his DNA with the hair. His reaction to that revelation would tell her, without a shadow of a doubt, whether he was guilty or otherwise. She could hardly wait.

'Aaron, where's Danny?' she said to the officer manning the phones.

'Archives room … again,' the man replied. 'He'll be setting up home in there if we're not careful.'

Mia nodded her thanks, then grabbed a blue plastic folder from her desk and hurried to the door. Hopefully, Danny would be alone and she could spring her trap immediately.

The archives room was situated on the ground floor, off the main corridor. It was a long, thin space: fifty feet by twenty. Floor-to-ceiling bookshelves ran almost the whole length of the room, with three-feet-wide walkways between. Those shelves were packed tight with documents going as far back as 1897, when Larchborough police division had first come into being. Overhead strip lights gave off a meagre glow and the air was musty and cloying. It caught the back of Mia's throat as she burst in, adrenaline pumping.

'Danny?' she said. 'Danny, are you in here?'

He appeared as if by magic from behind the furthest bookshelf, a fat folder of yellowing papers in his hands, the dust from it peppering the front of his brown jacket. 'Where's the fire?' he said, grinning.

'Skiving, are we, Danny? While the cat's away….'

He shrugged. 'Just doing a bit of research for my degree course. The DCI will never know … unless you tell him.'

'Oh, sod your degree course, Danny, I've got bigger fish to fry.'

'I'm so intrigued,' he said, feigning a yawn.

She held up the blue folder. 'Guess what's in here?'

'No idea,' he said, returning to the bookshelf.

Mia followed him, loath to let him out of her sight. 'It's your DNA result, Danny.'

He stopped in his tracks, his back towards her. Did he flinch, or had she imagined it? Very slowly he slotted the folder back into its spot, handling it as carefully as he would a new-born baby. Then he turned to face her, 'I didn't realize I'd given a sample for testing.'

'You didn't,' she said, grinning. 'I pinched a Styrofoam cup you'd used and sent it along to the Lab.'

His expression was stony, his eyes giving nothing away. 'Can I ask why?'

'I was following a hunch.' She laughed, the sound immediately deadened by the rows of tightly packed papers. 'Female intuition's such a wonderful thing….'

'I haven't got time for this, Mia. Things to do and all that.'

He made to leave, but she blocked his path. 'You're not going anywhere – not until you've heard me out.'

He spread his hands. 'Well? I'm waiting.'

'I worked it all out and now I've got the proof,' she said, tapping the blue folder.

He stood before her, hands on hips, and skimmed his eyes towards the ceiling. 'Worked out what?'

Her smile faded as she held his gaze. 'That it was you who killed Hannah Bates.'

It was his turn to laugh, but the sound held little mirth. 'You're mad,' he said. 'You're bloody mad. Go to DCI Wells with that and he'll have you committed.'

'Do you think?' she said, eyebrows raised. Once again she held up the blue folder. 'But I've got proof now – remember?'

He snorted. 'And I'm James Bond. Just go away, Mia, some of us have got work to do.'

'And I've got a witness who's willing to swear in court that he saw you with Hannah on that Friday afternoon.'

'You don't say….'

Her resolve was beginning to flounder. Had Tom Bates got it wrong? Almost throughout the whole of their brief encounter Danny had remained calm and unruffled; it was hardly the demeanour of a guilty man. True, he'd wobbled a little at her remark about the Styrofoam cup. But wouldn't anyone be annoyed knowing their DNA had been checked without their knowledge? It was hardly enough to convict the man.

And then his attitude underwent a startling change. He was glowering, his features distorted, and he rushed towards her. 'Get out of my way, Mia – now – and you'd better give me what's mine.'

Danny lunged for the blue folder but Mia held on tight, reluctant to let it go. If he got to see inside then the game was up, and that would be a shame because at last she seemed to have him on the run. Alarm was bright in his eyes and perspiration shone on his forehead. Could it be that Danny Rose was afraid?

And still they wrestled, but Mia would not give up the folder. Eventually, with a roar of frustration, Danny grabbed her shoulders and flung her against the nearest shelf. She suffered a glancing blow to her right temple, rendering her senseless for a fraction of a second; enough time for the folder to fall from her grip and slither unimpeded into a dusty corner. Danny stumbled after it, but Mia reached it first, falling heavily on to her side as she strove to cover the folder with her body. A fierce pain shot through her right shoulder, but Mia ignored it and grinned up at him. 'Got you … you weird bastard.'

'Bitch,' he spat.

And then he disappeared through the door, his urgent footsteps beating a rapid retreat towards reception. Mia reached for her mobile and tapped out the number for the front desk.

'Larchborough police. How can I help?'

'Stan … Danny Rose is heading your way. You mustn't let him leave the building. Keep him there. And watch yourself, Stan, he's dangerous.'

CHAPTER TWENTY-ONE

DCI Wells pressed the record button and lifted his gaze, disbelief still showing in his eyes. 'Time of interview … 2.15 p.m.…. on Saturday the second of March. Those present are DC Daniel Rose – the accused. Interrogating officers: DCI Paul Wells and DS Mia Harvey. Mr Charles Aldridge, duty solicitor, is attending at DC Rose's request.' He settled back, arms folded, long legs crossed beneath the table, and nodded for Mia to proceed.

She cleared her throat. 'Daniel Rose, we put it to you that between the hours of 5.30 p.m. and midnight on Friday the twenty-second of February, you unlawfully killed Hannah Bates. Do you have anything to say before we start the interview?'

Danny took in a breath, but before his lips could form a single word, the solicitor intervened. 'My client doesn't have to say anything at this stage,' he said, then turned towards Danny. 'In fact, DC Rose, I'd urge you to say nothing until we've had a proper chance to talk.'

Danny silenced the man with a dismissive wave of the hand. 'Guilty as charged,' he said, smiling.

The amusement in his tone brought goosebumps to Mia's arms and she shivered uncontrollably. Forcing herself to return his stare, she said, 'Why, Danny? Why?'

He gave a tight smile. 'Why not?'

She shot him a look of utter contempt. 'But you're supposed to uphold the law, you weird bastard, not flout it.'

Wells bristled beside her. 'We all share your sentiments, Mia, but kindly stick to procedure.'

'Procedure....' Danny snorted, skimming his eyes over the pair of them. 'That's what it all boils down to in the end, doesn't it, sir? It doesn't matter that we're not actually *doing* anything about crime in the UK today. It doesn't matter that crime figures are still rising. As long as we always stick to *procedure* then everything's fine.' He unbuttoned his jacket, took time to make himself comfortable in the chair, and all the while he regarded them with a mocking stare. 'I'll tell you something, sir – bloody procedure's stifling law enforcement in this country.'

'Save your speeches,' said Mia, 'and tell us what happened from the time you met Hannah.'

The solicitor leant forward and held up his pen. 'I strongly advise DC Rose to say nothing at this juncture.'

Danny let out a laugh. 'I've admitting killing the girl, Mr Aldridge, so perhaps I've said too much already. Still, thanks for the advice. Truth is, though, I don't really need your help. I only asked you to sit in because it's *procedure*. Do you see?'

Wells let out an impatient breath. 'You obviously think you're cleverer than the rest of us, Danny ... but you still got found out.'

'I know, sir. And by Mia Harvey, of all people.' He shook his head. 'I'll never be able to live it down.'

'Just go back to that Friday, Danny,' she said, trying not to gloat. 'Where did you take Hannah after you picked her up?'

'Back to my place. We got talking after I responded to that break-in call from the bike shop. I told her about my degree course in psychology—'

'You and that bloody course,' Mia muttered.

Danny looked from her to the DCI, shoulders lifted, hands spread. 'Do you want me to tell you what happened, sir? Or have we got to listen to her little put-downs all afternoon?'

'You'll both be languishing in the bloody cells overnight if you don't get a move on,' Wells bellowed.

Mia tried hard to hide her flinch. 'Right, Danny, you told her about your degree course. What, then?'

He folded his arms, his body language mirroring that of the DCI. 'She told me about Fowler in the remand unit, about her relationship with Chris Lennox. She asked if I could help get Fowler off the charges.' He gave a sardonic laugh. 'As if I'd help get that piece of shit back on the streets. Anyway, I said I'd look through my reference books, see if I could find some loophole, and she agreed to meet me after work on the Friday to discuss my results.'

'Friday came, and when we got to my house I just gave her a load of spiel ... made it up as I went along ... and she fell for it. Christ, she was so gullible.'

Wells gave him a no-nonsense glare. 'And?'

'I changed out of my uniform and we went to the Pig and Ferret on York Road to celebrate Fowler's imminent release. Hannah wanted to send Lennox a text, give him the good news, but I'd had the foresight, back at my place, to lift her mobile from her bag while she was using the toilet.' He stared into space, chuckling. 'I really did think of everything.'

'Wasn't she worried about where the phone might be?' said Mia. 'Wasn't she worried that Lennox might want to contact her? He told me they talked briefly at bedtime every night.'

Danny gave a couldn't-care-less shrug. 'She just thought she'd left it at work and wasn't too bothered. She said something about borrowing her brother's to call Lennox later, but I wasn't really listening.'

'OK, what time did you leave the pub?'

'About nine o'clock.'

'It was freezing that night. How did you get Hannah to go to the river with you?'

'Easy. I told her one of my tutors had offered to help. She thought I was driving over to his house. When we got past the Apollo nightclub I stalled the car and pretended I couldn't get it started again. She didn't panic. She felt quite safe. After all she was with a policeman.'

That chuckle came again, and Mia flinched at its pitiless sound. She said, 'Was that when you decided to kill her?'

'Christ, no. I decided on the Wednesday when I met her in the shop.'

'So it wasn't a spur-of-the-moment crime?'

Danny actually looked offended by the remark. 'Of course not, I'm not a spur-of-the-moment type of guy. I planned everything, down to the smallest detail. I decided where it was going to happen and I cleared the area of all vegetation ... you know, made it cosy. I'm a gentleman. One of a dying breed. Yes, I reckon I thought of everything.'

He'd fallen silent, seemed to be remembering events, and DCI Wells had to prompt him to continue. Blinking rapidly, he said, 'I told Hannah we'd have to walk the rest of the way. I said it wasn't far. And when we got to my chosen spot, I pounced.' He spread his hands, his smile triumphant. 'It was so easy ... like drowning a kitten.'

'Hardly,' said Mia, slowly shaking her head. 'The poor girl had to endure quite a bit of damage first. And procedure dictates that you list all that damage for the benefit of the tape recorder. So would you mind?'

He rolled his eyes, as though they were stupid. 'Bloody procedure again. Make doubly sure you've arrested the right guy. What's the point? Even if I hadn't killed her I know what her injuries were. I was at the post-mortem, I've read the crime reports countless times. And, anyway, you know I did it – you've matched my DNA.'

Mia made a face, shot him an apologetic look. 'I didn't actually, Danny. There was nothing in that folder. I was hoping you'd give yourself away and you did.'

'What?' he said, glaring at her. '*What*?' Very slowly Danny's face drained of colour as he moved menacingly towards the edge of his seat, his rigid stare glued to Mia's face. 'You tricked me? *You* tricked *me*?'

'You're not as clever as you thought,' said Mia, almost purring with pleasure. 'A bit more fine-tuning needs to be done.'

Wells unfolded his arms, sat upright in the chair, and said, simply, 'Why, Danny?'

'Because I want to be the best in my profession, sir. And to be the best you have to get *inside* the criminal's mind, find out exactly why he commits such gruesome crimes.'

Mia frowned, her jaw sagging. 'You mean to tell me Hannah's murder was a ... a bloody research project?'

'If you like,' said Danny, shrugging. 'I'd have had another go, as well – honed my skills a bit more – if it hadn't been for that bloody stomach bug. To be the best, Mia, you have to be willing to get your hands dirty.' He sneered. 'You'll never amount to anything. You haven't got the guts or the imagination.'

She offered him a smile. 'Don't forget, Danny, it's thanks to me you're getting life.'

'Why did you pick Hannah Bates?' said Wells. 'What was so special about her?'

Danny's laugh was short and forceful. 'There was *nothing* special about her, sir. That's the reason I chose her. She was spectacularly stupid ... *shallow* and stupid. I knew the universe wouldn't miss Hannah Bates. In fact I was doing the planet a favour. Her death would mean one less unnecessary encumbrance to be supported.' He smiled. 'I'm very ecologically minded, sir.'

'And clinically insane, too,' said Wells, getting to his feet and striding purposefully towards the door. 'But there'll be no cushy psychiatric hospital for you. No, Danny, if there's any justice in this world, you're going to rot in jail. Charge him, Mia.'

*

It was Mia's finest hour. A rumble of applause and a few salacious catcalls greeted her as she entered the board room later that day. Danny Rose had been formally charged and remanded in custody; and it had been her job to see that the proceedings remained low key. Superintendent Shakespeare, horrified by the news of Danny's arrest, was desperate to keep the facts from leaking to the press for as long as was humanly possible. He knew only too well that once it became known that Hannah's killer was a uniformed officer, all hell would break loose.

Hannah's parents, already aware of Danny's supposed involvement in their daughter's disappearance were nonetheless staggered at the news that he'd actually confessed to the murder. Shirley Bates, especially, was in a bad way. A doctor had had to be called and a sedative administered. The pair would need lots of help in preparing for the expected media frenzy and Mia had promised to be by their side every step of the way.

She was emptying the contents of her desk into a cardboard box – Shakespeare wanted his board room back – satisfied with a job well done, when Nick sauntered across. 'Congratulations, Mia. I didn't know you had it in you.'

She acknowledged the compliment with a brief smile. 'What did Lisa have to say for herself?'

'One of her regulars did it – a complete nutter….'

'It *was* you, then,' she said, keeping her voice low.

He had the good grace to smile. 'The bloke got demoted at work, apparently. He couldn't hit his boss, so he hit Lisa instead.'

'Think we'll catch him?'

'Lisa gave me everything apart from his shoe size, so, yes, I think we will.'

'I'm glad. I like Lisa. She didn't deserve it.' Mia looked away. 'But, then, she doesn't deserve a lot of what she gets, does she, Nick?'

He put a hand on her arm and forced her to look at him. 'I'm going to change, Mia. I swear to God I am. I'll make it up to her.'

'Good,' she said, grinning. 'I'd better get an invite to the wedding.'

'What? Fuck that.' He headed back to his desk, but not before treating Mia to another wide and genuine smile.

She was returning to her packing when the door burst open and Paul Wells made his customary sweep into the room. 'Good work, darling,' he called from the dais. 'You've redeemed yourself at last.'

Why didn't those words fill her with relief? They would have done yesterday. Yesterday, all she wanted was to get back into the fold. What had changed? She gazed surreptitiously at Wells and realized she no longer respected the man. He didn't care about her occasional sparks of inspiration. He didn't care whether she progressed at all, grew into the job. All he wanted her to do – all he wanted them all to do – was bolster his flagging ego. They were there to make him look good, that's all. Well, it wasn't enough for her any more.

Mia sighed deeply, suddenly drained. She'd finish her packing and then get off. Pulling open her top drawer she came across the pile of final demands and bailiff's letters she'd taken from Janet Munroe's desk. She was about to give them to Paul Wells when she suddenly stopped. Why make it easy for him? What was so wrong about believing Janet had actually helped the old lady to die? Would anything really be gained by Janet's languishing in a prison cell for a long stretch? That woman had done an awful lot of good over the past few years – more good than most people managed in a lifetime.

Mia made a quick decision: she'd put the papers back in Janet's desk and say not a word to Wells. She was planning to visit her mother the following day anyway. OK, so the truth about Janet's debts would probably come out at the trial, but Mia didn't want to be the cause of the disclosure. That decided, she continued to fill the box. And then Jack was beside her, his overcoat half on.

'Well done, partner. Brilliant....'

'Thanks, it was nothing,' she said, grinning. 'What are you up to?'

'Just on my way home, actually.' He gave her a sheepish look. 'Any chance of a lift?'

THE END

THE DS MIA HARVEY SERIES

Book 1: Desperate
Book 2: Obsessed

Please join our mailing list for updates on
DS Mia Harvey, free Kindle crime thriller, detective,
mystery books and new releases.

www.joffebooks.com

FREE KINDLE BOOKS

Manufactured by Amazon.ca
Bolton, ON